Southern
Fried
Plus
Six

SOUTHERN FRIED PLUS SIX

Short Works
of Fiction

by

**William
Price
Fox**

J. B. LIPPINCOTT COMPANY
Philadelphia and New York

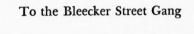

To the Bleecker Street Gang

Contents

Southern
Fried
Plus
Six

LOWER MULBERRY

WE LIVED ON the corner of Mulberry and Stewart in a small five-room clapboard house that had never been painted. The front porch was level with the clay sidewalk. A thick pea vine grew around the front porch and there were always peas in June. It was the only thick vine on the block, and on hot afternoons two and sometimes three of the hound dogs from down the street would sneak through the broken railings and sleep in the solid shade at the edge of the porch near the swing.

In the house next door the Mullinses lived. Mr. Mullins was a small thick man who smoked a pipe and never talked much. He wore a black leather band on his right wrist and a Mickey Mouse watch that never worked on his left. Mr. Mullins worked for the sanitation department. In the evenings he would park his big Mack truck right up on the clay sidewalk in front of his house. He always brought toys and things home from the city trash pile, and after supper me and Earl and Clyde and sometimes Lucy Mullins would climb into the rear of the open truck and toss everything out.

There would be bells and balls and skates and parts and wheels of wagons. There would be water-soaked Big Little Books, crushed model airplanes, wind-up toys with sprung springs and big china dolls with missing arms and legs and hands. There would be false faces, Zorro whips, xylophones and bits and parts of Tinker Toy sets. And nothing was good enough to work or bad enough to throw back in the truck.

And after we had inspected everything and returned what couldn't be used or sold or buried or given to the hounds, Mr. Mullins would appear in the doorway. He would be smoking his pipe and most of the time he would be barefoot. He would cough and he would always say the same thing, "All right, you kids, quit messing round that truck."

My buddy, Coley Simms, lived next to the Mullinses. His father Harlis had two jobs: he was a loom fixer at the Columbia Cotton Mill and in the evenings and on weekends he repaired automobiles in the open field across the street. His only advertisement was a big Seiberling Air-Cooled truck tire that had been painted white and hung from a link chain on the front porch. It read CAR REPAIRS—CHEAP. He had a fine collection of mechanic tools and the older boys would bring their cars in for repairs.

And there were automobiles. There were Fords and Chevrolets and Buicks and Hudsons. And before that there were A-models and before that there were T-models. And there were tires to be fixed and tubes to be patched. There were valves to be ground and carburetors to be cleaned and set. And gas lines to be blown out and radiators to be soldered. And when it was cool in the big field they would jack up the rear end of the car and prop it up on Coca-Cola crates or swing it on a hoist from the big limb of the chinaberry tree. And the rear end would be pulled and the clutch plate would be changed or the differential packed. And cars needed timing and fresh spark plugs and points had to be filed and cleaned and set and sweated over. There would be ring jobs and valve jobs and brake jobs, and special tools would be borrowed from the big Crescent station on Broad Street.

And the hard job, leading . . . Joe Snyder would bring a plumber's sink over and with a blowtorch melt the lead and prepare to wipe. And when the lead was right and Joe was ready he would fill the dips and curls and breaks in the fenders and in the roofs of the cars. And when he worked on the older cars he would say, "No sir . . . they don't build them like this any more."

Next to the Simmses were the Turners. They were bootleggers. Most of their customers were colored, and they would come in the back door to the kitchen. There a gray bucket sat in the middle of the table and a tin dipper floated and tinked at the edge. The whisky was strong and the smell would hurt your eyes when you stood close. The dipper had been marked on the inside with a metal scribe and for fifteen cents the men could buy a half of a dipper. They would drink fast and shake their heads as if they couldn't believe what was happening. And then they would smile and wipe their mouths with the back of their hands and leave. On Saturdays, when the neighborhood men got paid and there would be five or six of them in the kitchen, you could hear their shoes on the bare floor and the little house would groan under the shifting weight. And in the evening the colored men would go out into the field and rassel and sing and sit out in the dark and smoke cigarettes and tell lies. And every half hour or so a small skinny boy called Stutt (because he stuttered) would appear at the door for another spider-webbed pint of white whisky. And if Mrs. Turner was in the kitchen she would give Stutt an apple or a piece of cake or two or three slices of cold bologna.

Next to the Turners' house was the blind man's house. He had a son who led him up the street every morning to sell sheet-metal dustpans and broom holders that he made by hand. The boy was very small and when he played baseball we let him hit and let him score and gave him all the easy grounders.

Beyond the blind man's house and the open field was the Porters'. They were twin brothers and they were both blond and they both wore glasses. They were bad baseball players and someone was always picking a fight with them and they were always getting beat. One of them was named Carl and the other Herman. Later they both grew up very big and no one fought them. They got blonder and blonder and when they stood in the sun they looked like albinos. They never took off their glasses and they never unbuttoned their collars. Later they moved north.

Beyond the Porters' house was the colored section. There were no porches on the low shotgun houses and the women would sweep the flat clay yards as if they were an extension of the front rooms. Green cane chairs were placed on the ground and from a distance you'd think there was an actual porch there. They'd have iced tea in big-mouth Mason jars and lemonade in big-mouth Mason jars and water-cut whisky with a lemon floating in the middle in big-mouth Mason jars.

In the evening there was always a guitar or a mandolin. And someone would say, "Warm her up there, Claude," or "Play that thing," or "Make it talk," or "Make it moan," or "Make it go like the Orange Blossom Special." And "Let's hear 'bout old Staky Lee," or "How 'bout that 'Evil Woman Blues'?" And there would be a harmonica and they'd play the Freight Train Blues. And later someone would show up with a pair of bones and maybe a washboard and thimbles. There would be a jew's-harp and a paper and comb combination and the drinking would start and then the singing. And they all played rhythm and the sound would carry three and four blocks up the street.

And a tall skinny Negro called Dance would show up from the other side of town. He was over six foot five and couldn't buy clothes thin enough or long enough. His wrist bones stuck out way below his shirt cuffs and the bottoms of his un-cuffed pants legs were four inches above the tops of his shoes. He wore long wide yellow clipper shoes with three razor slashes at the sides to make room for his little toes. He never wore socks.

And he would come and say "Evening." And then he would start dancing. You couldn't see him in the dark but you knew he was out there. He'd pass before the kerosene-lamp-lit door and someone would say, "Now ain't he some-thin'." He'd have his eyes closed and he'd be smiling and he'd dance in a little small circle and then move back out into the shadows. And when he lit a cigarette he'd take two or three deep drags and then place it behind his ear. And you could watch the red ash burn out there in the dark even though you couldn't see old Dance.

And sometimes he'd keep dancing when the music was over and the men were drinking. He never talked much. He'd answer questions about what he was doing and where he'd been and questions like that. But most of the time he'd just listen and smoke. And when the music would start again he'd rise up, shake his arms and legs as if they were triple-jointed and move out.

And most nights a mockingbird, the same mockingbird, would fly out of the woods and sit on top of the porch where you couldn't see him and he'd imitate every instrument except the bones. And they'd all laugh at him and he would keep trying. But he never could do the bones. And then someone would say, "You got it now, Mr. Mockingbird. That's it. You got it right, now." But he wouldn't have it and he'd know he didn't and he'd keep on trying. And someone would say, "Man, but don't he work at it."

And off to school. They'd come out of the Bottom in a group of maybe nine or ten. There were overall pants with cream- or red-colored turned-down and buttoned pocket flaps. There were strapped overalls with big biblike pockets for pencils and baseball-player cards from chewing-gum packages, and brass rivets at the corners of the pockets and yellow leather labels. And homemade shirts with long banana-shaped collars. The shirts were blue and brown and sometimes gray. And they would always bulge and buckle at the seams from not enough sewing. And there were numbered baseball caps holding down long yellow and brown strawlike hair that grew three inches every two weeks. And when the cap was removed and stuffed into the rear pocket the water-combed hair would spring up like weeds in a wagon track.

And there were tennis shoes and twelve-cent socks. And wide black leather or brown leather belts still around from the First World War. Brass-bound and buckled and barely fitting through the wide belt loops, and folded under at the end with a quick series of ice-pick holes to hold the pants on the snake-thin hips. And marbles and baseball gloves and string and fishhooks wrapped in cigarette foil and ten cents for lunch.

There was the home room. The Pledge of Allegiance and The Lord's Prayer and the examination of fingernails. Earl Edge would be asked to stop picking his nose. And there were pictures. There was a picture of the Fifth Grade. Thumbs dug in under the wide belt, knees bagged and shiny from playing marbles, and always the water-combed and carefully held and quickly drying hair. And the sun. There was always the sun. Glaring in the clear sky, glaring in the white and eraser-chalk-dusted steps and flashing on the tiny mirrors of mica in the wide sidewalk between the two mognolia trees on the Bee Street side. And then the robed and hooded beetle man with the big camera would wrap himself in black and count. And he would say "Smile" and we would squint and then it was over. It was over and inscribed and already yellowing before the gray cardboard frame had had a chance to chip. The bare knees of the short girls in the front row. The reflected light from Carl Porter's glasses. His face was the first to yellow. The prim pursed unlipsticked mouth of the tall and shiny-elbowed teacher. Someone in the back row was making a face and Kirk Turner was looking down Lucy Mullins' dress collecting information. And the cardboard frame could be sprayed with glue and frosted with mica for five cents more.

And later there were autographs and no one looked like anything except the long rows of the same pictures that hung gloomily on the dusty wall of the principal's office. And when you stood before him wondering if you were to be talked to, screamed at or beaten, the sad yellow faces in leather frames standing against the same steps would stare at you. And if Mr. Jeffries kept you waiting long enough, and he usually did, you could see a boy in the class of 1929 with his tongue out. And in the 1921 photograph near the wall there is a beautiful finger gesture long before most of us knew it existed. . . .

WILMA

COLEY SIMMS and I had a tree house in the big oak at the edge of Cecil Malone's field. Beyond the field was Colored Town and the river.

Cecil Malone had two daughters, Elaine and Wilma. He ran an automobile repair shop in the garage behind his house on the corner of Cherry and Stewart Streets and had his junk yard in the field next door. There were all kinds of cars and parts of cars under his house and in the field and in the trees. There was an old Terraplane with orange supercharger pipes and a turtle-topped Chrysler siting low and flat in the tall sour grass with no wheels or engine. There were fenders leaning on the fences, and bumpers, radiators and gearboxes stacked under the house. Universals, brake drums, crankshafts and oil pans were everywhere and heavy rear ends were hanging like hams from the big limbs of the chinaberry tree. Red, black and orange paint-spray marks covered three sides of the garage and the back side of the house and two Fords were jacked up so high on railroad crossties they looked like tall dogs pissing on a flat rock.

Our oak tree was old and dead, and when a windstorm blew it down we shifted the clubhouse to the Chrysler. We cut back the weeds, cleaned it up and moved in our marbles, hubcaps, fishing tackle, rubber guns and a quart of peanut butter.

The week we moved in Elaine Malone ran off with a sheet-metal worker from Roanoke, Virginia. That left Cecil with just Wilma. But Wilma was a handful. At first no one paid much attention to her. She seemed fat and plain. And then one summer Wilma grew up.

She slimmed down and she started wearing tight sweaters and high heels. The older boys began coming by. T. D. Pettibone started taking her out first. Some evenings Coley and I would be sitting in the Chrysler and we could see them out in the field. If it was cool, T. D. would lay his head in her lap and make her squeeze his blackheads. T. D. had plenty.

Coley and I didn't know what love was that year but whatever it was we were pretty sure it had a lot to do with Wilma and T. D. and all those blackheads. T. D. lasted a month. He began losing weight and complaining about being tired.

Jack Hodges tried her next. He lasted about two weeks before he got the same run-down, weary look that T. D. had. When Jack eased up, the Porter twins took over. Mr. Porter was a railroad man on the Southern and he soon put a stop to this.

The uptown cars started coming down every night. Coley and I would be out in the old Chrysler and we would watch them turn off their lights a block away and come coasting in out of gear with their engines off.

There would be three or four boys in the big Buicks and Hudsons and they'd all be smoking. There wouldn't even be time for introductions and Wilma would go giggling off into the night in the back seat.

Wilma had two walks. One for walking and one for walking by the drugstore. She'd come by every day at three to catch the three-ten bus uptown to Morehead's Dinette. Someone would see her coming and he'd run inside and tell the Doc. It didn't matter what he was doing or who he was talking to on the phone, he'd cut it off and rush out front. And Wilma would come by. M. L. Anderson always sang out,

[19]

"Lordy, Lord. Here she comes."

Wilma would smile, shorten her stride and tighten her shoulders back.

"Oh, Wilma, you look so good."

Doc would crack every knuckle on each hand and shift back and forth like the ground was too hot to let him stand in one place.

Lonnie Register whispered loud enough for Wilma to hear, "Great God, look how it rolls." And then, "Oh, Wilmer, you're breaking my heart."

She loved this kind of attention and she'd smile and slow down.

M. L. again, "Look at it, will you. I say, look at it. It's like two bobcats in a croker sack."

Doc would be getting more and more nervous. He'd be sweating. "I can't stand it, I tell you. I can't stand it." He'd wipe his brow with his sleeve and go back inside.

Lonnie again, "Oh, Wilmer, please take me home with you. I'll just sit around and smile and wag my tail."

A half a block past the drugstore Wilma would ease up and go into her regular walk.

You'd think four boys would be enough but it wasn't. One night it was the five first-string men of the high-school basketball team plus the little runty team manager. They came by several times and one of them gave her his maroon varsity sweater. She deserved it.

Spring came and we cut the weeds back from the Chrysler and covered the seats with some old bed sheets. We were sitting there one night listening to the colored boys singing and arguing when we saw her cutting across the field. She'd just got off from Morehead's.

Coley said, "Let's call her over."

I said, "Okay."

"All right, you call her."

"No, you."

"Together."

"All right."

"Wilma," then louder, "Wilma!"

She came over. "Well, well, what are you two up to?"

She sat in the back seat with us and we talked. Later, she gave us cigarettes and lit them for us.

Well, we sat around and smoked and coughed and talked. Then we put the cigarettes out and started fooling around, and along about one o'clock right there in that back seat of that Chrysler, Coley and I found out that blackheads had absolutely nothing to do with it.

A couple of years passed and the Chrysler rusted out and the moths got at the upholstery. Coley and I graduated from junior high and were in first-year high school. Wilma had quit in the eleventh grade and become a full-time waitress.

Once a week and sometimes twice Coley and I would stop by Morehead's after the movie at the Palace Theatre. Wilma would signal us to sit in her area and we'd start ordering. We'd start off with a couple of club sandwiches, a side of French fries, and a malted. Then a Tin Roof or hot fudge sundae and maybe finish up with a banana split. Morehead's always had good food. After we'd rested a few minutes and looked over their funny books, Wilma would give us our check. It always read "2 Coca-Colas 10¢." Wilma wouldn't even let us tip her.

By this time, Wilma was in the big league. High-school football stars, college football stars, county representatives, senators, sheriffs. Once in a while she would ask if the old Chrysler was still our clubhouse and how many hubcaps had we stolen. We'd tell her everything and invite her out but she'd say she was too busy.

Two more years passed. Coley and I stopped by to see her. Wilma was a hostess now and wore a light blue uniform with white cuffs. The other girls wore white. We sat in her old area and she told the waitress she would handle our order. When she gave us our ten-cent check she said, "Meet me in the Chrysler at midnight."

Wilma arrived at midnight with a half pint of whisky, a pack of Camels and a quart of strawberry-ripple ice cream. We ate the ice cream first.

When it was over, we all stretched out in the tall grass and listened to the Negroes singing in the Bottom and the trains whistling down by the river. It was a beautiful clear night and I wanted to know the names of the bright stars. Wilma didn't know. But she began talking. She told us about making love to a senator from downstate. She liked talking about it and rattled off a list of names as long as the Richland County Confederate Dead. She got serious and told us how a Pentecostal preacher had slept with her at the King Cotton Tourist Camp. How all night he had tried to convert her. He kept asking her why she did it. She said she told him she liked it and that it brought joy to others.

There was a question-and-answer period and Coley and I really asked them. About Orientals, about fat people, thin people, old people. About dogs and animals, about dogs and people, about goats and sheep. And more, and worse than that and better than that. Nothing fazed her and the few answers she didn't know she said she would check. So we sat out there by that old Chrysler and smoked low down so no one could see us and listened to Wilma and watched the moon shining on the old cars and glistening on the chinaberry tree. It was a fine night.

And then Wilma fell in love. He was a guitar player with the Dixiana String Band. His name was Wade Harrison. He was tall and good-looking but he was always in trouble with the law for fighting, speeding, or drunken driving. All during the six months they went together Wilma wouldn't even look at another man. They almost got married, but when she discovered he wanted to take her back home to Georgia she refused. She said all her friends were in Columbia and besides she never did like Georgia. When Wilma turned Wade down he quit the band, packed his Hawaiian steel guitar and amplifier box and drove home to Valdosta.

A few months went by and Wilma got in trouble. A lawyer got her pregnant and when she had her abortion things got complicated. She was sick for about a month and when she recovered she married the first man that asked her. He was a sorry little pimple-faced fellow. He worked the big grill at the Dixie Bee. Why they kept him on the big grill I'll never know. Maybe he stayed sober. But he was jealous of Wilma and kept dogging her. He never gave her a moment's peace.

Wilma got fed up and left him. She went to Georgia for her divorce. When her papers came through she went to Valdosta and tried to find Wade Harrison. She met his folks. Wade had left two months before. He was somewhere in North Carolina or Tennessee. He had told them he was going back to Columbia. He didn't write much.

She came back to Columbia and got her job back as hostess at Morehead's. Coley and I had heard all the news from the drugstore crowd, so we went by one night to try and cheer her up. We sat in our old booth and she took our order for club sandwiches and cheeseburgers and chocolate sodas. A regular waitress served our order. When we looked in the back for Wilma we saw her crying by the Coca-Cola crates at the rear of the store. Coley went back to talk to her. He was gone a long time. He came back and said she had agreed to come out to the Chrysler that night after work. We bought the cigarettes and the whisky and the strawberry-ripple ice cream that night. We even stopped by a florist and got a small bunch of violets. We were very fond of Wilma.

She arrived around midnight in a taxicab. She was carrying cigarettes and strawberry-ripple ice cream for us. She laughed when she saw our ice cream and gave us each a kiss when we gave her the violets. We each took one drink and then she started crying. We patted her back. She cried for a long time. Nothing would stop her. Finally she began drying her eyes and telling us she was in more trouble. Wade Harrison was in town and he wanted to take her out. Coley asked her wasn't that what she wanted. She said it was but that there were complications. She was in trouble. Her ex-husband had been to see her and had given her a venereal disease. The State wanted her to go to a camp for two weeks for a cure. She said she wasn't afraid to go but that she just had to talk to someone. She didn't want Wade to know until she came back. She wanted us to get a car and drive her to the camp.

Next day, Coley borrowed his sister Helen's Chevy and we drove Wilma down to the camp in Florence. We brought along fried chicken and potato salad with little wooden spoons and nine bottles of Doctor Pepper. On the way down we kept the radio on a hillbilly station and we sang every song we knew. When we arrived in Florence she said good-by and gave us a letter to give to Wade Harrison. She said she had decided to tell him everything. We were to check the Dixiana String Band; they would know where to find him.

We located Wade late that night. He was playing Hawaiian guitar at a place in West Columbia called the Blue Light. It was a sorry, low, concrete blockhouse-type place with no sign on the door. During the intermission we went up to the bandstand and gave Wade the letter.

He read the letter in the red light from the men's room. He excused himself from the band and packed his guitar and amplifier and told us to follow him. Outside he told us he had rolled his Buick the week before and he had no transportation. Coley told him we had the Chevy but we didn't have any money for gas. Wade reached in his pockets and pulled out two tight four-inch rolls of money held together with thick rubber bands.

He grinned, "Don't worry about the mule. Just load the wagon."

He wanted to pay us fifty dollars to take him to Florence that night. We didn't want the money but we agreed to take him if he would buy us dinner and pay for the gas.

We had barbecue sandwiches, chicken-in-the-basket, a

malted milk and a butterscotch sundae at Holly Yates' and we started driving.

We liked Wade. He told us a few jokes and stories about the band and after a while he unpacked the guitar and we all began singing. Wade had a nice voice.

We stopped for coffee and gas at Sumter. When we got through Sumter and got back on Route 76 Wade turned the dome light on and reread Wilma's letter.

In the letter she told him everything. He read us part of it and then explained how the new penicillin drugs can cure anything. He wasn't mad at all about Wilma getting V.D. The thing that bothered him was her not telling him.

It was dark as pitch on Route 76 and Wade sat in the back seat smoking. He was tall and had his feet up on the edge of the front seat near the window. He seemed to be a couple of years older than Wilma. He hummed a while like he was thinking.

He was quiet for a long time and then he said, "Boys, I've just decided I'm in love with that little gal. I'm going to stay in Florence and wait for her. She'll like that. I'll take the bus up one day and pick up my car, but for right now I'm going to stick around and cheer her up. What do you say?"

Coley said, "Sounds fine to me, Wade . . . fine."

I said so too.

And that's what Wade Harrison did. He stayed in Florence and saw her every day during visiting hours. When she got out he drove her down to the Pee Dee River in his fresh-painted Buick and proposed.

She accepted and they were married right there in Florence, South Carolina, by the justice of the peace.

Two weeks later, Coley found five twenty-dollar bills in the glove compartment of the Chevy. We split it.

Wade and Wilma Harrison moved to the Santee River area where all the dam construction was going on. He picked up a string band and bought himself a little honky-tonk. Later he sold the club and the band, and with the money he and

Wilma went back to his home in Valdosta, Georgia.

He has a big night club now with a seven-piece band, a grill, a fountain, and white linen on the tables. They have two little boys and a girl and he says Wilma is prettier than ever.

Ten years have passed now and a wild morning-glory vine has wound around the old car out in Malone's field. In summer when the leaves are green and the big blue and white flowers are out you have to look pretty close to see there is an old Chrysler buried there.

PIT FIGHT

DURING THE THREE years we lived near Camden, South Carolina, my father owned a roadhouse. It was a big place with twenty-two booths for parking, a dance hall, six cabins, a barbecue pit, a red room for roulette, craps, black-jack and chuck-a-luck, and a blue room for poker. There were over a hundred lights burning at night. From Logan Watts' store a mile down Route 1 and across the field from the schoolhouse, you could see the big neon pig wagging his tail and the sign Bill's Place.

The roadhouse has nothing to do with the story but it will give you some idea of the kind of gambling that was going on in the late thirties around Camden.

The story starts at Watts' store. It was a long high-ceilinged building with a Southern Bakery sign stenciled in red and blue on the screen door. Inside the store three mule collars hung down from the center beam that ran the length of the room. Barrels of meal, smoked fish, pickles and hogs' feet were on one end of the counter; directly behind the counter, on the backboard, rows of rice, beans and sugar were neatly stacked in plain brown paper bags. Watts also sold fertilizer, clothing, beer, school supplies, and Texaco gas and oil.

Grady Lee was my best friend that year. We were both fifteen. The only thing you can't do in Kershaw County at fifteen is vote.

Watts had promised to take us to the pit fight.

The day arrived. We had been hanging around the store since eight-thirty. It was noon and Watts had said nothing. We were afraid he had forgotten or that he'd changed his mind. The fight was to begin at one-thirty in Claude Jenkins' pit.

Watts had a bad temper and we didn't want to remind him he had promised. We were afraid to ask and afraid not to ask. I decided I'd wait until he started. If he had said nothing by then I'd speak up. I rehearsed my brief speech as I paced back and forth between the stove and the fertilizer bags. Watts was in the back.

Finally Grady could stand it no longer. He sang out, "Mr. Watts."

I stopped breathless at the stove.

"Yeah, what is it?" He sounded irritated.

Grady chirped back, "Mr. Watts, you want us to sweep up for you?"

He grinned at me. Watts didn't answer. Grady's grin vanished. We knew that Watts had decided we were too young to see the fight. He came out of the storeroom hunching into the brown cardigan sweater he wore right through the summer.

"Where's my pipe?"

Grady leaped, "Right here, sir. Right here by the scales."

Watts grunted, took the pipe and started outside. We stood behind him on the gravel driveway as he locked the door. He turned and looked at us as he began lighting his pipe.

"Still want to come?"

I said, "Yessir." Grady nodded.

His pipe was lit. He shook the match out. "Okay . . . let's go."

Grady grinned and nudged me on the arm as we followed Watts down the path toward the woods.

Two hogs rooted in Joe Brown's old cotton patch. They had been field raised and in the distance their long legs and thin flanks made them look more like dogs than hogs. We passed through the small woods and out into Claude Jenkins' field.

The pit was on the far side of the field. We could see the crowd beginning to gather. Watts stopped and looked back at the woods. He had dark brown eyes and dark heavy brows. His hair was streaked with white. He looked serious.

"I'm going to put it to you straight. This ain't going to be a regular pit fight. Luke Finley's got himself a wildcat. It's going to be a slaughter and you might as well know it now. If I had my way this fight would have been called off. I don't care what they say about this Georgia dog . . ." He paused and then added, "Now if you boys want to light out back through those woods nobody is going to know a thing."

It was the longest speech I had ever heard from Watts. There was more. "What do you say?"

I spoke quickly, "We want to come."

Grady said, "Yessir, we want to see it."

Watts said nothing. He started across the field. We let him get five or six paces ahead of us. Grady showed me his crossed fingers. In the middle of the field Watts stopped again. He looked back.

"Goddammit. I knew that dog was around here some place."

We looked back toward the woods. At first there was nothing. Then we saw Red, one of Watts' hounds. Watts called, "Okay, Red, come on out."

The big dog passed the last scrub oak tree at the edge of the woods and started toward us. Watts walked back toward the dog and then stopped. The hound got closer and closer to the ground as he neared Watts. His long tail was chopping back and forth kicking up red dust.

He took the dog's head in his hands and said, "Red, damn your soul anyway. I told you I didn't want you along."

The hound's tail wound under his belly and the ears flattened sadly. Watts looked straight at Red. Red's head dropped lower and lower. He rasseled the dog's head in his hands.

"Now, boy, I want you to go back to the store and wait for me. And I don't want to turn around and see you sneaking back through them woods."

He turned the dog around and slapped him lightly on the rear. The big dog started back across the field. Once he paused and looked back but Watts, with his hands deep in the cardigan's pockets, was heading for the pit.

As we neared the pit, the Hall brothers and Earl Estee walked out to meet us. It was still early. Earl pulled his baseball cap lower as he said, "Watts, what do you think? What do you think about it?"

Watts said, "Not much to think. It's going to be another slaughter."

Earl paused and said, "There ain't going to be much of a fight then?"

Watts said, "That shouldn't be hard to figure out."

At twelve forty-five, Luke Finley's Ford could be heard behind the woods. It came into view at the south end of the field. Finley straddled the car over the old furrows that ran directly toward the pit and the crowd. He had a friend with him in the front seat. The wildcat would be in the back seat. After Finley and his friend parked and walked over to the water bucket, we moved in to look at the wildcat.

The back seat had been removed and the cane cage sat squarely on the steel floor. The cage was big but the cat made it look small as he moved back and forth. He was buff-colored and short. The shortness had packed his muscles together and they bunched at the hind quarters. His shoulders were narrow and solid and he carried his head low. He must have weighed fifty pounds. The trip had irritated him and his heavy breathing rocked the cage against the metal floor. I saw the fierce green eyes and knew the cat could never lose. And then, as we watched, the cat stuck a paw between the cane bars. The paw was small as it came out. Once out, it swelled up and he extended four long claws as if he were yawning. His claws were well over two inches long and they fish-hooked into fine points.

At the water bucket, I bit the tin cup to keep from shaking.

Parnell Taylor's pit bulldog was from Savannah. The dog was three years old and stood as if he were on show. He was beautiful. He held his head square and high and the sleek muscles under the brown coat glistened as he breathed. Most of the dog's weight was in the head and shoulders. The rear tapered back into smaller and smaller muscles to the short back legs. The dog had been bred to fight, and all during the confusion before the fight he stood like a rock by his master.

At one, Finley and his friend carried the cage to the edge of the pit. The cat had been in a pit several times and knew how to slide down the clay side. When the bulldog saw the cat he jerked himself up on his hind legs. He strained against the metal leash. Taylor held him firm.

It was quiet for a minute. The breeze on the back of my neck suddenly stopped. My heart pounded. The dog was unleashed. The metal click sounded like a hammer. As the leash dropped to the ground the dog's image blurred before me. The bull dog slid down the side and jumped the last few feet.

The dog hit bottom and started to charge. At first his feet slipped but then they took hold. He charged low and hard with his mouth opened up like a steam shovel. The lower jaw and the big teeth flashed as he crossed the pit bottom. The wildcat fell back from the heavy charge and rolled under the dog. In that second he raked his claws into the dog's stomach.

It was over before the dog knew what had happened. The brown dog didn't cry out. He sat down with his great mouth opened in confusion. He had no stomach. The dog's eyes searched the crowd above for his master.

He shifted his body as if to cover the darkening area beneath him. As he looked up again his eyes met his master's. A look of shyness passed over his face in profile as he curled tighter in the area in which he was to die.

No one spoke as we crossed back over the field toward the woods. It was hotter and the red earth held the heat close. I could barely walk. Grady said nothing. I kept swallowing and breathing through my mouth to keep from being sick. We shouldn't have come. Watts was right. Everyone was right. We shouldn't have come. If I could only get away from the men. If I could only crawl away somewhere and vomit. I would lie down and vomit and cry for that beautiful dog.

Earl Estee stopped at the fence post at the corner of the field and uncovered a spider-webbed pint of Kershaw County whisky. Earl drank and passed it around. As I raised the bottle to my lips, I wondered why they hadn't sent me home. The whisky was hot as coffee. My throat caught fire. My eyes filled and ran over. For an instant I couldn't breathe. I retched and began to gag violently. I didn't care who saw me.

Back at the store, everyone was talking at once. Suddenly Watts banged on the counter. The room quieted and a faint tapping of the screen door in the wind was the only sound.

"That settles it. I've had enough of these killings."

Earl Estee said, "Watts, you can't do a damn thing about it."

Watts shouted, "The hell I can't. You just wait."

Earl said, "All right . . . tell the sheriff. You think there's only one county in South Carolina? Johnson can't enforce a thing outside Kershaw County, and you know it.

Watts opened another beer. The cap bounced on the floor and rolled out toward the stove.

He said, "I'm not calling any sheriff."

Estee waited, then asked, "What are you going to do then . . . shoot the cat?"

Watts took a deep swallow of beer and said, "First, I'm going to Macon. I've got a cousin over there that you boys don't know."

He paused.

There was a scratching at the door. It was Red.

Watts said, "Let him in."

I pushed the screen door open and the dog came in. He went over to Watts and sat down at his feet. Watts was leaning on the counter now and the smoke from his cigarette was winding up and through the mule collar which hung above him.

He said, "Yessir, I should have done this a long time ago. Been too many dogs killed by that cat."

Watts wasn't in church the following Sunday. Monday, Len Bishop opened the store and announced he would be running it for three weeks.

August came. Now the sky was a paler blue, and nothing interrupted the sun. Between three and four o'clock the shade from the Coca-Cola sign in front of Watts' store spread over the long bench between the Texaco gas pumps. The men took their beer outside and watched the thin traffic coming down the road from Camden. No one had heard from Watts for three weeks.

Earl Estee said, "Maybe old Watts is in trouble. It ain't like him to keep so quiet."

He paused. "It could be the old buzzard had his shotgun out for Finley and was hiding in the swamp and a 'gator got him."

Joe Hall yawned and said, "Watts was weaned in that swamp. He knows every one of them 'gators by their first name."

Len was looking down the highway. "Isn't that Luke Finley's Ford?"

Joe said, "That's Finley all right. I'd know that engine knock anywhere."

Earl said, "Now I wonder what he wants."

When Finley got to Watts' driveway he steered around one of the big ruts and parked in the middle of the drive. As he crossed over to the men he relit his cigar. When he walked he didn't swing his arms. He moved along as if on oil.

He said, "I never seen it so hot. I had to prop up the hood to get circulation. Damn car is a hundred and eighty before I lay a hand on it."

Joe Hall stretched and stood up. "Finley, you haven't heard from Watts, have you?"

Finley smiled and said, "That's why I stopped by. I'll read this letter after I get some water."

He drank from the spigot. He didn't use his hands but put his lips around the filthy thing the dogs licked and drank. Wiping his mouth and leaning against one of the gas pumps he said, "Ah, that's better. I got this letter from Watts this morning. He's still in Macon."

Finley drew a folded sheet of paper from his trouser pocket. His eyes traveled down the single page. "Here, I'll read this part. '. . . And what's more, I have a dog that I am entering against that hell-bred means of support you are claiming is a pit-fighter. I am betting one thousand dollars. The odds are still four to one, so you had better start raising the four thousand. I will be in town Friday for the betting at twelve o'clock. After that, I don't want to see that face of yours until the fight at noon on Saturday.' "

Finley coughed and sat down. "The rest is of a more personal note."

He slipped the letter in his shirt pocket. "I'm covering all bets at four to one. Spread the word around. If I ain't around, leave the money at Bill's."

That Friday, Watts was in his store. All day long the men asked him what he was fighting the cat with. He wouldn't talk. During lunch when the men had all left I said, "Mr. Watts, where did you get a pit dog?"

He was tying rice packages. He had weighed a dozen half-pound bags and as he tamped the rice down tight he said, "Boy, I've had one. . . . I just keep him quiet. That's all."

He popped the string between his knuckles and reached for another bag. "Now get out of here and get your dinner. I'm not answering any more questions."

Later that afternoon, Len Bishop asked me if I wanted to walk with him over to Watts' house. The store had been closed at four.

As we crossed the yard, Watts' hounds raised their heads. The dogs all knew us. None of them barked. Only the small puppies of Belle made any noise. The rest were lying in the shaded corners of the fence and under the thick peach tree in the middle of the yard. There were three or four under the house sleeping against the cool bricks of the chimney. Red wasn't in sight. When he didn't come out to see us I figured he was under the house.

A hen fanned her brood of biddies toward the water trough. On the low clothesline a pair of overall pants and a blue work shirt hung motionless.

Watts met us at the door. "Hurry in, boys. Keep those flies outside."

We closed the screen door quickly.

Watts said, "How 'bout some iced tea?"

He chipped ice into two large glasses and sliced a lemon in quarters. Len pulled a cane-bottom chair away from the kitchen table. Len was slightly younger than Watts but he was taller and thinner. He sat down heavily. "Logan, I'm worried. I don't mean I'm worried about the two hundred I bet on your dog. I'm worried about you."

He stirred three spoons of sugar into his tea. "You know you said 'dog' in your letter to Finley. Now I want to know, Logan, and I want to know now, do you have a dog?"

Watts said, "I got me a dog, Len."

"Where?"

"Out in the yard."

Len stood up. "You mean to sit there and tell me you're going to let one of your hounds get in that pit with Finley's cat?"

"I am."

"You're kidding me, Logan. You're kidding."

"Len, I got three dogs in that yard that can handle that

cat. Sport could do it, Tag could do it, Red could do it."

I interrupted, "Is it Red?"

"It is. He's the strongest and I can count on him. He looked fine in Macon."

Len walked across the room. "God almighty, Logan, what in the hell could you teach him in Macon?"

"How to fight Finley's cat, that's what."

"Does Red know he's fighting a wildcat?"

Watts said, "He knows."

He got up and went to the screen door. He called the dog. "Red . . . come on, boy."

The big red and white hound slid through the screen door. His eyes were calm and brown. He looked sleepy. He had been under the house. He wagged his tail when he saw me but continued on to Watts. Red sat down and placed his head in Watts' lap. His long tail thudded softly on the floor.

No one spoke for a while. The water began to drip on an empty pan in the sink.

Len looked squarely into Watts' eyes. "Can that dog fight?"

Watts ran his thumb down the wet tea glass. "He can fight and he knows how to fight. Now that's all I'm going to say about it."

They talked about the betting, how over four thousand had been bet against the cat and how Finley had said he could cover it with sixteen thousand.

While they talked, Red came over to me. I made a fist and he opened his mouth and softly chewed on it. The mouth was tender and warm. As the dog rolled his mouth around my fist I thought of the biddies in the yard. The smallest weakest biddy would be safe in that soft retriever mouth.

That night I lay awake and tossed back and forth. I was perspiring and my heart was pounding. I watched the moonlight on the far wall and wondered if Red would cry out when he felt the cat's claws. The pit bulldog had made no sound, but they were bred and trained for fighting. Red had been trained for birds, for rabbits, for coons.

In the shadows on the wall I saw Red standing before the cat. It was raking its long claws over Red's lowered head.

I got up and went to the kitchen. Sitting down at the table I outlined a small square on the oil cloth. It was the pit. Would the sun be in all of the corners or would there be a spot of shade for the dog to die in? There would be flies if Red died. I'd make Watts let me bury him all by myself. I'd carry him from the pit, the blood would get on me. I wouldn't mind.

The jukebox was playing loudly in the dance hall and all the lights were on. In the distance an owl made a low sad noise.

Next morning Grady and I went to the pit early. We were going to build a shelter to protect Red from the sun. Grady had a short saw, I carried a hatchet. I cut down four small scrub oak trees. After sharpening the tops I gave them to Grady to square off. He laid the four pieces side by side and marked them with the saw blade.

When he had them cut, we drove the spiked ends into the ground. The rest was easy. Chipping away some of the long branches from the larger trees, we laid a roof over the four posts. We piled the roof higher and higher to keep out the heat and the flies.

When we finished I walked over to the pit. From the edge I could see the spade marks in the hard clay near the sharp corners. The red clay was firm and none had fallen from the steep banks. The bottom was clean and hard. I thought of Red and stared at the spot where the pit bulldog had died. The mark of the blood was gone. I wondered who had cleaned it up.

Watts arrived early with Red. They came through the woods and across Jenkins' field as we had done. The dog walked slowly behind him and when Watts stopped, he stopped.

Watts brought him over to the shelter. He said that the

shelter was a good idea and motioned Red under the low roof. Red scratched at the earth to scrape away the hot surface. He circled twice, as if he were looking for something, and lay down. He put his nose close to the fresh soil and in a few minutes he was asleep.

I didn't want to talk to Watts. I walked back to the pit. Nothing had changed except now there was a bucket of white lime at the edge. I stood there for a while and watched the crowd gather. I pulled a boll from a dead cotton stalk and walked between the benches and the soft-drink cases that would be used for seats, walked back toward Red. He was still asleep and Grady was shooing the flies away with a long pine branch. As I watched him sleep I broke the boll along the seam. Grady was quiet. I could think of nothing to say. I broke the two black pieces in half again and let them drop one by one to the ground.

The mule-drawn wagons and three or four cars had bumped and clattered over the old cotton rows, but most of the crowd came on foot. A few of the men had come from as far away as Charleston and Savannah. A rumor went around that a state senator was in the crowd but nobody knew him.

Watts had mentioned in his letter that he wanted to place a small stool right at the corner of the pit. Luke Finley had agreed on condition that Watts let himself be searched for a gun or knife. Everything was ready.

At eleven-fifty Watts took his seat on the stool. He called Red over from his shelter.

"Okay now, boy," he said, "I want you to jump down there."

He snapped his fingers once. Red slid down the pit side and jumped the last three feet. The pit was about eleven feet square and eight feet deep. Red moved into the shade cast by Watts' shadow. He sat still for a minute and then stretched out with his eyes closed.

"The son of a gun's going to sleep," someone said.

There had been rumors that some of the boys weren't

going to allow Red to fight. When Red stretched out Earl Estee jumped up.

"What the hell, Watts! Let's call this thing off! I've seen enough!"

Watts said, "It's my dog and I know what I am doing. Now don't bother me."

Len Bishop said, "Leave him alone, Earl."

Earl mumbled something and sat down.

Finley and his friend carried the cat's cage up to the edge of the pit. Finley stopped.

"Okay, Watts, I want to make sure you ain't carrying a gun."

Watts frowned. "Okay, Finley, but I won't have your filthy hands on me. Send one of your boys over."

After the search everyone leaned forward. This was it. Everything was ready.

Watts said, "Okay, Red, here we go, boy."

I looked down at Red's eyes and my heart almost broke. I felt as though the dog were my brother. I remembered the bulldog with no stomach.

Luke Finley took his hooked stick and raised the door at the cage. The cat was swishing back and forth. He was furious at the heat and the crowd and the cage.

For a minute he wouldn't come out, but then he saw the pit and he remembered. He slid down the side the way Red had and jumped from four feet. He landed in the middle of the pit and whirled to face Red. His back was hunched up and he was taller than Red. His claws were out on his front paws and they looked like razors.

Red was up. He started moving around the cat. He circled the cat while Watts talked to him.

"Easy, boy. Easy now . . . just like in Macon, boy. Just like in Macon."

Red moved around the cat counterclockwise. By moving this way he kept both eyes on the cat and avoided the sun's glare. The cat was ready. The thick muscles in his hind legs bunched and quivered. All he needed was one shot at the hound's belly. His thick back legs could do it in two seconds. The cat wanted Red to charge. Red might have charged, at least the crowd thought he might, but he didn't. He kept on circling with his head pointed straight at the cat.

Watts kept on in a low easy steady voice.

"Easy, boy . . . easy now . . . you remember . . . just like Macon, boy . . . just like Macon."

The pit had large splotches of lime around to kill the smell of blood. It was white but where the shade lay in the corners it looked gray. Red began to track through it. About the third time around a circle of tracks began to appear. The sun was overhead but the sharp shade line was beginning to soften.

There wasn't a sound. People were swallowing coughs and straining themselves not to shift on the hard seats. The hundred-and-one-degree sun meant nothing. No one was conscious of their soaking wet shirts or their limp collars—only of the two circles being slowly inscribed eight feet below on the lime-splotched Carolina clay.

Every minute or so Watts would come in with, "Good boy Red, . . . easy boy . . . easy Red, . . . just like Macon boy, . . . just ex-act-ly like Macon."

Red moved at the same speed, never gaining or losing a step. Slowly, methodically, moving around, listening to Watts for encouragement and keeping every muscle alive for anything. Red's eyes had changed. The soft brown had given away to a hard cold black. Red had class. When the cat would feint as if to attack, Red wouldn't even break his stride or blink his eyes.

And Watts was there all the time with his "Just like Macon Red, . . . easy boy."

The wildcat had won nine fights. Only one dog had lived more than two minutes. They all had died with the same wound—their stomachs had been opened.

The cat would trade anything—one, five, fifty of whatever Red had for that one shot at his stomach. One countermove was all he needed. His neck muscles, at first invisible beneath the short fur, now bunched and quivered.

He spat, bared his teeth, clawed the ground, shifted quickly, angrily. The spot he was in was heating. He had to jump. He had to do something.

He rushed forward two feet and braked. He spat, clawed at the air, and began hissing and backing up at the same time.

Red didn't miss a stride.

Finley shouted, "What the hell! What the hell's going on? This ain't no fight. This ain't nothing."

"Shut up, Finley."

"Shut up, hell. Look at him. He ain't fighting. Sic 'em, hound. Get him, you flea-bitten egg-sucker."

Red didn't hear Finley. Red only heard Watts who, through Finley's shouts, kept up his "Easy boy, . . . easy Red, . . . just like Macon boy."

And the big dog kept on. The thin white line was now solid. The sun had passed the point where it struck the pit bottom. Still Red circled with that same fixed, idiotic look, his head pointed in, his body out.

I wondered if Red's neck might not freeze in that position. Would he be too stiff to do anything if the cat charged? Was Red getting tired by now? Maybe they would call the fight a draw.

The cat still moved in his small circle. He was now sliding around rather than shifting around. His stubbed tail was on the ground and his front legs moved his body around. He had begun to wear the small circle of clay down to a slick finish.

The cat began to twitch violently. His nerves had taken over again and they were pushing him forward. He hunched up high, the long hair bristled all the way down his spine. He moved forward as if to spring. He feinted, spat and backed up again.

Ten more times, twelve more times around and still nothing.

Red looked calm, almost soft. His pace had never changed.

Some circles were larger than others, some rounder than others, but his stride, his speed, his position never changed.

Watts' voice sounded lower now. "Easy boy, easy now, . . . a little more time . . . a little more time boy . . . just like in Macon boy . . . just ex-act-ly like Macon."

The crowd said nothing, not one word. The tension was impossible, something had to break. Once more Red went around, slowly deliberately, head turned in, body out, eyes fixed, with Watt's low steady voice sounding like an incantation.

And then the cat decided to take a short cut. Instead of spinning his entire body around he moved his head to its farthest position without shifting his body and then whipped his head back to the other side.

Watts' voice, still steady . . . "Just like Macon . . ." but by this time everything sounded the same. The next time Red went around I saw a thin quiver behind his neck.

Then it happened. The cat did the same thing. He didn't move around but looked over his shoulder as far as he could and then whipped his head back to the other side.

I have never seen anything move as fast as that long hound moved in that split second. As the cat whipped his head back Red jumped. The position he was in was made for that jump. Everything was ready. By the time the cat had his head halfway around, Red had sunk his teeth into his neck. He leaped up over the cat and shook him three times with all of the strength from all of the hounds that ever crossed the Piedmont. The bone broke twice.

The cat was dead when Red dropped him. Watts let out a rebel yell that nearly broke my ear drums and dropped down into the pit and picked Red up in his arms. Watts was crying.

He tossed the big hound up to me.

"You're alive," I said to him and held his sleek, sweating, wiggling body in my arms. It was impossible to believe that he had actually killed the cat. It was not only impossible, it was unnecessary. My only thought was that he was alive.

He licked my face. I could feel the long tail slapping my legs. Someone taller took him from me and hoisted him up. They passed him around. The crowd had to touch him.

Red was great. Red was absolutely the most terrific dog in the world. His tail was flopping back and forth and he had that beautiful hound smile on his face. He couldn't have been happier. I have never been happier.

Watts chased me and Grady out of the store at suppertime. We came back after dark but the door was locked. From the rear window we saw them in there drinking "moon" and telling stories. Red was right in the middle gnawing on a big T-bone steak and flopping his tail back and forth. . . .

EUGENE TALMADGE
AND SEARS
ROEBUCK CO.

LET ME TELL you about Eugene Herman Talmadge. He's been dead a long time now and his son's a big man now, but the folks around here talk about Old Gene so much it's hard imagining him gone.

Everybody saw him and everyone remembers him and those that didn't see him will lie like hell and say they did.

But some nights when the wind is right and the air is right and the 'gators and the frogs are quiet and the Negroes aren't shooting craps and making a lot of fuss right under the window, you can hear Old Gene shouting out there on that flat red clay in front of the feed store, or else stomping back and forth in those steel-heeled brogans on Thompson's gallery.

But let me tell you about him. . . .

First of all, when he came to town the school and the poolroom and the feed store would close down. And then they'd start coming—through the windows and through the doors. I don't know where they didn't come from. There weren't too many roads then and every mule and buckboard and Ford would come flopping out of the back country and across the fields and through the drain ditch and up onto Route 1. Route 1 was narrow in those days, only two lanes and no shoulders, and some of those mules couldn't stand the sight of cars. And some of those Ford drivers couldn't stand the sight of other Ford drivers.

Well, the mules would start kicking the cars and there

would be the first fight. And then the Ford drivers would race across a fallow field or down the highway and, win, lose or draw, there would be another fight. And finally they'd lock front bumpers and see which six-cylinder engine was in better shape. They'd push one another back and forth until one would go skidding down into the drain ditch between the field and the highway. And then all the mules would be needed to come pull them out. The drivers would make up and they'd start drinking right down there in that drain ditch where the wives couldn't see them.

Gene usually carried a musician along. I guess you could call him a musician; he played a four-string guitar, which isn't much to listen at, and he had him a harmonica wired from his collar to his mouth. He'd play a hymn to get it started and then one of those freight-train songs with a lot of the same bass chords on the guitar and a lot of sucking noises on the mouth harp. You know what I mean. . . .

There wasn't much music around then and everyone would slap their hands and pat their feet. And somebody would say, "Lord, listen at him," and "It's exactly like a train," and "Will you study that man's fingers." And this fellow, he'd probably be from Macon or Valdosta, would grin like an ape and he'd play faster and louder and suck that fool mouth harp until you thought his eyeballs would pop right out. An if Old Gene wasn't there to stop him he'd play himself crazy.

But Old Gene was there and he'd come out on the gallery or else get up on the tailgate and he'd ease his hand onto the musician's shoulder. "Easy now, Sheldon, easy now. Let 'em down slow now. I'm here to get some votes."

And he'd smile out at the crowd and they'd grin right back. "I don't want these good folks getting all worked up and go dancing off into that swamp."

Then he'd laugh and they would laugh and then he'd say, "They can't vote from out there."

And old Sheldon would grin and he'd play a little more alto and no bass and all the time the train sound on the mouth harp would be getting fainter and fainter and farther away. And finally we'd listen at it disappear into some green hills or mountains and we standing right there on that flat clay in Calhoun County. I got to admit, he was pretty good when he did that. The men's eyes would be shining and some of the women would be in tears.

Old Gene would wait a while. One thing you got to say for Gene . . . that rascal knew how to wait. He had the longest pause in the state.

Then he'd stop waiting. He'd rare back on those steel heels and dig his thumbs into his wide red suspenders. He always wore a pair of overall pants and a blue shirt, big buck brogan shoes, a flat canary yellow wide-brimmed straw hat and those fancy loud orange-red suspenders with brass catches, latches and slides. Oh, he was something all right. He wasn't big but he looked big, you know what I mean? A big smile, a bright gold tooth and those blue eyes . . . he had the derndest eyes you ever saw. They sparkled when he wanted them to like he had just come from some secret war or something. Like he'd seen it all and heard it all and he'd kept it secret just for us. Like it had been a hard secret to keep but he had saved it for us and now that he was among his friends he was going to whisper it to us.

"Howdy, folks."

I know it sounds corny but that's where he was great. He could take those two words and make them into something personal, something so special you could feel the crowd kind of folding in towards him . . . no lie, I mean it. He could really do that thing.

Then he'd turn those eyes on and make them think some enemy was listening from the swamp or from the end of the drain ditch. The crowd would look over their shoulders and they'd move closer.

And now the crowd was ready and Old Gene was ready. Hell, I don't know why he ever had to speak around here. He never lost more than seventeen votes all total in all of

Calhoun County the whole time he was in office. I guess he just liked to feel that crowd around him.

Well, he'd start off with some mule or nigger joke and the crowd would laugh until he had to make them stop. And then his old routine . . . it went like this. . . .

"Everybody getting plenty to eat?"

A few people in the crowd would say, "We're all right, Gene."

"Well, let me hear it. . . ."

Then the whole crowd: "We're all right, Gene."

There were two men leaning on a buckboard about thirty yards back and two more sitting in a Ford by the drain ditch.

Gene raised his voice, "How 'bout you men back there? You, Peevy, what do you say?"

"We're fine, Gene."

"Now that's better. You know I got to save my voice for that Atlanta crowd. Now let's see. . . ." He'd hold up his left hand and start counting fingers with his right.

"You asked for a new road near Amos Jones' field and you got it . . . right?"

"That's right, Gene."

Second finger . . . "You asked for a new room on the school and you got that . . . right?"

"That's right, Gene."

"You wanted some help on the church and a coat of paint and you got that, and the crop dusting, and the poll tax . . . right?"

"That's right, Gene."

"And you got that new well and ditch up near Peevy's place and all that good, free, clean, convict labor . . . right?"

"That's right, Gene."

"Well then, everybody's all right then."

And he'd smile hard and his eyes would flash. He'd pull his suspenders way out and hold them out while he smiled. And he'd stand like that while the crowd roared. And then real easy-like he'd stop smiling and start easing up on his suspenders. The crowd would sense it and they'd start quieting down. Then Gene stopped smiling and turned his suspenders loose. The crowd grew silent. Gene looked serious, and then more serious. There would be no sound from the crowd. Small boys stopped moving, dogs stood still, Sheldon stopped picking his nose. Gene glared into the swamp at the enemy. The tension grew. You could have heard a grasshopper fart.

"There's some talk going on around this state. . . ." He stopped, looked at the swamp, at the field, at the drain ditch. He leaned forward and began talking low.

"There's a lot of talk going on now. A lot of talk. A lot of foul, filthy, low, rotten-egg-sucking talk that I'm stealing money. That I'm stealing money, lying, cheating and laying around in them (pardon me, ladies) Savannah houses. . . ."

Someone shouted, "All lies, Gene."

"Let me finish, Murdock. I want it all out in the open. Now I've always said that if it's the truth it will out. And if it's the truth and I'm guilty of all these things, I want you to know here and now that I'll step right down out of this office and let the accuser take over. Now haven't I always said that?"

"You have, Gene," Murdock said. "All lies, Gene, all damn foul lies. Tell us, Gene. Let's hear his name, Gene. Tell me the sonofabitch's name and I'll fix his ass."

"Hush now, Murdock. Excuse him, ladies. No, no more, Murdock. I want this conducted in an orderly manner. Well, I know you're my friends and probably my only friends. I tell you I get down in that Atlanta town and I can't tell who's biting me in the back. I know you want his name. I also know if I give you his name it won't go no farther than that drain ditch. No farther than my own people."

"Tell us, Gene."

Gene folded his hands in front and stared the crowd down again. "How many of us are blameless?"

[48]

He found Preacher Stuckey in the crowd and talked right at him. "How many of us are blameless? How many of us have laid awake thinking of ways to sin?"

Stuckey said, "Amen."

"Thoughts of anger, lust, greed. I say all of us. You and me and all of us. Every man jack one of us is guilty—and I mean we know it. How many men right here, right now . . . how many women right here, right now, can raise their hands and say they have a clear conscience—right now at this moment?"

There were no hands.

"I say very few, very few. Indeed, very few."

"Amen."

Gene bowed his head. "I'd like to mention this fellow's name but it ain't fair. I am guilty of so many things before God. I don't want to add the sin of informing on one of my fellow men. I am guilty of so many things but I try to overcome them. Lord, I keep trying and I'm going to try now. I don't believe I can reveal this man's name and consider myself a good Christian."

"Amen."

Gene paused again and then finished up with: "All I ask is that when these rumors start spreading over this fair county, I want you to think back to this day when Old Gene stood before you and begged for your forgiveness and your understanding."

Great burst of applause. . . .

"We're with you, Gene. . . . We're with you, Gene."

Gene let them settle down and then he waved Sheldon back on with his music. And then after the music . . . the grand finale.

Gene stood in the very center of the gallery and rared up as tall as he could and snapped his suspenders. He addressed the men and the women in the back row,

"You got three friends in this here world and I want you to know it."

"Tell us, Gene."

He raised one finger, pointed it at the sun and spoke to the back row and the two men leaning on the buckboard.

"You got Sears Roebuck Company—and I want you to know it."

"That's right, Gene."

A second finger . . . a louder voice to the back row . . . the two leaning on the buckboard and the two seated in the Ford by the drain ditch drinking corn whisky out of a mayonnaise jar.

"You got God Almighty—and I want you to know it."

"That's right, Gene."

And then he crashed his steel heels into the gallery boards, snapped his suspenders, rared back like he was going to lift a whole bale of cotton single-handed and roared to the men by the buckboard, the men in the Ford, to the sky, the swamp and down the drain ditch the length of Calhoun County. . . .

"And you got Eugene Herman Talmadge of Sugar Hill, Georgia, and I want you to know it."

THE ORDEAL
OF LONNIE REGISTER

WHEN LONNIE REGISTER came into the drugstore and casually announced that he'd just drunk a pint of rubbing alcohol, everybody got pretty excited. Doc Daniels took his pulse, checked his pupils, and crouched down and listened to his heart for a full three minutes.

Doc kept shaking his head and saying he couldn't understand it. He finally stood up and said that Lonnie was all right. Lonnie is a short little fellow no more than five foot five, but he's hard as stone. He has a horseshoe of black hair around the back of his almost flat head and a few strands on top that he combs forward into a fine point. He has fierce bushy eyebrows and small black eyes.

The rubbing alcohol hadn't made him drunk and he strutted up and down the counter eating Lance's peanut-butter-and-cheese crackers.

M. L. Anderson came in and Lonnie sang out, "How 'bout it, M. L.?"

"How 'bout what, Lonnie?"

"Me knocking down a pint of Rub and ain't even sweating."

"That's pretty good, Lonnie. But you better keep out of that sun. . . . What did it cost you?"

"Fifteen, maybe seventeen cents. You can't beat that, can you?"

"I guess not."

Pig Hobson stood at the end of the counter near the potato chips. He waited until Lonnie was through talking. Pig cleared his throat and called Lonnie down to the end. "Lonnie, you feel kinda raspy down in here?"

He pointed to a spot on Lonnie's cowboy scarf three inches below his large Adam's apple.

Lonnie said, "Yeah, Pig. Right there. How'd you know?"

Pig lit his pipe, paused a minute. "Next time you drink Rub you add in a stick of cinnamon and a pinch of chicory."

Lonnie looked puzzled for a minute. He raised his fist and slammed it on the counter. "Goddammit!"

The potato-chip rack fell over. Pig picked it up.

Lonnie shouted, "Dammit, Pig. Why come you do that?"

"Do what?"

"You know what. Always low-rating my stories. That's what."

Pig looked serious. The lids were half closed on his big eyes. "I was merely trying to be helpful."

Pig and Lonnie were door-to-door salesmen for the same company. They sold kerosene lamps, chenille bed spreads, hairbrush and mirror sets, and religious statues and plaques that glowed in the dark. They called on the colored trade and the mill hands that lived in the Strawberry Hill district and down along the canal banks. In order to demonstrate their lamps and phosphorescent articles, they had to make their calls at night.

Lonnie worked six times harder than Pig or, for that matter, anyone else, but he always sold less. Some nights he'd make as many as twenty calls down the dark streets without a sale. Pig would make two calls and he would make two sales.

Anyhow, it was kind of funny and kind of sad about Lonnie Register. The pressure of selling and of selling against Pig would get him, and every six or seven weeks he'd cut loose and start drinking. It would be that spitting-in-the-dirt, below-the-belt, loud, wild-type drunk. The police would have to hit him in the head or strap him down to get him to the jail. He'd get fined fifty dollars and have to work ten days on the gang. He didn't have to wear stripes or hook on to the chain, but there would be a man in a black hat on shotgun and a couple of sleepy-looking bloodhounds out there panting in the heat.

The road gang was doing a lot of work along Mulberry Avenue right in front of the drugstore and about four houses from Lonnie's house. Well, one morning we look out and there's Lonnie on rake with his head down low and his cap down low. He had one eye on his front porch and one eye on the drugstore. His wife had the front door closed. The kids were shut up in the back.

Pig got his name because of his eyes being so small. He didn't have much distant vision. He didn't see poor old Lonnie out there and no one was about to mention it to him. Well, it looked like Lonnie was going to escape detection when all of a sudden his big Labrador rushed through one of the hedges and ran up to Lonnie and jumped all over him. Lonnie tried to shoo the dog away but you know how Labradors are. Well, when Pig saw that he squinted his eyes up and started smiling. He stepped to the front of the store and cupped his hands.

"Hey, Lonnie. Lonnie Register. I thought you were up in Walterboro on business."

Lonnie figured he had to beat Pig down because of the road-gang embarrassment. It was on a Saturday around six. Everybody was in the drugstore. Lonnie told how he had drunk a full quart of Old Crow. How two cops beat him on the head and beat him against the curb and how he had laughed at them. They had to get two more cops to drag him in. How he set fire to the mattress in jail, pulled up the toilet and flooded the floor and shouted so loud they had to put him in a straitjacket and tape his mouth.

Lonnie Register finished his story and stepped back. He looked at Pig. We all looked at Pig.

Pig smiled. You know, that no-teeth, soft, rubbery smile when they're holding four of a kind?

"That's pretty drunk, Lonnie. That's pretty drunk."

We all got in close.

"Yessir, that's what I call a pretty good drunk."

Lonnie's face began to fall. He could read the "but I remember" in Pig's smile. Pig lit his pipe, rolled his eyes around to make sure everyone was present.

"But I remember once . . . it was down in Mobile, Alabama. Any of you boys been there? Yeah, down in Mobile. I'd been drinking that absinthe. You all know that absinthe isn't allowed in the country. But you can get it down in Mobile and a couple of places in New Orleans. I mean you can get it if you know the right people. Anyhow, you know how drunk I got on that absinthe?"

"How drunk, Pig?"

"I got seat-stabbing drunk. That's how drunk."

"What's that?"

"Well, I came out of this absinthe house. Been there a couple of days or so. I came out and I couldn't tell if it was sun or moon."

Lonnie eased out of the crowd and went over to the beer case. He didn't want to hear the rest.

"I got me a cab and sat back. Next thing you know I've got my pocketknife out and I'm down there stabbing the leather seats. That absinthe was driving me crazy. You all know I'm a quiet sort. But man, I got loose on that stuff. Whup —whup, up to the hilt. I stabbed a while then slashed a while. When I finished up on the seat I started working on the door paneling and the roof. The cab driver saw me but he was too scared to do anything."

"So that's seat-stabbing drunk?"

"Yessir, that's what it is. Every now and then you'll hear about it. But not very often."

Lonnie came back. He was lipping the bottle of beer and

had a funny look in his eye. He counted on his fingers to eight.

He shouted, "Damn you, Pig. Damn you anyway."

We grabbed him. Lonnie's voice was strained, hysterical. "Don't worry, I ain't going to swing at that lying bastard. Listen, you, Pig. You listen."

We cleared a path. They were facing one another. Lonnie was hysterical and jumping. Pig was calm and packing his pipe.

"Maybe you've been drunker than me. Maybe you've done more and better of everything than me."

His face was white, his upper lip was wet. He set his beer on the counter. He was shaking. "But I've got you now, Pig. I've got you."

He counted quickly on his fingers to eight. "Okay, Pig, if you win this one . . . I won't give you any more trouble."

Pig lit his pipe and closed his eyes. "All right, Lonnie. What you got?"

Lonnie smiled, "I slept in worse places than you."

He was too nervous to pause for an effect.

"One . . . on a pool table with my feet in the end pockets.

"Two . . . in a goat pen.

"Three . . . under a car with the grease dripping on me.

"Four . . . in a chicken coop."

He screamed these last four together: "In bed with four gypsies and a dog. In a bowling alley gutter. . . . In . . . in . . . in . . . in a refrigerator car at thirty-two degrees Fahrenheit from Mobile to Atlanta. On a slant tin roof with my feet in the drain gutter!"

We almost applauded. Lonnie was sweating and his teeth were chattering. He drank his beer and ordered two more.

We asked him questions. How he got out of the refrigerated car. How he got on the roof. He answered them all and kept looking at Pig. We ran out of questions. Lonnie began repeating himself. He ran through the list again. . . .

And then Pig coughed. "I don't suppose any of you fellows every stayed at the Rope?"

"The Rope? What's that?"

"A hotel."

"Where?"

"In Charleston."

You could hear the beer-cooler motor going.

"The Rope is a very famous hotel in Charleston. I'm surprised Lonnie here hasn't stayed there. . . . Well, I mean it's like a hotel in that they charge you. The rates vary. It's thirty-five cents in the early evening, but as it gets later the rates gets lower. Around about midnight you can get a place for a dime."

"A dime?"

"A dime."

"A dime for a room?"

"Well, it's not exactly a room. It's more like a place. The room is long. Oh, say, about seventy feet long, maybe even eighty feet. The best places are in the middle. Cost thirty-five cents to a quarter there. The dime places are all towards the end. It isn't so bad in the middle. It's kind of level there."

"What's kind of level, Pig? You lost me."

"The Rope. This big six-inch hawser line. You know the kind they tie the big ships up with. That's what you sleep on. It runs the length of the room."

"How do you sleep on it?"

"Simple. You just lean over it. Nothing to it. Of course it's easier when you're pretty drunk or pretty tired. It's best when you're both. But you pay the man and you go in. First come, first serve. The dime places are pretty close to the wall and the rope is on an angle. It gets pretty bad out there.

"I was lucky. I got in early and got near the middle. I didn't care much for the clientele but I must say I did get me a pretty good night's sleep. . . ."

We looked around for Lonnie. Doc said he had gone out the back way.

FAST NERVES

WHEN THE SHERIFF of Four Holes, South Carolina, broke up Greenwood Keho's poker game, he took all the money on the table and all Grennwood's cards. The cards were Bee Brand strippers from a magician's mail-order house in Chicago and cost thirty-five dollars a deck.

Greenwood got mad. He stormed outside to his car, got his .38 Colt automatic out of the glove compartment and started for the sheriff. Between the top step and the screen door someone hit him in the head with a piece of stovewood.

He awoke in the morning with his friend, Chauncey Jones, watching over him.

"I'm sorry, Greenwood," Chauncey said. "I didn't mean to hit you so hard."

"You did right, Chauncey. You did right."

"Does it hurt, Greenwood?"

Greenwood looked up and squinted his blue eyes. "I'll be all right, good buddy. Don't worry so." He groaned, "I go crazy like that . . . happens every once in a while. Too much tension."

Chauncey said, "You did look a little tense."

Greenwood sat up and looked at Chauncey. "I wouldn't tell just anybody about it, Chauncey, but you're my friend. And you might as well know."

"Know what?"

"I got fast nerves."

"No lie?"

"No lie."

Greenwood lay back down. "How'd you like to leave this town, Chauncey?"

Greenwood and Chauncey stopped in front of the sign: WELCOME TO FOUR HOLES, S.C., POPULATION 492. Greenwood got out of the car with a black crayon in his hand. He changed the numeral "2" in "492" to a big zero, pissed on the signpost, and after kicking the post where he'd pissed he limped back to his 1948 Ford, gunned the engine, and roared off down Route 78. . . .

He drove fast. Chauncey kept looking at the speedometer and smoking black cigars.

Greenwood said, "Chaunce, you know what they say about Charleston?"

Chauncey watched the needle on 68. "What they say?"

"They say Charleston is when the Ashley and the Cooper Rivers come together and form the Atlantic Ocean."

"How 'bout that."

They hit Charleston going seventy miles an hour and didn't make a dent. They checked in at the De Soto Tourist Camp, cooked their meals on a hot plate, and began looking for work.

Chauncey looked all day and Greenwood looked all night. Chauncey picked up a job as a mechanic for the OK Chevrolet Company and Greenwood got a foot in the door of the Blue Moon dealing blackjack on the twenty-five-cent table.

Greenwood dealt blackjack for two weeks and then he got a break. The shell-game operator had to leave for Tacoma, Washington, one night and Greenwood was promoted.

He liked the feel of the walnut shells and he was good. He moved them slow with the tips of his long fingers and never talked much. People trusted him behind the table and he knew how to treat the big losers.

Greenwood knew that no one works a shell game long.

After he had put two thousand dollars in a sock and put the sock in a shoe and the shoe in his suitcase, he figured he'd had enough. But the manager liked him and before he knew it he was dealing on the big poker table with a take-home, tax-free salary of three hundred a week.

And the games were big. Big pot limit, sky limit, games with every big gambler in the country. Big men from Miami, San Francisco, Las Vegas, and New York City. There were big stud-poker butter-and-egg men from Milwaukee, a big butcher from Des Moines and a man who they claimed had inherited Chicago from Al Capone.

Greenwood's take went from three hundred to five hundred a week, but he wanted more and he wanted it faster. . . .

Chauncey plugged away doing ring jobs and carburetor jobs and finally worked himself up to hydramatic clutch service. He came home filthy every night. He had to wash himself with gasoline and Ajax cleanser. While Greenwood would be combing his black hair into a careful pompadour and roughing up his long sideburns, Chauncey would be scrubbing away with a stiff bristled brush.

One night Greenwood said. "Next week, good buddy, you tell that OK Chevrolet man to kiss your ass."

He shook some Old Spice after-shave lotion into his hand and patted it onto his face.

Chauncey stopped brushing, "What's up?"

"Next week I open my own place and you become my manager."

"Man, what I know about managing?"

Greenwood laughed and placed his hand on Chauncey's shoulder.

"Back there in Four Holes, that piece of stovewood alongside my head . . . that's managing."

So Chauncey quit the OK Chevrolet job, bought and put on a Hart Schaffner & Marx suit, lit up a Corona-Corona and became Greenwood's manager.

And Greenwood needed a manager. He quit the Blue Moon and took a suite of rooms near the Battery at the Pinckney Arms. He opened his own game. It was a big sky-limit game with free whisky, beer, and French cooking.

He hired a girl named Mildred Oakes as a manicurist at a hundred dollars a week for five settings. She did his nails long and narrow and used a transparent polish with a little green in it. She was good and she was careful. She used a magnifying glass when she worked on his middle fingers. Here she had built in a little nick for clipping cards that was as sharp as a razor. Greenwood could mark a fresh deck of cards as quick as he could get his hands on it.

Greenwood bought a black, bullet-proofed, custom-made Buick with super-chargers, twin carburetors and velvet curtains. It looked like a hearse and drank gas like a tractor. Chauncey could fill up the twenty-eight gallon gas tank, go across town twice and have to stop at the Esso station on the way back for another tank.

At the Pinckney Arms, they took a whole floor and a private elevator. Greenwood had a round bed, a round mirror up on the ceiling directly above the bed, a French chandelier, French furniture and telephones, and two rooms carpeted wall to wall in a long white hair that looked like Persian cat.

Greenwood kept Stella here. When he got tired of Stella, he moved her out and moved Gladys in. And then Ava. And then Mimi. And each one got a big bankroll, a mink coat and a ticket to New York City. . . .

In the center of the living room on a high marble pedestal stood a twenty-inch solid gold statue of Greenwood. In the statue he wore a derby hat, cutaway and tails, and he carried a straight cane. He was smiling. . . .

Greenwood had a roomful of suits, more shirts than he could count and more shoes than any man in Charleston. He had blacks, browns, and whites. He had brown and whites, black and whites, about seven shades of yellow, and one pair with seed pearls on the toes. Some looked like arrows, some like knives and some were so long and dagger-shaped that he could only wear them for thirty minutes at a time.

But his nerves started acting up and Chauncey had to watch him every minute. He began arguing with his women. His hands began to tremble. He couldn't sleep at night and he was too restless during the day to stay in the apartment. He began going to the movies; the Ritz, the Strand, the Century. Some days he'd see all three and then start back over. He saw *Godzilla, the Monster* seventeen times.

Greenwood Keho went to the top of the mountain, planted the flag, climbed the pole, grinned and leaped off head first. . . .

It happened in the Century Theatre. The matinee went on at ten-forty-eight. Greenwood sat in the third row. He had to tilt his head back to see all of the screen. The feature was Joseph Cotten in Jules Verne's *From the Earth to the Moon.*

Greenwood hadn't slept the night before. He was nervous. He clicked his long green fingernails on the chair arm and did a little toe-tapping shuffle with his dagger shoes. He had to keep moving his head back and forth to see all of the action on the wide Vista-Vision screen.

Joseph Cotten was showing a great crowd of people his new fuel, Power X, which was to take him to the moon and beyond. The scene was set. Power X was loaded and ready. Joseph Cotten waved the crowd back another thousand yards, unfastened the safety device and pulled the trigger. An atomic explosion filled the theater and the entire width of the Vista-Vision screen became a giant revolving ball of flame.

The trigger that Joseph Cotten pulled was connected to Greenwood Keho of Four Holes, South Carolina.

He rose up, stood in his seat and turned and faced the small prenoon crowd in the Century Theatre. Against the red flame and the crashing noise, he raised his arms and shouted: "My God, what a terrible explosion. . . . What a fantastic explosion. . . ."

"Down in front! Get that nut out of here!"

He shouted louder and stepped over the seat backs until he was in the middle of the crowd.

"Why, with that power I could rule the world. Rule it, you hear?"

Two ushers threw him out into the hot street. Chauncey was waiting in the Buick. In the ride back to the Pinckney Arms, Greenwood raved about being Joseph Cotten, Huey Long, Billy Sunday. When the car stopped he emerged Billy Sunday. But he was grander, wiser, more benevolent than Sunday. He could raise the dead, fertilize the land, cause fish to bite and most of all he could give away money.

He withdrew all of his money from the bank in five-dollar bills and started passing it out in front of the Francis Marion Hotel on Battery Park. Four thousand, ten thousand, twenty thousand, on and on . . . up and up . . . faster and faster. He gave to the old folks, the young folks, he gave it to the bums and the children and the mothers and if the dogs could have carried it they would gave gotten it.

He gave away his money, his clothes, his jewels, and his shoes. He fired his tailor and his manicurist and broke every mirror and piece of glass in his apartment. On the day before he was committed he had Chauncey drive the Buick down King Street and he sat up on the radiator. He shouted that he had control of Power X and that they should pay attention to him.

When they let Greenwood out of the home four months later, Chauncey was waiting. They drove up to the De Soto Tourist Camp and checked back into their old cabin.

Chauncey had his job back at the OK Chevrolet Company. He fed and took care of Greenwood and in the evenings he read him the news from the Charleston *News and Courier*. Three months passed and while Greenwood looked better and never talked about Billy Sunday or Power X he still couldn't hold a deck of cards.

"It's those fast nerves again, Chauncey."

"Take it easy, Greenwood."

"No, man, I tell you, they're back. I can feel them. They're like rubber bands all set to break."

Chauncey took him to the clinic and then to a doctor. Nothing worked. Finally they went to a psychiatrist. After two weeks they tried a shock treatment.

The next day Greenwood was a changed man. He could fan a deck of cards with one hand and could deal seconds and bottoms with no strain.

"Man, Chauncey. This is it. Look at those hands."

He held them out. They were as steady as ping-pong paddles.

"Looks good, Greenwood. Deal me a hand."

He dealt four fast hands of poker out on the coffee table. Chauncey turned his cards over. "Nothing."

Greenwood laughed, "I got them all. First time."

He turned over a royal flush of hearts. He went to the mirror and began practicing while Chauncey ran out and bought beer and barbecues.

Two nights later Greenwood was dealing dollar poker at the Blue Moon. He dealt a week and made two hundred dollars and stole two hundred. In the second week his hands felt clammy and began shaking. He had to have another shock treatment.

It got better and then it got worse. Every dollar he made went to the doctor. There was no getting ahead. He quit stealing. He began to worry. He lost his confidence and began playing honest poker. He wouldn't mark the cards or use strippers. He was too nervous to deal seconds or bottoms and anything really fancy was out. The Blue Moon manager began to watch him and he got more nervous. He kept a towel on his lap and kept drying his hands.

"Chauncey, I'm losing it all. I can feel it."

"You'll be all right, Greenwood. Relax, lie down a while."

"No, my hands feel like I got gloves on. The feeling's all gone. I tell you, it's those fast nerves again. They got me running. Did I tell you the manager's been sitting in on my games?"

"No."

"Well, he is."

Chauncey was scrubbing his hands with gasoline. "That's no good."

"If I could just get some money ahead and get about five of those shock treatments, I'd be set. I'd be all right then."

Chauncey poured the gasoline down the drain and shook Ajax on his hands.

"He give you any credit?"

"Hell, no. It's worse than dope. He knows I deal at the Moon and he wants cash every time."

Chauncey had the stiff-bristled brush going on his hands.

"How many volts they give you up on that table, Greenwood?"

"I don't know. Maybe a thousand."

"You know how many amperes?"

"You know I'm no electrical man. How would I know? All I know is that I jump up ten feet in the air when it hits and if it wasn't for those leather straps I'd be on the next floor."

Chauncey dried his hands carefully and began skinning out the rinds of grease under his fingernails with a matchbook cover. He studied his fingernails.

Chauncey opened the door. "You come with me."

He led him out to the Buick and patted the winged figure on the radiator.

"This old horse will kick up a thousand volts if I put her on the floor."

"Whoa now, Chauncey. If you think you're going to lash me to that hood you better think again."

Chauncey said, "No man, I wouldn't do it like that."

Greenwood said, "You aren't going to do it anyway, good buddy."

"Greenwood, you got to trust me. I know what I'm doing. I've taken a thousand volts before and I'm all right. Tell you what we can do. I'll rig up a little test and give you a couple hundred volts. No more than that. If it works, I'll gradually build her up to a thousand."

"You can do that?"

"Sure."

"How does a hundred volts feel?"

"Greenwood, it isn't any more than like tipping your tongue to a flashlight terminal."

"And if I say 'no more,' you can stop at a hundred?"

"I can."

Chauncey trotted into the cabin and brought out the Ajax cleanser. He got his tool kit out of the car trunk and placed it on the fender.

"Steady now, Chauncey, I didn't say I was going to try this."

Chauncey pulled a big roll of black electrical tape out of the kit. He stripped off four long lengths and hung them from the car fender.

"What's that Bull Dog tape for?"

"That's for contact. You'll see."

He unrolled two eight-foot lengths of copper wire and dropped them on the ground.

"Greenwood, you see these shears?"

He held out a rubber-handled pair of electrical shears.

"If there's any trouble, I mean any trouble, I just clip the wire. It's really very simple."

"I declare, Chaunce. I trust you and all that and you know it. But, Lord, I just don't know about this. I don't know anything about electricity but it seems to me I'm liable to burn up or have a stroke before you can cut that wire."

"Listen, Greenwood. A hundred volts is just going to maybe tickle you. That's all. Anyhow I'll be right by your side. I mean it. Now Greenwood, you got to trust me or I'm not going any further."

Greenwood smiled like a zipper being opened and then closed.

"All right, Chauncey. I guess you know best."

Chauncey sprinkled Ajax cleanser on the fender. "Here, rub your palms in this."

"What for?"

"Gives you a good even contact."

Greenwood patted his hands in the white powder.

"Oh Lord, Chaunce. I'm still not sure."

Chauncey tied a wire to the car frame for a ground. He wound the other wire around the top of a spark plug. "Don't think about it, Greenwood."

He began backing up with the two lengths of wire. "Think about those good poker hands you'll be able to deal."

He took one of the long pieces of Bull Dog tape and reached out for Greenwood's hand.

"Okay, Chaunce."

He placed the copper wire in the Ajax cleanser in Greenwood's palm and began strapping it up.

"All right, make a fist now."

Greenwood closed his hand around the wire and Chauncey began winding the black tape tight. He used two long pieces on each hand.

"Chauncey, you sure this isn't too tight?"

"No, it's right."

Chauncey looked at Greenwood. "How do you feel?"

He took his handkerchief out and wiped the sweat from Greenwood's face.

"I'm scared, that's how I feel."

"I'll take care of you, Greenwood. Don't you worry."

He got in the car. He checked to be sure the emergency brake was on and that the car was out of gear. Greenwood was white and Chauncey could see him trembling. He turned the switch and pushed the starter.

Greenwood screamed and waved his taped hands.

Chauncey let the car idle and got out. Greenwood was vibrating and doing a little fast dance on the grass.

Chauncey had his shears ready.

"You all right, Greenwood?"

His teeth were chattering. He was pale.

"Okay, Chaunce. Okay."

He jumped again and did a little fluttering movement in the air. "I'm okay."

Chauncey said, "I'm going to give you a little more power. I'll be right back."

He took his tool kit into the car. He pushed the engine faster and faster until the accelerator was flat on the floor. Greenwood leaped higher and danced faster. He was shouting but Chauncey couldn't hear him. Chauncey locked the accelerator down with his tool kit. The voltmeter was on maximum. The car was shaking and thundering and a great drift of black oil smoke was rising in the pine trees of the motorcourt yard.

Greenwood was screaming, "Stop it. Stop it."

He tried to tear loose from the wires. He was confused and trying to run and jump and tear away all at the same time.

Chauncey ran to him with the shears and looked. His face was red with purple spots. His teeth were chattering and his eyes looked like they were going to pop right out. He bucked up three feet in the air and came down dancing. It looked like a triple-time Charleston dance. His feet and hands and hair were flying. The dance stopped. He fell down, spun and jackknifed back up into the dance again.

"Now Chaunce! Now! For God's sake now!"

Chauncey studied his frantic dance and checked his watch. One minute.

Greenwood's eyes were wild.

He went to his knees, bounced up and jumped toward the car. He pounded his taped fists on the fender. He leaped again with his knees high and fell over backwards.

Chauncey cut the hot wire.

He rolled over on his stomach and stared at the grass. He couldn't focus his eyes. He groaned.

Chauncey turned the engine off at the carburetor and came back to Greenwood. He rolled him over on his back.

"How you feel, Greenwood?"

His eyes were closed. "Oh, Chaunce. That was terrible . . . terrible . . . I think I'm dying."

"Don't talk now."

He fanned his face with an Esso road map. In a few minutes Greenwood's eyes began to focus. His color returned and he sat up.

Chauncey stripped off the tape. His hands were red from the wires but they weren't burned. And then Greenwood stood up and grinned. He stretched his arms wide and then studied his hands.

"You know something, I do feel better. As a matter of cold fact, I don't believe I've ever in my life felt as good as I do right this second."

Chauncey laughed and began gathering his tools. He pulled the wires off and closed the hood.

"I figured this old deep breather was good for something."

Inside the cabin Greenwood began dealing poker hands in front of the mirror. He dealt fast and the cards worked for him.

He smiled. "Chaunce, why don't we put that can of Ajax up here by the after-shave lotion?"

Chauncey laughed, "That's a good idea."

Greenwood shuffled with his left hand. He began dealing one handed and with his right hand he began carefully shaping his big pompadour. . . .

RAZOR FIGHT
AT THE
ST. LOUIS CAFÉ

DIDN'T MATTER WHAT you said to Round House Brown. All he'd ever answer was, "That's right . . . that's right." Unless he was in a talkative mood. Then he'd say, "You are right about that." That's the way he was . . . quiet and secret. He had a jut jaw, and there wasn't a mark or scar on his dark brown face.

Round House wasn't very tall and he had to scramble up on the pool table when the cue ball was in the middle for corner pocket shots. But he held his own in the eight-ball games and always managed to win himself fifteen or twenty dollars in the big games on Saturday at the St. Louis Café.

Oh, he'd talk a little bit now and then. Like he'd tell you he got his name because he was born near a round house, and things like that. But not much else. He wouldn't say where he came from or what he did for a living or even tell where he got his fancy orange neckties.

Round House always dressed in the very latest style: wore bright narrow yellow clipper shoes or else Chicago flats, tight pants, and most of the time he had himself this wide orange necktie that glowed in the dark.

He was a regular Beau Brummel and everybody liked him but he just wouldn't talk. He'd stand around and shoot his cuffs and smoke and every now and then he'd smile and say, "That's right."

Like the time he won a lot of Bad Dave Harper's money

and Dave started giving him trouble outside in front of the St. Louis Café. . . .

Dave spoke loud and everybody in the café and the poolroom came out to see what was going on.

Dave said, "Round House, I don't mind you winning my money, but you getting to be a first class pain in the ass."

Round House said, "That's right."

"Round House, how you like it if I got mad at you?"

Round House looked at the crowd gathering and mumbled, "That's right."

Dave rubbed his right fist into his left hand. "Well then, suppose you start talking and start clearing up all this mystery about you."

Round House was quiet. He kept his eyes off Dave and started fingering his necktie.

Dave Harper had a bad reputation and Round House knew about it. It was quiet for a minute and then Dave reached over and grabbed him by the shoulder.

"Round House, you are no doubt familiar with the fact that I carry a custom-made razor in my back pocket."

"That's right." He looked at Dave's hand on his shoulder.

Dave turned to the crowd up on the cafe front. He wanted them all to hear. "Well, unless you start talking, I'm going to get that razor out and go to work on you. And you know how I'm going to cut you?"

Round House kept looking at Dave's hand on his shoulder. He touched his necktie knot again and said, "That's right."

Dave spoke slowly so everyone could hear him. "Round House, I'm going to cut a four-inch strip under each one of your left ribs and a four-inch strip under each one of your right ribs. And you're going to run around here looking like a zebra."

He squeezed Round House's shoulder, "What do you think about that?"

"That's right."

"What's right?"

Round House didn't want any trouble from anyone.
He said, "You right about me looking like a zebra."
The crowd laughed. Dave Harper didn't laugh.
"Round House, you think that's funny?"
Round House looked at the crowd and then at Dave's hand
still on his shoulder. "That's right. . . ."
Now Bad Dave Harper is a big man. He's big and he's
black and he's fast, but most of all he's mean. Bad-mean.
That low-down-below-the-belt-type mean. He'd just as soon
swap licks with a police officer as he would spit on the street.
And that isn't all . . . besides being mean, he is one tough
man.
One day a big white police officer accused him of resisting
arrest and rapped him across the head three or four times. I
mean hard, with one of those eighteen-inch hickory billies.
Dave blinked his eyes real hard and kind of shook his head.
He was hurt, all right, but he was just too tough to go down.
He started getting his razor out and he looked at the police
officer and said, "You . . . should have never done that."
And if that police officer knew one thing in his life he
knew that was a fact. And what's more, he knew Dave knew
he knew it. He must have figured the rest of his life was
about as long as Dave's arm and Dave's six-inch razor.
That police officer left his billy right there on the ground
and took off like a new Ford. Dave sat down and someone
gave him a drink and after he'd rubbed his head and shook it
a little more he was all right. . . .
Now that's how tough Bad Dave was and here he's standing about a head and a half taller than Round House.
Dave said, "Which side you want me to start cutting on?"
Round House looked him right in the eye, "That's right."
Dave reached in his back pocket. He pulled his razor out,
slow-like, and then gave it a little flip and the long blade
dropped open.
The crowd sighed and began moving in close. The St.
Louis Café was empty.

Dave grinned, "Ain't you going to fight?"

"That's right."

Dave stepped close and picked up the end of Round House's orange necktie. "How about for a little fun I cut this necktie off?"

"I'd be obliged if you didn't."

"Why is that?"

"That's an expensive necktie."

The razor flashed and Dave laughed. He handed Round House most of the tie. He'd cut it off right below the knot.

"How much it cost, Round House?"

Dave and the crowd laughed. The crowd stopped laughing before Dave did.

"That necktie cost me two dollars and fifty cents in New York City."

"Well, my, my. . . ."

Round House smiled. He had four gold teeth right in front. "But you know how much I'm going to charge you?"

"How much?" Dave began laughing again.

Round House waited until it was quiet again. "I figure that necktie plus all this embarrassment should run you about one hundred dollars."

Everybody laughed again. Dave had to wipe the tears out of his eyes. "Tell me, Round House," he was talking loud again so everyone in the back row could hear him. "Exactly how do you propose to collect this one hundred dollars?"

Round House was serious; "Do you have a hundred dollars?"

Dave didn't like this at all. He slapped his razor in the palm of his left hand. "I got two hundred and fifty dollars if you got some way of getting it."

Dave began loosening his necktie. The crowd didn't move or say a word.

Round House said quietly. "Then I'm raising the price to two hundred and fifty dollars."

Dave put the razor in his left hand and began drying his right hand on his trousers. "How much you charge me if I cut off that necktie knot and tickle your Adam's apple a little bit?"

Round House took two long steps back. "There wouldn't be any charge for that, Dave."

Dave shifted the razor from his left hand to his right. "You know what you're doing, Round House?"

"That's right."

Nothing from the crowd.

Dave took two quick steps forward.

Round House went sideways and backwards at the same time and came up in a crouch with an open razor in his hand. His arm whipped out like a snake's tongue and before Dave could move Round House had removed two buttons off his coat and the long right lapel was hanging by a thread.

The crowd sighed. Somebody whistled, and a high-pitched older voice said, "Good God Almighty . . . did you see that?"

Dave ignored the lapel and jumped again. He faked a lunge and then swiped a whistling backhand at Round House's head. Round House got under it quick and came up fast. He leaped back before Dave could catch him.

Dave circled . . . Round House circled . . .

Dave faked and stopped. Round House picked up Dave's timing. He made a little fluttering movement, faked and the arm flashed again. The blade came back tipped with red. The long lapel fell away from Dave's coat. The shirt lay open and a fine line had been drawn down his chest. It was a light cut and barely bleeding.

Dave was quiet now. He was sweating and his face looked lighter. They circled again. Slowly, right arms out, blades up, left arms balancing in the air like fencers. . . . Slowly, quietly—like it was a secret. . . . No noise from the crowd. No noise from the shoes. No noise from the St. Louis Cafe.

They kept their bodies as far back as possible and made little jiggling movements with the razor points. Nothing is as quiet as a razor match. . . .

Dave faked twice, then again, then rushed and hooked the blade up for Round House's throat. Round House rolled to the left and spun back. He began to smile. They circled again. . . .

Round House began to hum. . . .

Dave was getting madder and madder. He wanted to kill Round House and nothing else. The sweat glistened on his forehead and on the back of his hands.

Round House stopped and stepped back and dried his hands on his pants. Dave did the same thing. Dave flexed his shoulders and moved in.

He stopped, shuffled and moved in, bobbing on three levels at once. He shouted and slashed at Round House.

Round House moved with him. "That's right," he said. He went sideways again, spun away from two slashes and came up under the fourth. They collided and Round House leaped away as Dave's blade swished again.

The crowd sighed—moaned—and shook their heads. Dave's coat and shirt were laid open again. This time across the top of both pockets on the coat. The skin showed through. An eight-inch slice had crossed the other cut and a perfect cross had been cut through Dave's Hart Schaffner & Marx suit coat and his wet skin.

Dave must have felt the draft because he stepped back and looked at the cuts. Round House couldn't have done a better job with a good pair of scissors.

Dave studied his skin . . . traced his finger across one cut and down the other. He closed his razor. When he put it in his back pocket, he pulled out his wallet.

"You pretty good with that steel."

Round House was serious. "You right about that."

THE BUZZARD'S LOPE

SATURDAY NIGHT square dance at the Irmo High School Gymnasium. Crowd mostly mill workers and farmers, a few local merchants, mechanics and about a dozen students.

Maurice Haynes and his younger brother Billy are on guitar. Cedric Foster on banjo and harmonica combination. Claude Brightwater calling.

Big promenade ends and Claude is wiping his face with his handkerchief and shouting for attention.

"All right now. All right now. Let's have your attention, please. We got a main attraction coming on."

The crowd bunches down close to the platform. The gymnasium is small. The foot-high platform and microphone is underneath the basketball backboard and net.

"Ladies and gentlemen from Shell Bluff, Georgia, the pride of Horse Creek Valley, none other than the master of barnyard impersonations . . . Slim Odell Roach."

Slim Odell is six feet, six inches tall. He tries to stand shorter by hooking his neck and shoulders down. He is embarrassed and shy and Claude has to pull him across the platform to the microphone.

"Come on, Slim. You among friends."

The audience laughs and applauds. Slim's face is red and he keeps staring down at his long shoes with razor slashes at the sides. Claude tries to pull the microphone up higher.

"Well, I reckon that's about as far as it'll stretch."

Slim nods his head and stands a little shorter by bending his knees. He looks at the basketball backboard and the rafters up under the roof.

Someone in the front row says: "How's the weather up there, Slim?"

Slim can't think of an answer. He blushes again and grins from ear to ear. He has long arms, long legs, a long red neck and a small head. His eyes are set close together and his shiny black hair is parted in the center with greased spit curls at the side.

Claude says, "Slim's got a case of the shys. He wants me to announce his first number."

Slim loosens the knot on the red bandana at his throat and looks back down at his shoes.

Claude says, "For his first selection Slim's going to try a Dominecker hen laying an egg."

Slim wipes his hands on his trousers and closes his eyes. He tilts his head into his cupped hands:

"Cwuk . . . Cwuk . . . Cwuk . . . Cwuk . . . Cwuk . . . Cwuk." Slow, measured, even. Pause. Eyes still closed. "Cwuk . . . Cwuk . . . Cwuk . . . Cwuk." Faster now with a little sob in it. "Cwuk . . . Cwuk . . . Cwuk . . . Cwuk." Sound rises with a jerk and a questioning: "Cwuk? Cwuk? Cwuk? Cwuk? . . . Cwuk?"

Slim fans his right hand up. His eyes are closed as he speaks, "Here it comes now."

Faster and faster, rising and falling, but now more positive. "Cwuk . . . Cwuk, Cwuk, Cwuk." Rising sharply in surprise and accomplishment. "Cwuk, Cwuk, Cwuk, Cwuk." Settles down in a throaty, proud, curdling. "Cwuk. Cwuk. Cwuk. Cwuk. Cwuk."

Slim Odell opens his eyes, steps back and begins to smile. He is still embarrassed.

Audience applauds and whistles.

"Well, I'll be dogged if he didn't fool me."

Mary Jo Finley, the Queen of the Square Dance, says, "No

reason for a boy with all that talent to be shy."

Slim looks at her, and when she smiles he begins examining the basketball netting.

A tight-lipped man with a black hat on in the second row says, "Mister, I liked that. I know chickens and I really liked that. You got any more with chickens in it?"

Slim speaks in a whisper. "Same chicken only more this time. They up on their roosts in the hen house."

"What did he say?"

"What did he say?"

"He says they're settling down for the night."

Slim closes his eyes, "Cwuk . . . Cwuk . . . Cwuk . . . Cwuk." Slow muffled dreamy. Slim speaks through his hands, "Mister Rooster now, he has to get last word in. Cwok—Cwok —Cwok.

"All right, now we got 'em all sleeping. A little time passes and directly here comes a weasel tipping in. Our Dominecker hen, she sees him first. Cwak. Cwak. Cwak. Cwak. Cwak. Now the rooster. Cwok-a . . . Cwok-a . . . Cwok-a . . . Cwok-a. Listen close now, you can hear them flapping around trying to climb up higher. Cwak-a. Cwak-a. Cwok-a. Cwok-a."

Slim looks up from his cupped hands. He stands up over the microphone now.

"Mister Weasel selects himself a hen and drags her out. All kinds of racket now. Rooster flopping around crowing and screaming. Hens falling down and running into one another. Going out of their minds. Cwak-a-Cwak-a-Cwok-a-Cwok-a. Mister Weasel gets the hen through the hole. The rooster, he's rushing around wailing and trying to calm the hens down. After a while he has to scold them to make them straighten out. A little time passes and they begin settling down. But they're still pretty nervous . . . Cwuk-Cwuk-Cwuk-a-Cwuk-a Cwuk. . . . Finally they all asleep . . . Cwk, cwk, cwk. . . . All except one. Our Dominecker hen friend, she's got one eye closed and one eye on that weasel hole. But pretty soon she begins to doze . . . Cwuk, cwk, cwk . . .

Every minute or so she shakes herself awake and checks that hole, Cwk, Cwk-a, Cwk, cwk. Finally she's too tired and she drops off to sleep cwk . . . . cwk . . . . owk."

Long applause and whistles. The man in the black hat says, "They ought to put that man in a Hollywood movie show. That's what I call first-class entertainment."

A woman near the rear has a buzz-saw voice that cuts through the noise. "All I got to do is close my eyes and I seen it. Ain't he something, though? I tell you, I just had to close my eyes and I seen it."

Mary Jo Finley smiles at him from the first row.

From the back, "That rooster rushing around took all the doubt out of my mind."

Slim's face is about a foot from the basketball net. He is smiling slightly and examining the cords in the net. He takes a glass of water off the small table at the edge of the platform. He drinks it all down without removing it from his mouth. He wipes his lips carefully with a new red handkerchief, folds it and puts it in his back pocket.

"Mister, for a man with the shys you do all right."

The audience is still murmuring. Slim dries his hands again on his trousers. The crowd is quiet. He steps back and looks at the back of the backboard. His face is tight and serious. His eyes are flashing. He bites his bottom lip, takes a deep breath and shouts, *"Hawg-a-rootin'."*

He buries his face in his cupped hands. Only his eyebrows are showing. He is in a deep crouch around the microphone. His elbows are jammed into his stomach.

"Umkha—Umkha—Umkha—Umkha—Umkha. . . ."

His whole body shakes. He stays in the crouch but looks up.

"Two hawgs in same pen: Umkha, Umkha, Umkha, Umkha. . . ."

Faster now, platform shakes. He stops, heaves for breath. Face wet, face red, eyes like new dimes.

"Same two hawgs in slop trough: Umpka, Umpka, Umpka, Umpka."

A slick, wet, slapping sound.

Slim speaks through his hands, "Getting near bottom of trough. Here comes a small shoat trying to get at his mother while she's eating: Umpka—Umpka—Umpka . . . Sqwee—Sqwee . . . Umpka—Umpka . . . Sqweeeee. Umpka Umpka . . . Sqweeeeeeeeeeeeeee."

Slim jumps back waving his hands free. He cracks his hand sharply on the backboard.

Crowd bursts into applause and swamp shouts. Someone bangs a dipper on a tin bucket.

"Great God in the morning, ain't he something, though?"

"He's something else!"

A rebel yell, more applause.

"That small shoat cutting in there like to broke my heart."

"Yeah, that shoat shore do make it nice."

"That man's a genius. A genius, I tell you."

Claude Brightwater jumps up on the stage and slaps Slim on the back. "You're great, man, great. Look at them out there, they love you."

Slim's face flushes. He can't speak. He holds his hand and looks back down at his shoes.

Claude says, "How's the hand?"

"It's fine, sir, fine . . . It's fine."

The man in the black hat says, "They ought to put that man in a Hollywood movie show."

"I once saw a fellow do a bitch dog in heat with a bo-dog sniffing around up near Macon. But he couldn't hold a candle to Slim here."

"All right, folks, Slim's going to do one more. He tells me this is a serious one and it's dedicated to our boys overseas."

The crowd is quiet again.

Slim Odell Roach drinks another full glass of water without removing the glass from his mouth. He wipes his lips carefully as if they were some delicate reed. He reaches into the table drawer and pulls out a pair of snare drumsticks and a whistle. He places the whistle in his mouth and flexes the drumsticks. Smiling around the whistle, he says, "The Stars and Stripes Forever."

He raises his arms high and begins tapping on his head. The sound comes out through and around the whistle. Slow at first and low. Then louder and faster and then faster. Harder and harder. Louder and louder. Faster and faster. The whistle shrills at every bar and you can see the columns of soldiers marching along. When it seems he can beat no harder, absorb no more, whistle no more, his speed increases, his range becomes louder and the big room and the yard is filled with Slim's music.

No one claps their hands, no one pats their feet. The only noise is from Slim Odell marching in place, knees high, eyes straight and shining bright, elbows high and flashing and the drumsticks tattooing away on his small tone-true head.

And then he stops. Pushes his hair back, squares his sticks, and steps back. He stands at attention.

The audience goes wild. Shouts, screams, rebel yells, more applause.

"Lordy Lord, Lord, Lord."

"Jesus, that man is great!"

More yells, swamp shouts. Distant dogs join in.

"He's a cold natural-born genius. There's no denying that."

"I know a lot of them Horse Creek Valley boys and every dern one of them's got talent."

"And no instrument either. Right out of that scutter's head."

"I swear I tell you that boy ought to be in a Hollywood movie show."

Mary Jo Finley has metal heel and toe taps on her shoes. She jumps up and down and shouts, "More, more."

Claude rushes over and hugs Slim.

"Slim, you really done yourself proud tonight. You really did. All right, folks, let's have one great big hand for our friend, Slim Odell Roach from Shell Bluff, Georgia. . . ."

When the applause stops, Claude holds onto Slim. He tries to pull away and get off the stage but Claude holds on.

"Folks, Slim here says he has to go home. What I say is he should stay and dance with us. All right, I want one of you pretty girls out there to step up here and be Slim's partner in the next dance."

Five girls get up on the platform. Slim tries to pull back.

"Please now, Mister Claude. I got to go home now. Besides I can't dance."

Claude laughs. "Well, little Mary Jo Finley here's going to show you how."

He places Mary Jo's hand in Slim's and pushes them down onto the floor.

The audience clears a path as the music strikes up. Mary Jo is excited about being chosen as Slim's partner and she pulls him toward the center of the floor. She has a red dress on, a white bow in her black hair, white shoes and white socks. She does a little running tap dance as they reach the middle of the floor. Mary Jo leads him into a simple two-step dance. He crouches down so he won't be too tall for her. He dances clumsily with long strides and doesn't seem to know what to do with his neck and head. His right hand is on her shoulder.

In the middle of the dance the music stops. Maurice Haynes, his younger brother Billy, and Cedric Foster are talking. They nod, smile, and rip into a fast version of "The Rabbit Ain't Got No Tail at All."

Slim Odell suddenly jerks up to his full height. He knows the music. He looks eight feet tall. He grabs Mary Jo and they begin a fast walking dance. Mary Jo is quick and she follows close.

"What's he doing?"

"I don't know. Looks like he picked up some trail."

Slim Odell spins the girl out and leaps up in the air. He comes down hard on one knee with his head back.

"I ain't ever seen dancing like that before."

"Somebody go ask Maurice what it is."

"You reckon he's been taken hold of?"

Slim whirls the girl out and dances by himself. He dances in a small circle with his heels coming down hard on the floor. He is at mid-court, his eyes are on the ceiling. His knees are pumping high. He raises his arms like wings and leaps high. He shouts as he leaps. It's a weird, wild, almost birdlike noise. He comes down hard. He drags one foot and then the other as if he's wounded.

Mary Jo is petrified but she manages a little tapping shuffle during the long break. Slim grabs her and they whirl around. Each time around Mary Jo goes higher. Her feet leave the ground the second time around. Her feet touch the ground on the sixth time. The floor has cleared and they are using most of the mid-court area.

Slim spins Mary Jo out again. She is too dizzy to dance. She watches him proudly. Slim leaps and yells again. He cracks down on the floor on one knee, then rises straight up and comes down on the other knee.

He squats and dances in the squat. He rushes foward in a high head-back screaming leap. The floor boards make a crashing noise and the audience goes wild. Black rubber heel marks are all over the mid-court. Some are long, some are short. All are heavy and solid.

Mary Jo joins him and they do a fast head-to-head heel dance.

"Stay with him, Mary Jo!"

"He's been taken hold of, I tell you."

"No sir. . . . That's some kind of dance. I know it is."

"Here's John now."

"Maurice says it's Horse Creek Valley, all right. Claims they call it the Buzzard's Lope down there, only he ain't ever seen it done so extreme-like."

"He does take up a lot of room."

"You shore he ain't been taken hold of? Keep an eye on his tongue when he comes by."

The music is mostly banjo now. Loud and fast and nasal.
Slim Odell goes into a short fast heel-and-toe jig. Mary Jo
steps aside and watches him. His feet and hands are flying.
The audience is applauding and keeping time.

Claude Brightwater leads the musicians out to Slim at mid-
court. Slim smiles at Maurice Haynes. "Call 'em, Mister
Haynes."

Maurice squats down and watches Slim's feet. He shouts,
"Heel and Toe Breakdown."

Maurice, Billy, and Cedric are playing as fast as they
can.

Slim bends down deep and studies his flying feet.

Maurice shouts, "Heel and Toe Cutaway."

Then, "Brogan Stomp."

"Buck and Double Buck."

"Candydance."

"Chicken and the Hawk."

Slim slows down, "How about this one?"

Maurice looks and smiles. His fingers are rippling up on
the high notes, "Don't know it."

Slim shouts, "Jenkins County Hell Dance."

Mary Jo is clapping in time and tapping her feet. Slim
Odell calls out, "This here's a Saluda County Breakdown—
Heel Stomp with a Buzzard's Lope thrown in at the end."

Someone shouts, "Keep that music going. We're seeing
dancing tonight. Don't let Maurice stop."

"The Buzzard's Lope. I'll be dogged. I've heard of it but
I've never seen it."

Slim dances back to the center circle in the middle of the
floor. There are big rubber marks everywhere. He wants
plenty of room. The musicians are squatting down around
Maurice and playing faster than ever.

Slim dances in a fast, jerky, elbow-pumping, heel-thumping
stomp. His eyes are closed again. He is transported.

"Boy, you're seeing dancing tonight."

"Yessir."

"They don't dance like that any more."

"No sir."

Slim Odell works his way backwards. He has his eye on a spot near the center circle at mid-court. He goes to one knee, then the other. He bends backwards until his head is almost on the floor. He pushes himself up with one hand. He rushes forward. He screams as he leaps as high as his long legs and arms will take him. He seems to hang in the air while the noise bounces off of the walls. He crashes down in a full leg split and bows his head as the music ends.

He's soaking wet. His hair is in his face. The last two heel marks run the width of the center circle. He stays in the full split with his toes tucked down and his head bowed while the crowd screams and thunders and the puzzled dogs in the distance answer.

Finally he gets up. "Thank you. Thank you, folks."

The man is the black hat takes him by the elbow. "Son, that's what I call dancing. I'm telling you, you ought to get taken up by one of those talent scouts and gotten into a Hollywood movie show."

Mary Jo Finley holds both of his hands. "Slim, I know a lot of boys from Horse Creek Valley, but ain't none of them near as talented as you."

Claude Brightwater laughs, "Well, Slim, I see you gotten over that little case of shys you had."

Slim smiles down at Mary Jo and says, "Yessir, Mr. Brightwater, I just reckon I have."

LEROY JEFFCOAT

ON LEROY JEFFCOAT's forty-first birthday he fell off a scaffold while painting a big stucco rooming house over on Sycamore Street. Leroy was in shock for about twenty minutes but when the doctor brought him around he seemed all right.

Leroy went home and rolled his trousers and shoes into a bundle with his Sherwin-Williams paint company cap and jacket. He tied the bundle with string to keep the dogs from dragging it off and put it in the gutter in front of his house. He poured gasoline over the bundle and set it on fire. That was the last day Leroy Jeffcoat painted a house.

He went uptown to the Sports Center on Kenilworth Street and bought two white baseball uniforms with green edging, two pairs of baseball shoes, a Spalding second baseman's glove, eight baseballs and two bats. Leroy had been painting houses at union scale since he got out of high school, and since he never gambled or married he had a pretty good savings account at the South Carolina National Bank.

We had a bush-league team that year called the Columbia Green Wave. The name must have come from the fact that most of us got drunk on Friday nights and the games were always played on Saturdays. Anyhow the season was half over when Leroy came down and wanted to try out for second base.

Leroy looked more like a ball player than any man I've

ever known. He had that little ass-pinched strut when he was mincing around second base. He also had a beautiful squint into or out of the sun, could chew through a whole plug of Brown Mule tobacco in four innings, and could worry a pitcher to death with his chatter. On and on and on . . . we would be ahead ten runs in the ninth and Leroy wouldn't let up.

But Leroy couldn't play. He looked fine. At times he looked great. But he knew too much to play well. He'd read every baseball book and guide and every Topp's Chewing Gum Baseball Card ever printed. He could show you how Stan Musial batted, how Williams swung, how DiMaggio dug in. He went to all the movies and copied all the stances and mannerisms. You could say, "Let's see how Rizzuto digs one out, Leroy." He'd toss you a ball and lope out about forty feet.

"All right, throw it at my feet, right in the dirt." And you would and then you'd see the Old Scooter movement—low and quick with the big wrist over to first.

Leroy could copy anybody. He was great until he got in an actual game. Then he got too nervous. He'd try to bat like Williams, Musial, and DiMaggio all at once and by the time he'd make up his mind he'd have looked at three strikes. And at second base it was the same story. He fidgeted too much and never got himself set in time.

Leroy played his best ball from the bench. He liked it there. He'd pound his ball into his glove and chatter and grumble and cuss and spit tobacco juice. He'd be the first one to congratulate the home-run hitters and the first one up and screaming on a close play.

We got him into the Leesboro game for four innings and against Gaffney for three. He played the entire game at second base against the State Insane Asylum . . . but that's another story.

When the games ended Leroy showered, dried, used plenty of talcum powder and then spent about twenty minutes in front of the mirror combing his flat black hair straight back.

Most of the team had maybe a cap and a jacket with a number on it and a pair of shoes. Leroy had two complete uniform changes. After every game he'd change his dirty one for a clean one and then take the dirty one to the one-day dry cleaner. That way Leroy was never out of uniform. Morning, noon, and night Leroy was ready. On rainy days, on days it sleeted, and even during the hurricane season, Leroy was ready. For his was the long season. Seven days a week, three hundred and sixty-five days a year, Leroy was in uniform. Bat in hand, glove fastened to belt, balls in back pocket, and cut plug going. And he never took off his spikes. He would wear a set out every two weeks. You could see him coming from two blocks away in his clean white uniform. And at night when you couldn't see him you could hear the spikes and see the sparks on the sidewalk.

The Green Wave worked out on Tuesday and Thursday in the evening and we played on Saturday. Leroy worked out every day and every night. He'd come up to Doc Daniels' drugstore with his bat and ball and talk someone into hitting him fly balls out over the telegraph wires on Mulberry Avenue. It could be noon in August and the sun wouldn't be any higher than a high foul ball, but it wouldn't worry Leroy Jeffcoat. He'd catch the balls or run them down in the gutter until the batter tired.

Then Leroy would buy himself and the batter a couple of Atlantic ales. Doc Daniels had wooden floors and Leroy wouldn't take his baseball shoes off, so he had to drink the ale outside.

Doc would shout out, "Leroy, damn your hide anyway. If you come in here with those spikes on I'm going to work you over with this ice-cream scoop. Now you hear?"

Leroy would spin the ball into the glove, fold it and put it in his back pocket.

"Okay, Doc."

"Why can't you take those damn spikes off and sit down in

a booth and rest? You're getting too old to be out in that sun all day."

Leroy was in great shape. As a rule, house painters have good arms and hands and bad feet.

He would laugh and take his Atlantic ale outside in the sun or maybe sit down in the little bit of shade from the mailbox.

Later on, he would find someone to throw him grounders.

"Come on, toss me a few. Don't spare the steam."

He'd crowd in on you and wouldn't be more than thirty feet out there.

"Come on, skin it along the ground."

You'd be scared to throw it hard but he'd insist.

"Come on, now, a little of the old pepper. In the dirt."

Next thing you'd be really winging them in there and he'd be picking them off like cherries or digging them out of the dust and whipping them back to you. He'd wear you out and burn your hands up in ten minutes. Then he'd find somebody else.

Leroy would go home for supper and then he'd be back. After dark he'd go out to the street lamp and throw the ball up near the light and catch it. The June bugs, flying ants and bats would be flitting around everywhere but he'd keep on. The June bugs and flying ants would be all over his head and shoulders and even in his glove. He might stop for a while for another Atlantic ale, and if the crowd was talking baseball he'd join it. If it wasn't and the bugs were too bad he'd stand out in the dark and pound his ball in his glove or work out in the mirror of Doc Daniels' front window. In front of the window he became a pitcher. He worked a little like Preacher Roe but he had more class. He did a lot of rubbing the resin bag and checking signs from the catcher and shaking them off. When he'd agree with a sign he'd nod his head slow . . . exactly like Roe. Then he'd get in position, toss the resin aside, and glare in mean and hard at the batter. He took a big reach and stopped and then the slow and perhaps the most classic look toward second base I've ever seen—absolutely Alexandrian. Then he'd stretch, wind, and whip it through. He put his hands on his knees . . . wait. It had to be a strike. It was. And he'd smile.

And read a sports page? Nobody this side of Cooperstown ever read a page the way Leroy Jeffcoat did. He would crouch down over that sheet for two hours running. He'd read every word and every figure. He went at it like he was following the puzzle maze in *Grit,* trying to find the pony or the seventeen rabbits. He had a pencil about as long as your little finger and he'd make notes along the margin. When he finished he'd transfer the notes to a little black book he carried in his back pocket. Leroy would even check the earned run average and the batting and fielding average. I don't mean just *look* at them . . . he'd *study* them. And if he didn't like them he'd divide and do the multiplication and check them over. And if they were wrong he'd be on the telephone to the *Columbia Record* or else he'd write a letter.

Leroy was always writing letters to the sports writers. Like he'd read an article about how Joe DiMaggio was getting old and slipping and he'd get mad. He'd take off his shoes and go inside Doc Daniels', buy a tablet and an envelope, get in the back booth and write. Like: "What do you mean Joe DiMaggio is too old and he's through. Why, you rotten son of a bitch, you just wait and watch him tomorrow."

Next day old Joe would pick up two for four and Leroy would take off his spikes and get back in that back booth again. "What did I tell you? Next time, you watch out who you're saying is through. Also, you print an apology this week or I am going to personally come up there and kick your fat ass. (Signed) Leroy Jeffcoat, taxpayer and second baseman, Doc Daniels' Drugstore, Columbia, S. C."

This would be a much better story if I could tell you that Leroy's game improved and he went on and played and became famous throughout the Sally League. But he didn't.

He got a little better and then he leveled off. But we kept him around because we liked him (number one), that white uniform edged in green looked good (number two), and then, too, we used him as an auxiliary man. A lot of the boys couldn't make it through some of those August games. When you start fanning yourself with a catcher's mitt, it's hot. All that beer and corn whisky would start coming out and in most games we would wind up with Leroy playing.

One game, Kirk Turner, our right fielder, passed out right in his position in the short weeds. We had to drag him into the shade and Leroy ran out to right field and began chirping. He caught a couple and dropped a couple. At bat he decided he was Ted Williams and kept waiting for that perfect ball that Ted described in the *Saturday Evening Post*. The perfect ball never came and Leroy struck out twice. In the seventh he walked. It was his first time on base in weeks and he began dancing and giving the pitcher so much lip the umpire had to settle him down.

Our last game of the year and the game we hated to play was with the South Carolina State Penitentiary down the hill.

First of all, *no one* beats The Pen. Oh, you might give them a bad time for a couple of innings but that's about all. It's not that they're a rough bunch so much as it's that they play to win. And I mean they really play to win.

Anyhow, we went down and the game started at one-thirty. The high walls kept the breeze out and it was like playing in a furnace. Sweat was dripping off my fingertips and running down my nose.

Billy Joe Jasper pitched and in the first inning they hit him for seven runs before Kirk Turner caught two long ones out by the center field wall.

We came to bat and Al Curry, our catcher, led off. Their pitcher's name was Strunk and he was in jail for murder. The first pitch was right at Al's head. He hit the dirt. The crowd cheered. The next pitch the same thing; Al Curry was as white as a sheet. The next pitch went for his head but broke out and over the inside of the plate. Al was too scared to swing and they called him out on the next two pitches.

Jeff Harper struck out next in the same manner. When he complained to the umpire, who was a trusty, he went out and talked to Strunk. It didn't do any good.

I batted third. It was terrifying. Strunk glared at me and mouthed dirty words. He was so tall and his arms were so long I thought he was going to grab me by the throat before he turned the ball loose. I kept getting out of the box and checking to see if he was pitching from the mound. He seemed to be awfully close.

I got back in the box. I didn't dig in too deep. I wanted to be ready to duck. He reached up about nine feet and it came right at my left eye. I hit the dirt.

"Ball one."

From the ground: "How about that dusting?"

"You entering a complaint?"

"Yes."

"I'll speak to him."

The umpire went out to see Strunk and the catcher followed. They talked a while and every few seconds one of them would look back at me. They began laughing.

Back on the mound. One more beanball and once more in the dirt. And then three in a row that looked like beaners that broke over the plate. Three up. Three down.

At the end of five innings we didn't have a scratch hit. The Pen had fourteen runs and the pitcher Strunk had three doubles and a home run.

We didn't care what the score was. All we wanted to do was get the game over and get out of that prison yard. The crowd cheered everything their ball team did and every move we made brought only boos and catcalls.

At the end of seven we were still without a hit.

Leroy kept watching Strunk. "Listen, I can hit that son of a bitch."

I said, "No, Leroy, he's too dangerous."

"The hell he is. Let me at him."

Kirk Turner said, "Leroy, that bastard will kill you. Let's just ride him out and get out of here. This crowd makes me nervous."

But Leroy kept on insisting. Finally George Haggard said, "Okay, Leroy. Take my place." So Leroy replaced George at first.

Strunk came to bat in the eighth and Leroy started shouting, "Let him hit! Let him hit, Billy Joe. I want to see that son of a bitch over here."

He pounded his fist in George's first baseman's glove and started jumping up and down like a chimpanzee.

"Send that bastard down here. I want him. I'll fix his ass."

The crowd cheered Leroy and he tipped his hat like Stan Musial.

The crowd cheered again.

Strunk bellowed, "Shut that nut up, ump."

The umpire raised his hands, "All right, over there, simmer down or I'll throw you out."

The crowd booed the umpire.

Leroy wouldn't stop. "Don't let him hit, Billy! Walk him. Walk that beanball bastard. He might get a double; I want him over here."

Billy Joe looked at Al Curry. Al gave him the walk sign. Two balls . . . three balls. . . .

"You getting scared, you bastard? Won't be long now."

The crowd laughed and cheered.

Again the Musial touch with his cap.

Strunk shouted, "Listen, you runt, you keep quiet while I'm hitting or I'll shove that glove down your throat."

Leroy laughed, "Sure you will. Come on down. I'll help you."

Four balls. . . .

Strunk laid the bat down carefully and slowly walked toward first. Strunk got close. The crowd was silent. Leroy

stepped off the bag and Strunk stepped on. Leroy backed up.
Strunk followed. Everybody watched. No noise. Leroy
stopped and took his glove off. He handed it to Strunk.
Strunk took the glove in both hands.

Leroy hit him with the fastest right I've ever seen.

Strunk was stunned but he was big. He lashed the glove
into Leroy's face and swung at him.

Leroy took it on the top of his head and crowded in so fast
Strunk didn't know what to do. Leroy got him off balance and
kept him that way while he pumped in four lefts and six
rights.

Strunk went down with Leroy on top banging away. Two
of us grabbed Leroy and three got ahold of Strunk. They led
Strunk back to the dugout bleeding. He turned to say something and spat out two teeth. "I ain't through with you yet."

The crowd went wild.

Someone shouted, "What's his name? What's his name?"

"Jeffcoat . . . Leroy Jeffcoat."

They cheered again. And shouted, "Leroy Jeffcoat is our
boy." And then, "Leroy Jeffcoat is red hot."

Leroy tipped his hat Musial-style, picked up George Haggard's glove and said, "Okay, let's play ball."

Another cheer and the game started.

The Pen scored two more times that inning before we got
them out. We came to bat in the ninth behind 21 to 0.
Strunk fanned me and then hit Coley Simms on the shoulder.
He found out that Leroy was batting fifth so he walked the
next two, loading the bases so he could get a shot at him.

So Leroy came up with the bases loaded and the prison
crowd shouting, "Leroy Jeffcoat is our boy."

He pulled his cap down like Musial and dug into the box
like DiMaggio. The crowd cheered and he got out of the box
and tipped his cap.

Strunk was getting madder and madder and he flung the
resin down and kicked the rubber. "Let's go, in there."

Leroy got in the box, whipped the bat through like Ted

Williams and hollered, "Okay, Strunk, let's have it."

Zip. Right at his head.

Leroy flicked his head back like a snake but didn't move his feet.

The crowd booed Strunk and the umpire went out to the mound. We could hear the argument. As the umpire turned away Strunk told him to go to hell.

The second pitch was the same as the first. Leroy didn't move and the ball hit his cap bill.

The umpire wanted to put him on base.

Leroy shouted, "No, he didn't hit me. He's yellow. Let him pitch."

The crowd cheered Leroy again. Strunk delivered another duster and the ball went between Leroy's cap bill and his eyes. This time he didn't even flick his head.

Three balls . . . no strikes.

Two convicts dropped out of the stands and trotted across the infield to the mound. They meant business. When they talked Strunk listened and nodded his head. A signal passed around the infield.

The fourth pitch was right across Leroy's chest. It was Williams' ideal ball and it was the ball Leroy had been waiting for all season. He hit it clean and finished the Williams swing.

It was a clean single but the right fielder bobbled it and Leroy made the wide turn toward second. The throw into second was blocked and bobbled again and Leroy kept going. He ran in spurts, each spurt faster than the last. The throw to third got past the baseman and Leroy streaked for home, shouting.

He began sliding from twenty feet out. He slid so long he stopped short. He had to get up and lunge for home plate with his hand. He made it as the ball whacked into the catcher's mitt and the crowd started coming out of the stands.

The guards tried to hold the crowd back and a warning

siren sounded. But the convicts got to him and paraded around the field with Leroy on their backs. The game was called at this point and the reserve guards and trusties came out with billy clubs.

Later Coley and I learned from The Pen's manager that the committee had told Strunk they wanted Leroy to hit a home run. We never told the rest of the team or anybody else about that.

After we showered at The Pen we all went back to Doc Daniels' Drugstore. Everyone told everyone about it and when Doc Daniels heard it he came outside and personally led Leroy into the store with his spikes on.

"Leroy, from now on I want you to feel free to walk right in here anytime you feel like it."

Leroy smiled, and put his bat and his uniform bag up on the soda fountain. Doc bought Atlantic ales for everyone. Later, I bought a round and Coley bought a round.

And just as we were settling down in the booths with sandwiches, potato chips, and the jukebox going, Leroy picked up his glove and started spinning his ball off the ends of his fingers and said, "I'm getting a little stiff. Anyone feel like throwing me a few fast ones?"

DEAR DIARY

TODAY IS MARCH 20, 1943. It has stopped raining. It is hot. I bought a diary. Am sitting in deep concrete drain ditch at Fort Jackson, South Carolina. First day in Army. A horrible mistake.

I gave my bike to Bob. Schwinn bike, sixty dollars, in great shape. Hated to leave Western Union job. Don't mind quitting school. Mr. Dodge said job at Western Union will be waiting for me when I return. Will save my number thirty-three, uniforms also. Best job I ever had. Clean, nice crowd, wonder if Mr. Dodge is lying.

Hated school, teachers. Like sports. Coach Stevenson great. Said I was a natural. Too bad I wasn't bigger. Good on defense. Longest punt eighty yards with roll. Longest pass forty yards. Favorite player Stan Stasica of U.S.C. Have copied his walk. Columbia High colors maroon and gold. Basketball, highest score in one game twenty-two points. Good for my height, five feet seven and a half. Can jump high. Good fast break man. Will probably grow more. Am only seventeen. . . .

Air Corps thinks I'm eighteen. Also think I finished one year of college. If they discover I finished one year high school, will be washed out, sent home. Maybe should tell them now. Get bike back and go back to Western Union. Homesick already.

Ate four Mr. Goodbars, two Bit-O-Honeys. Candy only

three cents at P.X. One Peter Paul Mounds. Some boys wearing suits and hats, some wearing neckties. I have on crepe-soled blue suedes. Western Union brown socks. Blue saddle-stitched slacks. Clean white T-shirt and blue checked sports coat. No necktie. Can't tie necktie. Western Union had clip-on black ties. Wonder if aviation cadets wear clip-on ties.

At least no more school. Really hated school. Principal, teachers hated me. Took me out of academic studies. Said teach him a trade. Develop his hands. I told him I had a trade building bootleg stills. Told him it was called whisky plumbing. Principal said not to get smart. Transferred to Manual Arts. Woodwork, metal work, machine shop, drafting. Some art. Made bread board in woodwork, failed course. Made poker and whisk broom holder in sheet metal work, failed course. Passed machine shop. Liked working on South Bend lathe. Hated all other courses. Hated all school except sports. Maybe I will grow three or four more inches. Now weigh 152½. If I can make 175 will play pro ball. Baseball in summer . . . football in fall . . . basketball in spring. If not tall enough for basketball will play golf. Lowest score seventy-three at Trenholm Road Course. Long off tee, good short game. Favorite club, 9-iron.

Hope there is no manual arts in Air Corps. Dream of piloting P-38 or P-40. Swastikas or rising suns under canopy window. Ace at eighteen. White scarf, fantastic reflexes. Maybe missing in action. Principal, teachers sorry then. Would blame themselves. Deserve it. Feeling homesick.

Had lunch. Good food. Had two helpings of everything. Nice cut of ham with raisin sauce. Potatoes, beans, ice cream and coffee. Had to wash own tin plate. Don't mind at all. Bought two more Bit-O-Honeys, copy of Batman and Robin. Back down in drain ditch out of the sun. Not homesick now. Wonder what we'll have for supper. Figure Bit-O-Honeys develop firm jaw, neck muscles. Good for spotting FW-190's . . . Messerschmitts.

March 25, 1943. Arrived Gulfport, Mississippi. Flat land

close to sea. Tourist homes with high porches, cane furniture facing ocean. American Flag in center of town.

Arrived at field. Hot, humid. Glare on white sand hurts eyes. Will need sun glasses. Will wear them on belt like B-25 pilots at home. B-25 bad plane. Many crashes in Lake Murray . . . "One A Day In Murray Bay". . . .

First day in Gulfport sat under lister bag shack outside Recreation Hall.

Second day did nothing but sit and smoke. Daydreamed of flying. White scarf at throat, sun glasses. Smiling into Movietone newsreel, nineteen swastikas on side of shark-painted P-38.

Thought of childhood dreams. Wanted to go to orphanage. Wear little green suit like all the others. Had dreamed of falling in love at orphanage. She had worn same type uniform: skirt instead of short pants.

Thought of cadet uniform, then lieutenant's uniform. Dreamed about standing at bars in New Orleans, Gulfport, San Francisco, Shanghai, Paris . . . home to Columbia. No bars in Columbia . . . would stand at soda fountain. Hero. Would frown and look older. Would drink rum and coke . . . good taste. Smoke a lot, talk out of side of mouth. Favorite movie star man or woman James Cagney. Wonder if my reflexes are as fast as Cagney's. Reflexes, eyes, depth perception very important in flying.

Third day went into Recreation Hall. Played ping pong. Great backhand from left to right. Good forehand but not same quality as backhand. Slammed every shot. Aggressive from first point. Played close to table. Never on defense. Nothing cozy. Everything bold. Most players play defensive. Can't handle my speed. Beat five men in row. Beat a boy from Atlanta eleven to nothing.

After lunch. Played Chinese cadet. Great defense. Unable to break through. Returned my backhand and forehand smashes. Returned everything I hit. Got mad, played too hard. Made mistakes, missed back edge over and over again. Was losing badly. Hated defensive players, wondered when he would attack. He didn't attack. He returned and kept scoring. Wondered if Chinese wasn't Japanese. Lost game. Two out of three. Lost second game. Convinced he is Japanese.

Thought of Terry and the Pirates description of Chinese and Japanese and how to tell them apart. Had forgotten difference. Would have to learn again. Know your enemy. Always smiling, always apologizing, always winning. Mysterious East. Lost three games in row. Question: if he was a Japanese spy wouldn't he have let me win one game? Gain confidence, gain friendship, get information later. Tried to remember Cagney movie about Shanghai, China.

May 26, 1943. Transferred to Sioux City, Iowa, for Aviation Student training.

December 1943. To Santa Ana, California.

January 1944. Classified as Bombardier-Navigator. Most of class has washed out.

March 1944. To Kingman, Arizona. Gunnery training.

May 6, 1944. Lower ball turret. Bad experience. Hatch opened up at twenty thousand feet. Hung by heels and gun sights. Sergeant in charge glad I wasn't killed. Hugged me when I returned. Lucky to be here. Good reflexes. Could have slipped out.

November 1944. Transferred to Victorville, California. Bombardiering School. About two-thirds of original class has washed out. Boys from colleges, necktie wearers, etc. I attribute success to fast reflexes, good physical condition. Long hours from five a.m. till midnight. Eat Mr. Goodbars and Bit-O-Honeys in bed at night. Older boys, twenty-five, twenty-seven, very weary. I never tire. Tell jokes, dance and entertain at night. War is a young man's game. Reflexes, good vision. Candy for energy, clear head, strong neck muscles.

December 1944. Graduated as a flight officer. Absolutely delirious with joy. Can't believe it. A commission at eighteen. Can't wait to strut into classroom back home. Class is now in eleventh grade. Thirty day furlough.

Spent four days traveling from L.A. to Columbia. Four hundred dollar wardrobe, three hundred dollars in pocket. Flight officer at eighteen . . . Lord, let the war last forever.

Arrived home for thirty day furlough. Folks met train. Mother crying, smiling, kissing. Dad standing behind her looking good in Navy uniform. Shook his hand, embraced. Smelled Sen-Sen. Banter about whether he should salute me.

Walked up Cedar Street to Broad. Hands filled with luggage. Enlisted Army men everywhere. Men salute me. Dad returns salute saying, "At ease, doggies. Smoke if you got them." Everybody laughed. Great moment.

Front room—nothing changed from last time. Same cane furniture, same floral pattern on slip covers and linoleum. Everything pointing toward the stove. Looked like enlisted men's room but no ping pong. Outdoor type cane furniture, green and red floral pattern still holding up. Always hated cane furniture. Cane marks stay on face or forehead if you sleep against it. Linoleum floor covering.

New dog behind stove under stove pipe. Heavy with litter. Sleepy eyes. Slept under pipe. Would probably throw litter under pipe.

Only new things in room were dog and mementos lined across mantelpiece. Will list in minute. View of used car lot from sofa. Back to mantelpiece. A real treat. Spotless cloth under objects. Shrinelike. At left end an ashtray from Carson City, Nevada, in form of a gray and black coiled rattlesnake. Real rattlers. (I mailed this.) French monkeys—brown, dwarflike. See no evil, hear no evil, speak no evil, from Casablanca. (Dad mailed this.)

Picture of me squinting into sun. Picture of Dad squinting into sun. Photograph of Dad a collector's item. It had been enlarged from a much smaller shot. Photographer had painted in blue eyes that weren't in register. (Dad's eyes were gray.) Had dabbed cheeks with red. Red was in register. Looked like rouge. Had on full-dress Navy uniform. Holding left sleeve around full face like a beer advertisement to show label. When photograph was made Dad had three stripes, now only one. Leaning on something. Probably bar. Photographer-Artist had coiled and furled yards of American Flag bunting behind him. Same reds and blues as on cheeks and eyes. Entire work of art in mica-covered frame. Frame in shape of horseshoe with two miniature flags at top corners. Shamrock only thing missing. Mother thought it beautiful. Had had the highly successful Photographer-Artist do one for me. Same as hers but more red in cheeks, more blue in eyes and flag. Mother kept saying how the man was an artist and describing how small original photograph was.

Photographer was not only an artist but a smart man as well. Left large flag entwined space at bottom of frame for dedication, inscription, etc. Mother had written a simple "From the Sailor" on her photograph. Not so on the one to me. Had spent night worrying the phrase out. Inspiration must have come with morning birds. Had printed in beautiful curling scroll "To My High Flying Son From His Sea Going Daddy."

Back to mantelpiece. Center of mantel large clock that worked but wouldn't chime. No glass on face, no minute hand. On right of clock gift from me from Needles, California. "Home Sweet Home" carved by hand on wood frame in shape of small cottage. Above mantelpiece gift from me from Gulfport, Mississippi.

Pillowcase. Rich thick silk, Air Corps Song in gold against blue background, bordered in heavy gold braided cord. American Flags embossed at each corner. Clouds behind Air Corps Song. Mother said it was so beautiful she had cried when she first saw it. Too good for pillowcase. Had taken Norman Rockwell print down and tacked it up above mantelpiece. Could be seen from any point in the room.

Remember buying it with tears in my eyes and lump in throat. Am proud of Air Corps. If killed in action or training want my head lying on this pillow. Only paid three ninety-eight for death pillow. Would have paid fifty.

Rest of mantelpiece filled with postcards from Dad and me. Views of Casbah (his), Gulfport (mine), Cannes (his), Mobile (mine), The Straits of Gibraltar (his), Main Street in Snapping Shoals Alabama (mine), Arc de Triomphe (his), Cactus plant in Yucca Arizona (mine). All humorous cards in pile not displayed. Colored boy on pot, colored boy in pot, full house at outdoor privy, Watermelon Jones . . . all old standbys.

Books at far end. Complete Works of Poe, Modern Screen, Modern Romances, tracts from Holiness Church, sheet music and words to "There's a Star Spangled Banner Waving Somewhere."

Looked out window: 1934 Chevrolet "A Steal at $250." Dad in kitchen getting beer for all; Mother in kitchen frying something, baking something, singing something:

"There's a star spangled banner waving somewhere
O'er a distant land so very far away.
Only Uncle Sam's brave soldiers get to go there. . . ."

February 17, 1945. High School class glad to see me. Low, eleventh grade. Teacher glad, but suspicious. Calls principal. Principal checks my A.G.O. card to see if I'm impersonating an officer. Class very impressed with my nonchalance. Girls in class seem younger than I remembered. Bobby socks, short dresses, pony tails. Will look over twelfth grade. Maybe young teachers. Take six classmates to lunch. Pick up a few salutes on way to S and S cafeteria. Columbia full of enlisted men from Fort Jackson. Infantrymen, Tank Corps, Artillery, etc.

March 1945. Pinetree Texas transitional training in B-29's. Large sluggish plane. Many malfunctions. Colonel a demon on flying every plane every day. He has bet with other Air Field Colonels. Who can fly most planes. Many accidents. Much drinking. Very little time for basketball.

May 1 to 3, 1945. Roommate in Pinetree, Texas, Jonathan Gates from Texarkana. First lieutenant . . . pilot on B-29.

When sober gentle as spring rain. When drunk, fights. Loves to fight. Will fight anybody. Usually men much larger. Gates is tall but thin. Wears pants low on hips. Claims men in Texarkana wear them low with gun belts. Believe him.

Rattlesnake, Texas, nine miles from Pinetree. Bus runs back and forth. Takes men in sober, brings them back drunk. Rattlesnake small, three street lights. Two honky-tonks: the Black Cat and the Green Light. Both serve food and beer. No whisky. Have to bring own. Can buy setups. Black Cat has black cat on black fence against white wall. Mirrored chandelier spins around producing different colors on floor and walls. Booths along both walls. Jukebox at other wall. Green Light has no chandelier. No real atmosphere. Urinal long folded, ridged, galvanized steel. Three twenty-five pound blocks of ice. Will stand ten men. Sign in toilet: "Don't piss on seats." Green Light doesn't have class of Black Cat. All hillbilly records. Merle Travis, Sons of Pioneers, Ernie Tubb. "There's a Tear in My Beer, Little Darling" . . . big hit with the gunners and the ground crews.

Gates plays "Smoke on the Water" record over and over. Stays sober.

May 4th. Black Cat. Fried chicken, biscuits, honey, beer, ice cream with chocolate sauce. Good meal. Farmers and low type enlisted men in other booths. I go to john. Return, find Gates in fight with another lieutenant. Quick fight. Lieutenant out cold. Gates drags him into latrine. Lays body in urinal. Water running, ice, very messy. Gates told to leave the Cat. Told never to return. Bad for Gates. Can only go to Green Light. Had better be careful.

May 5th. Green Light. Gates drunk. Wild, fighting drunk. Walks to middle of floor. Invites anyone to fight him. Sorry sight. First lieutenant. Disgrace to uniform. Most of crowd enlisted men. No one volunteers. Gates throws blouse on floor and invites enlisted men. Big corporal steps out. Gates smiles, tears into him. Great fight. Neither man moves from center of dance floor. Head to head. Toe to toe. Hard shot to heads, to bodies. No ducking, no feinting. Only short and long shots. Both good in-fighters. Blood flying. Still toe to toe. Not a glass broken. Not a chair overturned. Under chandelier, red, green, purple, blue. Chandelier spins slowly. Fight is slow, then fast again. Sound of heavy breathing and thumps of blows. Corporal seems to be ahead. Says, "Had enough?" Gates grunts, "Shit, no."

Fight continues. On and on. Much blood. Shirts ruined. No one stirs to break up fight. Corporal is favorite. Everyone wants Gates beaten. Both stop at once. Smile at each other. Gates looks happy, ecstatic. Got worst of fight but enjoyed himself. Puts arm around corporal's shoulder. They walk outside into night. Someone takes four beers to them. They sit on step and talk. Probably about fights. Talk from ten to one. Great friends. Management throws blouses and hats out door. Says Gates is through at Green Light.

May 7th. Gates and Corporal Joe Daniels from Stanley's Store, Georgia, not admitted at Green Light. Hang around yard. At first asking, then begging. Later cursing and threatening to break door down. It begins to rain. They begin shouting for justice, shelter, food. Long after dark, long hard rain. Shouting, pleading, cursing. Two brickbats slam against the building. Threaten to smash windows. Rain soaked, probably cold, probably sober. Have no place to go. Black Cat and Green Light only honky-tonks. Drugstore no seats. Post Office closed. Hardware and feed store closed. Two more brickbats probably same ones. Leave in rain for Black Cat. Gone thirty minutes. Come back. . . . "Have a heart, Sam. Where can we go? We'll be quiet." . . . Pause. Long pause . . . thinking . . . "We'll be quiet, Sam. Word of an officer, Sam. Going overseas pretty soon, Sam. Probably Iwo Jima. . . ." Sad but everyone laughs. Sam laughs. "We're going to fight for bastards like you, Sam." . . . Two more brickbats. They were drinking. Where did they get setups?

May 10th. Gates and Daniels sit on front steps of Green Light. Sam tries to chase them away. They claim they want to sit on steps and listen to music. No harm. Don't want ice or setups.

May 15th. Gates and Daniels sat still for four nights. To-night great dancing. Wacs from Big Springs. . . . Gates and Daniels break through screen door and start dancing. Won't leave. Sam calls MPs. Big fight with MPs. Gates court-martialed next day. Thirty day restriction, a hundred dollar fine, no promotion for six months. Corporal Joe Daniels gets stockade for sixty days . . . probably hard labor. Noblesse oblige.

June 16th. Gates first day out. "Have a heart, Sam. Let's let bygones . . . sorry as hell. Terrific case of war nerves . . . B-29's unsafe . . . make anybody jumpy." Sam lets him back in.

June 20th. Raining hard. Big night. Floor crowded. Women are in from Eureka. Wac officers in. Late in month enlisted men are broke. Mostly officers in Green Light. Whisky and fried chicken everywhere. Things too good for Gates. Wipes the ice and setups out of two booths. Three men jump him at once. Two hold me. I'm easy to hold. Can see handwriting on wall. Three men beat him. More standing around waiting for the three to get tired. Throw Gates out into rain. He lies on steps. Water from drain pipe falling on his head. Finally goes back to base. Sam is through with him. Everybody is through with him. Except me. I have to live with him.

July 1st. Saturday, pay day. Off at noon. Line up for bus to Black Cat. Gates in line. Everybody wonders where he is going. Black Cat west of town. First stop. Everybody off but Gates. Time is one-thirty. Where will he go. Someone says back to base. Bus stops at drugstore. Gates gets out. Watch him from steps of Black Cat. Goes to whisky store next to drugstore. Then back to drugstore for cokes. Loves cokes with whisky. Comes outside sits in outdoor phone booth. Must be 120 degrees in booth. Sits on stool looks up road. Route 66. Nothing up road but tumbleweed and jack rabbits. Nearest town Eureka, sixty miles. Same road goes to Dallas. Same road goes to green hills in the east of Texas near his home. Maybe he sees home. Continues staring. Continues smoking, continues drinking.

July 15. Except for small scar over left eye, Gates has healed from last fight. Duane Wallace, navigator, Atlanta, Georgia, and I have dates with Blanche and June Elroy. Girls own mattress rejuvenating factory near Rattlesnake. Girls have arranged date for Gates. He is enthusiastic. Wild with joy. Getting out. Date. First date in months. Whisky, maybe dancing. But where? Eureka, Texas, too far. Black Cat, Green Light still off limits for him. Blanche and June know Gates' problem. Very understanding girls. Salt of the earth.

Meet at Elroy sisters' house. Gates' date late. Probably waiting for darkness. Start drinking at once. Living room covered with cotton lint and round cotton balls for ticking mattresses. Shop out back. Four Roses. Three Feathers, PM, Schenley Red Label. Salami, cold chicken, crackers, olives, peanuts. Discuss where to go. No place. Too many to sit in Blanche's Ford. Blanche suggest sand pits. Says there is light there. No one has been there but Blanche. Blanche says she likes it fine.

Blanche likes everything fine. Mustn't be critical of her. Real sport. Cold chicken, salami, olives, crackers, everything provided by Blanche.

Knock at door. Gates answers. Later he said he thought she was panhandling. Announces she is Gwendolyn Hornsby. Gates crestfallen, but revives quickly. First woman in months. Beggers, choosers. Small talk with Gwendolyn . . . weather, roads, crops, mattress rejuvenating business. Lights her cigarette. Makes her big drink. Schenley Red Label. Perfect gentleman. Flatters her. Over forty. Stout but merry. Big legs, small feet. Black curly hair close to face. Perspiration above lip. Twinkle in eye. Light on feet. Probably good dancer. Dressed in shiny green silk type dress. Solid color makes her look larger than she is. Already large enough. Picks up food lightly with first two fingers. Makes small roselike mouth. Has high voice. Chews daintily with front teeth. No neck. Very fond of salami. Very fond of cold chicken. Lines up olive pits in ash tray. Artistic maybe. Gates switches to gin after Three Feathers and Schenley Red Label. Gwen still eating with back to us. Says Gin on Whisky Makes you Frisky. All encouragement Gates needs. Kisses place where neck should be. Touches her back and slides hand down. Gwen laughs and pushes him away. Gates comes back. Grabs her with two hands. Very crude. Blanche and June pretend shock. Pretend they are blushing. No luck. Gwen is mad. Mouth is full. Face red. Pushes Gates back hard. Threatens to slap him. Swallows hard. "Can't you see I'm eating."

Girls pack food in shoe boxes. Carry whisky, ice, cokes to car. Off to sand pits. No moon, warm. Rough dirt road to pits. Jack rabbit cuts across headlight beams. Sand pits. Five lighted gas pipes burning off gas pockets. White sand far as eye can see. Steep bank. Great place for sliding. Unpack car. Blanche in charge of refreshments and snacks. Very neat, wants a table. Gates takes spare wheel out of car. Blanche sets refreshments on wheel. Gates and I slide down bank. Sand dry, soft . . . marvelous. Go again. Blanche serves drinks and snacks under gas pipe. Duane and Gates wrestle at edge of slide. Fall over laughing. Blanche has peanuts and olives in little paper cups. Demon on neatness. Much drinking. Blanche complains about not wearing slacks. Wants to slide down. Says doesn't want to skin ass. Gates takes off pants gives them to Blanche. Puts pants on over dress. Slides down screaming. Comes back up. Arranges table, serves olives.

Takes another big drink, slides down again. Gates slides down after her in his shorts. Long silence. Dark at the bottom of the slide. Doesn't take much imagination. After a while, they climb back up. Blanche takes a big drink. Four Roses all gone. Gwendolyn afraid of the slide. Duane takes her to car. Blanche pushes June down slide. Gates pushes me after her.

Finish the PM and the Three Feathers. Gwendolyn eats

last of olives. Claims she wants a Bar-B-Que. Wants to go to the Black Cat. Very funny. Even Gates laughs. Everybody drunk. Who decided to leave? Who drove? Someone dragged mattresses from shop into living room. Girls in one room. Duane, Gates and me on mattresses. Remember Gates getting up in night and going into girls' room.

Early in morning sun coming up Route 66. Lying awake on mattress. Gates and Duane talking. Duane didn't like getting stuck with Gwendolyn. Gates is quiet goes to table. Drinks Schenley Red Label out of bottle. No chaser.

I tell Gates to lie back down. Let's sleep late. Girls will cook big breakfast. Time for argument later. Wants to argue now. Stands by table in olive drab shorts, nothing else on. Starts shouting at Duane. Says he deserved Gwendolyn. Duane covers head with sheet. "Later, Gates, Later." "No, not later—now." Calls Duane a yellow dog. Duane gets up fast. No one calls him yellow. Fight. Fight all over the room. Break a chair, glasses. Bottle of Schenley Red Label doesn't fall.

Blanche comes in . . . calm, collected. Aims a .45 automatic at Gates. He stops and backs toward the door. Through door. Blanche throws him clothes and shoes. "I keep a respectable house here. Don't ever bring him back."

Gates dresses in bright yard. Starts walking toward Rattlesnake. Schenley Red Label in middle of table. Duane and I take a drink. No chasers. Hear Gates whistling as he walks away. Will never understand Gates. Schenley Red Label very rough in the morning.

DEAR DIARY: WANDA

DEAR DIARY—OCTOBER 6, 1944. Tonight I met Wanda Cole. Drum majorette at Eureka, Texas, High School. Blonde hair, dimples, blue eyes, long legs . . . met her during last half after band left field. Cold night . . . I give her my trench coat. Hugh Evans and three girls from band get in car. Drive to Black Cat for rum cokes and dancing. On way back to town, girls begin singing "March On, Eureka High." . . . Can't get Wanda alone. Consumed with lust.

October 7. Attempt to bank fire of lust in movie. Alan Ladd, "This Gun for Hire." Veronica Lake stands round with hair over one eye. Can't get arm around Wanda in show. Popcorn, Snickers, Ju-Jy Fruit. Will permit only hand holding. Settle for hand holding. Smell of buttered popcorn. Hands slick with butter and salt. Try to touch her breast, casual-like. Stupid. Pinched my arm with fingernails. Still have red mark. Curfew at eleven in movie. Lights go on with last ten minutes of "This Gun" left. Management announces All Out. Wonder if Ladd makes out with Lake. Make a nice couple.

October 8. Hugh Evans, Dolores, Wanda and me. Hugh is B-29 co-pilot, 1300 hours. Hugh drives car fast. Flat country, no curves, heading for the Cat. Dark night, no stars, jack rabbits cut across light beams, look like airdales. Big rattlesnake lying in road soaking up heat from asphalt. Must be 15 feet long. Hears car. Hugh says they can't see in winter. Snake coils. Rares up maybe five feet. Frightening. Rocks head

[109]

back and forth. He hears tires singing on road. Prepares to strike. Girls scream. Strikes. Flops around wheel. Car bounces. Terrible noise. Terrible feeling. He's thrown under car. Back wheel catches him again. I feel awful. Nervous, need drink. Wanda is trembling in my arms. Smile and thank dead 15-foot rattler. Wait till trembling stops. Her cheeks are cold. Her hands are cold. Kiss her hands. Kiss her cheeks, face, eyes, lips. Kiss her again and again and again. Her arms are around me. Birds sing, bells ring, and the molten lava of love is rumbling. I have never been more tender. A newer, softer, finer, smoother skin now covers my body. Rise and soar and do slow rolls and figure eights above the dirt of lust. No longer want to get her in bed. Want to kiss her, hold her, protect her from all enemies seen and unseen—burning houses, sinking ships, spinning planes. Imagine sky writing across west Texas: I love you Wanda . . . I love you Wanda. B-29's would have hard time doing the W's. I keep telling her I love her over and over and over again. Same words different voices. Mean it . . . mean every word. Mean everything . . . very serious, very dull.

The red neon of the the Black Cat interrupts thirtieth I love you. . . . The Cat—long room, chrome and vinyl seats at counter, bad food, plastic covered menus, individual juke boxes in front of each seat. In back, dance hall—long room, booths at each side, juke box against far well, twenty-four records, good music. Wanda wants to dance. I want to say I love you, do you love me. Want to hold hands and make plans for future. We dance to "House of Blue Lights," "Summit Ridge Drive," "Cherokee." Great music . . . no hillbilly records.

Later, take her home. Long burning kisses on porch. This is girl for me . . . "My Ideal" from song of same name. I propose. She wants to talk about Ray Smith, the fullback for Eureka High. I keep proposing. She says I'm getting dull. Used to be a lot of fun. Now too serious. I leap off high porch and spread-eagle into a low pine tree to show I am still as funny as ever. Successful but very painful. Tear pants and shorts, sustain severe crotch burns from rough bark of tree. No matter, love had conquered lust. Love has won the day. . . .

October 9. Same as October 8. Go to the Cat. Wanda great shag dancer. Sinatra makes her cry. Very sensitive girl. Will make excellent wife, mother. Dance some more. Sinatra sings "Nancy." Wandy goes to washroom. Stops crying but starts again when I whisper one thousandth proposal. Hugh and Dolores go to motel. I feel superior to Hugh and Dolores. Very tender on porch. I hope Alan Ladd makes out with Veronica Lake—both have same straight blond hair. Faces a little alike too. Everyone should marry. Go up town alone. Look in stores at diamond rings. Very expensive. Will buy ring no matter what cost is. Will marry and go to engineering school on G.I. bill. Visions of wearing ex-officer uniform on campus. Combat jacket with B-29 on back, slide rule on belt, Wanda at side through thick and thin. Look forward to thin days. Will live on love. Homework late at night with slide rule. Advanced mathematics. Wanda serving coffee, eggs, grits and bacon (maybe no bacon—love and tenderness require no bacon). This is a corny thought, not in keeping with present state of mind.

October 10—morning. No sleep all night. Toss and turn. No dreams of sex, only hand holding, sunset, birds, bowers of flowers. Made pillow into Wanda. Held her tenderly, protected her from flames, floods, famine. No sleep but wake up cool and refreshed. True test of love. . . .

October 10—afternoon. Must keep diary notes up to date. Wanda and I will one day sit before fire and read them. Will plant seeds of love now, harvest in years to come. Silver anniversary. Wanda's yellow hair now tinged with gray, skin and eyes and long legs still perfect . . .

October 10—night. Long entry, many pages . . . will report as it happened.

Take cab. Pass motel where Hugh and Dolores are staying.

See car. Feel sorry for Hugh and Dolores, but maybe they will marry. Have double wedding. Go to Wanda's house. Meet father. Good man, stands straight, looks me straight in the eye. Texan, oil field work, pioneer stock, backbone of America. He has small feet. Like him. Will make good father-in-law.

He questions me about school, home, money, etc. Only natural—a father has to look out for only daughter. Says wife left him, has had to raise Wanda by himself. Doesn't want her getting involved with any white trash. Adds that anybody can be an officer these days but war won't last forever. Men and boys will be separated when country gets back on feet.

I answer all questions, look him straight in the eye. Honorable intentions, all trace of lust gone. I will stand any test. Pure heart, spotless soul, unblemished love.

Have drink with Mr. Cole while Wanda dresses. He drinks straight bourbon, no chaser, no ice. Drinks and shakes head a little. Good man, strong man. I like to see a man who can handle his liquor. Hear Wanda singing in shower. Soft, lovely voice, pretty song, "Oh, What It Seemed to Be." Hold glass in both hands, look into whisky. Perfect happiness, cup overfloweth. Will call Mr. Cole "Dad" tomorrow. Will ask for hand. I have four hundred dollars, and another three fifty on the first. Can get ring, trip to Mexico City. "We'll Settle Down Near Dallas" song. Drive image of Wanda nude in shower out of mind. Man is born in sin. Wanda will be big hit on campus with other G.I. wives. She will be younger and they will show her housekeeping methods. See small apartment . . . in the whisky . . . see embroidered silk pillow-case. "Pinetree Army Air Base," "God Bless Our Mortgaged Home"—Wanda would like that. Toaster, coffee table, maybe navigation sectional maps on wall, leather chair, me studying advanced mathematics, thermodynamics. Slide rule, sharp pencils, late hours studying. Sacrifice for security later. Wanda on chair arm, stroking my hair, serving coffee. All is love. . . .

Look up from whisky into future Dad's eyes. His smile

seems to have changed. Licks his lips. Question: "Are you getting it?" Repeat Question: "Are you getting it?" Unbeliev-
able, but by now unmistakable. "If you aren't, you're the first
one."

Want to hit him, want to turn kitchen table over on him
and give him a John Wayne overhand right with the follow-
through.

He says she has had many proposals. Attracts men (mostly
officers) like bitch dog in heat. Men keep hanging around,
circling house, sniffing, waiting until his back is turned so
they can break in through screen door. Claims she has had
many affairs. I have sudden flash . . . future Dad is still
future Dad. He is merely testing me. I laugh inwardly . . .
look him in eye. I say nothing matters, I love her. And what
she's done in past is her business.

I've passed test magnificently. One hundred percent. A.
Head of class . . . Summa Cum?? Inwardly talking rapidly:
nothing matters, my love, we'll be together for eternity. Will
take her away from crude, stupid, uneducated father. Test is
passed but I don't like method.

Wanda ready, comes out. Dressed in blue suit, white shoes,
and hat. Stunning, hair bright, skin radiant. Never such
beauty. Beautiful, beautiful girl and she's all mine. Consider
taking her away tonight. Can catch Greyhound or "All American" bus tonight from Eureka to Dallas . . . "We'll Settle
Down Near Dallas" song, our song, she doesn't know it yet.

Take cab to the Cat. Eleven dollars, could buy toaster with
that but no matter. Put her white hat on back window shelf
of car and begin kissing her. "I love you, do you love me?"
"Yes, I love you, do you love me?" Marriage? Yes. Honey-
moon? Yes. Love and marriage. G.I. Bill, engineering. Yes.
Yes. Yes. Yes.

Stars low on black horizon. Milky Way bright like illumi-
nated lace. I point out Orion and the Little Bear. Tell her
about Magnetic North Pole, size of Betelgeuse. No, I'm not a
genius. I'm so happy I keep talking about navigation, B-29

procedure. Actually want to delay talk of marriage, too sweet, too unbearably sweet to discuss right now. Tears are in eyes as I tell what co-pilot does during landing and stalling speed of B-29.

Approach the Cat from south. Wanda begins putting on lipstick. Pocket flashlight for making-up. Round O with mouth while applying lipstick. Sweet lovely girl. Touch the hem of her dress. Tell her about night clubs in Columbia. How we'll live on the sixty-five dollars a month and have money left over for dancing, movies, State Fair, Clemson-Carolina game in October. . . . Eleven dollars cab fare. Will cut corners and save money later.

Dance until 2 a.m. Take eleven dollar cab ride back to her house. Lights are on. Future Dad drunk. Hasn't stopped drinking since we left. Wanda cold. Put trench coat over her. Take her inside. Kiss her good night.

Future Dad insists I take one drink with him. Do so. Look at him . . . ugly, drunk, small mean hands, insensitive. Has weak eyes and mouth, licks lips before speaking. Uses vile, crude language. I realize there has been no game or contest to test my integrity, intentions, etc. Future Dad is a sorry man. True white trash.

He wants to talk. Great deal of lip licking. Makes little sense. Asks me again if I have had relations with Wanda. I'm shocked. Say "No, sir." He sits down at kitchen table. I sit across from him. Bottle in middle. He slaps table for effect, upsets glass, laughs.

"Thought you were a brighter boy than that. Guess it's like I said," he mumbles. "Anyone these days can be an officer."

Says he has no use for women. No women. Even own daughter. Claims he had a miserable wife, nagged him, dogged him, bored him. Finally told her to pack her rags and get out. He had thought she would take Wanda along. No luck.

Throws glass against wall. Doesn't break. Drinks out of bottle, lips the neck. Looks like he's drinking out of a tube.

Starts talking about screwing. Very crude. Hope Wanda can't hear him. Says wife miserable, always tired, always cold, menstrual period once a week . . . no quality. Prefers colored girls, or wetbacks, around El Paso. Eager, wild, cheap, pneumatic. Claims man works all day on a rig needs big meals, good whisky, good woman in bed. Says Wanda probably bad screw like mother. Runs in family. Asks me again if we haven't had relations. Very crude. Feel sorry for Wanda. Know her life has always been this way. How could my gentle flaxen-haired love stand all this. I will take her away as soon as possible. Tomorrow. Will get advance on money and we will go tomorrow. Won't write bastard father. Plan to never see future Dad again.

Mr. Cole finishes bottle, sets it down carefully and starts leaning back in straight cane chair. Falls over backwards. I make no attempt to catch him. Hope he kills himself. His face is relaxed as he goes down. Falls hard but no pain. Slight smile around weak lips, small hands at side. Evil, crude, stupid man. Decide to leave. Hear Wanda crying in bedroom. She has heard father fall. Go in to see her. Cover her up. Says he does this all the time. Will be out for twelve to fourteen hours.

Wanda shivering. Covers do no good. Wants me to crawl in bed with her and keep her warm. She is having chill. Take off shoes, socks. Take off blouse, shirt. Leave pants on. She insists I take them off. Will wrinkle. Do so from other side of bed. Very modest in front of future wife. Slide into warm bed with just shorts and T-shirt on. She is in slip. We hug. Slip is all she has on. Feel body pushing against me. Poor thing cold. Hold her tight. Kiss her tenderly. Kiss her gently. Kiss her neck, ears, throat, eyes. Kiss her mouth over and over again. She presses against me. Slides against me. Pants. Kisses hard. Touches me. Wants me. What to do. Lust vs. Love. I hold her close whispering "We'll be married tomorrow." She says Fine, but now is all right. Wants me now. Rubs hands over my body. Pushes sheet to bottom of bed. Little light from street. Can see breast through slip. Runs her hands down her own body. I wonder where she learned that. Only natural I tell myself. Natural instinct. Takes my knee. Places it between legs and squeezes. I'm sweating. Can feel hair between legs with knee. Both panting. What to do? Try to explain about marriage. How we'll screw every night. Don't say word screw. Say relations. Her slip slides way up above knees. Shoulder strap off shoulder. Can see tip of breast. About to go out of my mind. Roll to side of bed. Hear father snoring in kitchen. Wanda pursuing. Touching, pressing, showing. If only I wasn't in love with her. What a strange thing love is. Think of popcorn, movies, handholding, where did all this come from? Are women like this? Grab her fiercely. She relaxes. All mine. I say, "My darling bride, you'll thank me in the morning. I want ours to be a perfect marriage." Kiss her savagely. Shorts soaked. Final kiss. Get out of bed. Dress in hurry. She has turned back to me. Kiss her on ear and leave house. Brave, courageous, love inspired idiot.

October 11. She won't see me. I call eighteen times. Go to house. Door locked. Record player on. Glimpse officer's blouse hanging in front room. Enraged. Have never been so mad. Break out back window. Crawl in. Officer still dressed. Wanda in night robe. Maybe not guilty but no matter. Beat hell out of tall skinny first john. He's poor fighter and can't duck or hit. Goes down three times. Father staggers out. "What the hell is going on here?" Wanda won't look at me. Picks up funny book of Superman and turns back and reads. First john still on floor. I storm away. Should have at least screwed her. Probably have been the forty-fifth. Probably terrific. Probably never got enough. Probably make a terrible wife. . . . Turn down Rose Street and walk toward town. Go to first bar and drink beer until can barely walk. Pick up fat woman. Must weigh two hundred and forty. Small furnished room. Bare light hanging in middle of room, frayed cord hanging from light with rabbit's foot on end. Bed in middle of the room. Can reach light from bed. Chenille spread long over the hill. Pillow cases dirty and greasy. White cartons everywhere. Says she likes Chinese fried shrimp and curry sauce. Claims a little place around the corner delivers it for a dollar twenty. Send out for some. Eat in bed. Very squalid. Feel superior to fat girl but to little else in the world. She licks her fingers daintily. Small smile. Wanda. Wanda, how I loved her. It would have been so easy too.

Make some weird sort of love to fat girl. Even bigger than I thought. I ask old question about how fat people got together. She smiles and demonstrates. Very crude. Love over. Fat girl gives off musky smell. Faint but terrible. Go to sleep thinking about Wanda with the light burning directly over us. Wake up later. Have slid down to woman. Her great weight had caused the mattress to pitch in that direction. It is either sleeping on the steep hill or against her. Faint musk smell woke me. Look up at light. Almost obscured by giant hulk of woman.

Frightening at first, then funny. Think of description: White Whale, The Great Barrier Reef, La Obese. Like The Great Barrier Reef best.

Climb up steep angle of mattress and get out of bed. Dress in john. Cover up Great Barrier Reef and leave. Light still on. Musk smell still in air. Man is born in sin. Have black and white soda and go back to base.

A long, trying, educational, tragic day. . . .

Recall line from Merjekowski: Choosing a wife, oh Calendrino, is like plunging one's hand into a box of snakes hoping to draw forth an eel.

But still she was a lovely girl. Already the process of forgiving setting in. Will phone her in a few days. This time we'll crawl into bed and I won't need any encouragement to take off pants.

Never get chance, though. She won't see me again. Tell her I have diamond ring with no obligations. For old times sake. Pull out all stops. We'll go to movie. Popcorn, hold hands, etc. No soap.

And to think of that divine creature lying there before me in the moonlight with a slip barely on, squirming and asking for it. That's right, squirming and asking and begging for it, and me so goddam full of love and horse shit, I didn't know what to do.

Live and learn. . . .

October 12. No entry.

THE B-FLAT
CORNET

OLD JOE BONAPARTE was talking and I was listening.

"Some mornings I wake up feeling so good I sit on the edge of the bed and shout hoo-ray. That's right, that's how I feel. Other mornings I just lay there and stare up at the ceiling and don't care about nothing. Rain or shine, it's all the same."

Joe held on to the rocking-chair arm and began poking the fire with a long forked stick. He pushed a big pine log over. When it stopped smoking and began to burn he moved it to the back of the fireplace.

"You see that calendar back there?"

I looked back at the wall behind us. On the wall above a mahogany dresser was a 1941 calendar with a picture of Joe and his band grinning out.

Joe said, "What year that calendar say?"

I said, "Nineteen-forty-one."

"That was taken in New Orleans. We had a good group all during that time."

He looked at me and then back at the fire.

"You say you're Ben Hunnicutt's son?"

"Yes."

"And you work for the *Record?*"

"That's right. And if you don't mind, Joe, I'd like to ask you a few questions."

"What kind of questions?"

"Oh, about how it was then. About the band. Just general things."

He was quiet a minute. "I don't know. I don't like letting out too much information."

He began poking at the log again. I looked back at the calendar. The light was bad but I saw Old Joe's face shining out and right across his chest he had his cornet. The rest of the wall was covered with sheets from *The Afro-American News,* news clippings from *Variety,* and a big sepia-colored double page from the *Atlanta Constitution.*

I thought Joe had forgotten I was there but after a while he began to talk.

"It's no good when you stop playing music. 'Cause the music don't stop, it keeps on going and going. . . . Do you play anything?"

"Little trumpet."

"You any good?"

"Pretty good."

He paused and carefully laid his stick down. "You know how the lip works then. Well, mine went out in New Orleans. Let's see . . . it was about four, five years after that picture. I guess it had gone before but it always came back strong. This time it was different and I mean I felt different all over. . . .

"It came back all right, but it came back cold. It felt like ice and it scared me to death. And I mean I just couldn't get up enough steam to make it work. I reckon I could have stayed around and sat most of the tough numbers out . . . or else I could have pretended I was playing. It was my band. I owned it. I could have made them carry me. But that ain't no good. That ain't no good at all."

He picked up his stick and aimed it at the log.

"Naw. That ain't no good at all. It's no good because you know there's some young one out there in the audience waiting on you. I know, 'cause I did it too. I used to sit out there and pray that the cornet man would have a stroke or that he'd just get up and walk off the stand. And the leader would say 'Hey out there, are there any cornet players out there?' That's the way it goes. So when you start playing bad and splitting the long ones or shading them you can feel those young bucks crowding in close.

"I mean they'd be watching you and watching you close. They don't have to hear much, 'cause they've been listening too long and you can't fool them. And a lot of times when you're playing into the lights, it's worse. You can't see them but you know they're out there watching and grinning.

"My musician friends tried to help me out. But it wasn't any use. They keep saying, 'Ease up, Joe . . . don't push it, Joe. You got it now. Don't work so hard, you're still in charge' . . . and things like that. But it wasn't any use. No use at all. 'Cause when they tell you to quit leaning on it you lean that much harder. And you try to make it look casual-like, but just the same you're leaning on it and the music doesn't come out right. It comes out different and I mean it ain't worth a damn. . . .

"You care for a drink?"

He got up and moved over to the table and unscrewed the lid on a half-gallon Mason jar of white corn.

I said, "Looks good. Yes, I'd like one."

He began pouring the whisky into two tall glasses.

"Anything you want to know in particular?"

I got up and took the glasses. "Yes, how about Ethel Brown?"

Joe pulled a fresh lemon out of a bag on the table and sliced it in half.

"So you're Ben Hunnicutt's son?"

"I'm the oldest."

"Well, I'll be dogged. Boy. I knew your Dad when he wasn't any higher than this table."

We went back to the fire and sat down. He handed me half of the lemon and we both took a drink. It was good whisky.

"Yeah, I remember Ethel Brown all right. Let's see . . . I

think I met up with her in Vicksburg. Man, that was way back there before the big war. Lot of whisky and good times around then and everybody was playing banjoes. Oh, Ethel she was something all right. The Lord never made a finer girl than Ethel Brown. . . .

"Yeah, Ethel Brown . . . yeah, I liked that little girl. And she had herself a sweet voice too. I had me a Martin B-flat cornet about then. That was a good instrument . . . yessir."

He took another drink and leaned his elbows on his knees and looked at the fire. He put the glass on the floor and held up his hands as if he were measuring a small fish.

"Wasn't no longer than that. Not one inch longer. But it had a big bore, a solid gold mouthpiece and the sweetest middle-register tones you ever heard."

He looked at his hands, brought them in another inch and shook his head.

"Man, I miss that little rascal. I used to play that little thing just as natural as breathing. Never no strain. And when I went for a high note or a hard one it was always there waiting on me like it was expecting me.

"That little Martin got broke up several times and I'd keep soldering her up and taping her up until she looked more gray and black than brass. And I'd play it all night, and I mean strong. Most nights when the place closed I'd go outside and sit back of a bale of cotton and mute her down or else I'd get out in a drain ditch and I'd keep playing and messing around with that little scudder until the sun came out. Lord . . . I loved that little horn. I really did."

He took a big drink and then a small drink and got up. He went back to the calendar picture on the wall and stood there looking. And then he came back. He was smiling.

"I don't mean to brag but I was something of a sport in those days. I was making a lot of money and I had me a pretty fancy collection of shoes and suits. I got my suits straight from New York City. There were always a lot of ladies around then. High-class Creoles from downtown New

Orleans and French and several local ones that just kind of followed us around. Man, them were some good good times. They just don't have those kind of times any more. I'd be playing, see, and I'd play that little horn with one hand and that would leave me with my other hand free to play with the ladies."

He took another drink. His glass was empty.

"Ain't nothing a good woman likes better than a good cornet player. I'd play those soft blues right at them and let that Martin horn do all the courting. Like I said, I don't like to brag, but some nights, and I mean early some nights, say after the first set, I could pick out the lady I was going to go home with. It didn't matter who she was with . . . it didn't matter 'cause I'd let her know I was playing just for her."

He got up and went to the table. He brought the jar and another cut lemon back.

"We shore had ourselves some fun then. Yessir, we shore did do it up right. Like we'd come into a little town like Hattiesburg, Mississippi. You know where that is?"

"I think so. . . ."

"It ain't no more than a couple crossroads and a feed store. Wasn't much jazz around in those towns; mostly skiffle music and gandy dancers. The crowds would really turn out. We might play from a buckboard or a store front or if the notion hit us we'd just take those cane chairs out under a tree and set up right there. And the crowd would come and we'd play real good. They'd commence whipping those pints of whisky around and then the dancing would start. I mean, right out there on the grass and in the weeds. Right out there in clear view of the church. But the preacher knew he couldn't stop it so he'd make himself scarce.

"We had 'em dancing their heads off. Then we'd try a few things out. One Eye was on guitar and Old Claude was on bass. Yeah, that's the way it was. And me and Charley Nelson.

"Well, One Eye and Claude would grab that rhythm and

hold her by the neck and me and Charley would light out. We'd take that melody and counterpoint and run off with it. Sometimes we would race or do little corkscrew things. Other times we'd go off into the bushes and up into the trees. We'd get ourselves way out. We'd get so far out One Eye and Claude would start worrying and try to bring us back in.

"But it would be nice out there and Charley and me knew what we were doing. We didn't even want to come back. And One Eye and Claude would hold on. And it would be me and Charley. The cornet and the trombone. I can still hear it. We'd meet up in the top of those trees and begin chasing each other up one limb and down the other. Finally we'd surprise One Eye and Claude and come charging back down into the melody.

"They'd see us coming and there'd be a welcoming committee for us. And then all natural hell would break loose. We'd be bobbing our horns up and down, fast-like, like the law was on our tails. And play? Great God Almighty, we played like we were clean out of our minds. And the crowd would be going wild. Doing crazy dances and drinking that liquor like it was Doctor Pepper's. Vicksburg, Hattiesburg, Muscle Shoals . . . it didn't matter where we played, 'cause when we played we played it right and like it should be played. Man, we played it like we were up on Lake Michigan and playing for Mister Al Capone himself."

He took another drink.

"Drink up there, boy. You know, it's kind of nice talking to you like this. . . .

"Yeah, them were good, good times. We'd maybe get a small room or a packing house and we'd set up and start playing. It didn't matter where; it didn't matter when. 'Cause when that music started the crowd just naturally came. They'd be coming through the windows and coming through the doors and if the walls and floors weren't solid they'd be coming through them.

"And that little Ethel Brown, she was right there with us.

One Eye discovered her up near Vicksburg but after we traveled down to New Orleans she became my girl. No trouble
between One Eye and me at all—she just became my girl and
that was that.

"She was something nice too. And had a sweet voice. It
wasn't all messed up like these modern-day singers. She sang
'em straight. If she couldn't get a few high notes she wouldn't
let it worry her. Wouldn't bother her at all; she'd just put
her hands back on those little hips of hers and wait till it got
back in her range. She'd stand there with her little tail sticking out like a chicken. Yeah, that's right, that's what we used
to call her—Chicken. And I mean she knew why and she
liked it. That's the kind of girl she was and I mean I really
liked her."

Joe looked at me.

"Come on, boy, drink that stuff up. Here I am doing all
the talking and you not even drinking."

He drank again and rolled the glass back and forth between his hands. The fire was burning right.

Joe rocked back in his chair.

"Yeah, I really liked that little girl. She was my little girl
and no mistake. . . .

"And we had ourselves a good bunch of musicians. All first-
rate men. I liked them all, every one of them. One Eye,
Claude, Charley, Shag, Rabbit—all of 'em. Drunk or sober,
they were all fine boys. . . .

"Like another drink?"

"A small one."

Joe was getting drunk. "You don't need much of a fire
when you got plenty corn around . . . right or wrong?"

"Right."

"And I got plenty in the back and when that's gone I got
money to get plenty more. Like some more lemon?"

"No, I'm okay."

"You know," his voice was thick now, "I always figured a
good musician has to keep trying stuff out. If you got a big

background there ain't much new stuff you can't cut. But just the same, things can happen fast in this field and it's best to keep the pressure on. Our whole band was like that. Always trying things out and whenever some fellow with an instrument would show up from out of town, say like California, or Chicago, or even Mobile, we'd let him sit in and we'd listen pretty close for the new stuff."

Joe shook his head. "Man, I'm getting too drunk to talk. Man, I'm getting old."

"Joe, what band was that you had in Savannah?"

He looked at me and smiled and then looked into the fire. "Let's see here now. I've gone and forgot what year that was. Hold her now. I remember we called it 'Joe's Group.' Ain't that a name for a band?"

"I like it."

"There was a skiffle band in Monroe County about then. They used to run around in an old Hupmobile. Had themselves a washboard, a bass, a couple guitars and a jug. Now that crowd had themselves a real name. And they painted it on the side of that old Hupmobile. Yessir . . . 'The Mobile Strugglers.' Now that's a real name."

He took the stick and punched the fire again. "How's your Dad?"

"He's fine. Says hello."

"That's nice."

Joe reached over and patted my hand. "Boy, I'm getting too old. I got to quit drinking this stuff."

"You look fine, Joe. . . ."

"Sure I do." He was tired now and he talked slowly. I thought he might go to sleep.

"You know, if you were to ask me how old I was I'd have to tell you I don't know and that's a fact. I figure it's around eighty but I ain't certain. All I know is that it's old as hell and all the boys and girls I grew up with and played music with are all long gone.

"So I just sit here and think back to those days with Ethel

Brown and One Eye and that little old Martin cornet and wait. He'll come pretty soon now and I won't give Him no trouble. I figure the next time I leave this house they'll take me out and put me in the ground. But I won't give Him no trouble. I had myself a nice life and I played a lot of good music and I had a lot of real nice friends. . . . You know, that's about all you can ask."

"You're right, Joe."

"I know I'm right. And I know I've been lucky having all that music in me. You know I haven't hit a lick at a horn in eight or ten years. But I don't have to any more. I don't have to. It's still inside me and I can still hear it. So I just sit here and mess around with the fire and drink a little corn and listen.

"Sometimes I can hear Ethel Brown and Old One Eye doing the blues. But most of the time I hear that little B-flat out in that drain ditch and it's sweet and fine."

His head nodded.

"And, oh yeah, something else. I suspect you heard that I was never much of a religious man. Well, lately I been praying a lot and trying to catch up. I keep asking for the same thing over and over again. I figure the Lord will get tired of hearing me and might just give it to me to shut me up."

He was almost asleep now. . . .

"I keep saying . . . 'Lord, I don't care where you send me and I don't care if I'm black, brown, green or white when I come back and I don't care where I come back, but Lord if you have any openings and you can see yourself clear, I shore would be obliged if you let me come back as a cornet player. . . .' "

And then he slept.

THE HAIR
OF THE DOG

No ONE in Clovis cared if Elmo Roosevelt Todd got drunk on Monday, Tuesday, Wednesday or Thursday, but everyone who had money down on the Columbia Green Wave baseball team began worrying if he took a drink on Friday. Elmo could only pitch when he was drunk, and if he had a hangover on Saturday from the night before, he wasn't able to pitch.

It was Friday and Elmo spread his long legs and crouched down level with the pool table at the Blue Velvet Café and Poolroom to line up a bankshot. He drilled the ten ball into the side pocket and thumped his cue stick on the floor. "Hey, Willy! Bring me a beer back here!"

Willy Jessup the counterman came back with a bottle of Budweiser and slid it onto the dusting-powder shelf. "This is number two, Elmo."

"I know. I know." Elmo was circling the table looking for an open shot. He was wearing his white coveralls from the Mason Dixon Air Conditioning Company and two baseball caps sewed together at the crown. The cap bills pointed forward and backwards and from a distance you couldn't tell which way he was heading. "It's my last one. Come on, move out of the way."

"Listen, El, why don't you let me take it back and get you an R. C. or an Orange Crush?"

"Will you hush up! I done told you it's my last one; now

leave me alone." He missed a combination shot and reached for his beer.

Willy went out front to phone Maynard Latimer, the coach of the Green Wave and Elmo's boss at the Mason Dixon Air Conditioning Company. Maynard spoke in a calm voice. "Steady, Willy, don't carry on so. I tell you he's going to be all right. I'll have him so worn down when the day's over he won't be studying no honky-tonking."

Willy put his foot up on a Pepsi-Cola crate behind the counter. "He's already had two beers with his lunch!"

Willy Jessup was short and dark and the long hair on his arms and hands came right down to his first knuckle. While he was tall enough to rack the pool balls and work the counter at the Blue Velvet, he was so short he could hang his pants on a door knob and not have to worry about the cuffs getting dirty. Willy played second base for the Green Wave. He was a poor hitter, only batting .110 for the season, but he was a good glove man and he was Elmo's best friend and the only person who could keep him sober on Fridays.

Maynard said, "Willy, you don't know the first thing about dealing with people. I told him to have a couple. That way he won't be building up no craving."

A customer was at the cash register. Willy talked faster. "Okay, Maynard. I guess you know what you're doing. But keep calling him. If he knows you're watching he'll be careful. And listen, check his toolbox. He'll probably be trying to sneak a six-pack along."

It was two-thirty when Willy called Maynard again. Maynard said, "He's okay, Willy. Sober as a pallbearer. I sent him out to Joe Tatum's house to fix their Westinghouse."

"You been calling him?"

"Just hung up. It couldn't be better. I got him covered like a stove lid till you pick him up."

At Joe and Mabel Tatum's house on Hudson Street Elmo unscrewed the Phillips Head screws on the three-quarter-ton window unit in the living room, pulled the pump and condenser out from the casement and lowered the heavy unit onto a newspaper on the floor.

Mabel had come home from her and Joe's novelty and notion shop in the Woodlake Shopping Center to let Elmo in the house and to defrost a pork loin she was cooking for dinner. She squatted down, and tucking her dotted Swiss dress around her ankles so Elmo couldn't see anything, she peered into the air conditioner. "Mind you don't go dripping that oil on my rug."

Mabel was a thin, tidy little woman who wore her frameless glasses on a black velvet ribbon around her neck. Her hair had been rinsed blue. "Push those draperies back so they'll be out of your way. There, that's it. I just finished hanging them last week. Don't you think the yellow with that little green worked in there picks up the sofa color nice?"

"Yes, ma'am, it looks real good."

Mabel touched the greasy condensor plate with her fingertip. "I swear if the dust and the filth in this town isn't getting so bad a person doesn't know what to do." She wiped her finger on a piece of Kleenex. "Maybe if you just cleaned it up it would work."

Elmo tightened his gas gauges onto the compressor head with his crescent wrench, smoothed a kink out of the brass hose and opened the valve. "She needs a charge of gas, that's all. I'll have her cooling in no time."

"But aren't you going to clean it? I bet you'd be surprised at the difference it would make if you got that filth out of there."

"No, ma'am, that grease don't bother nothing."

"Well, it couldn't do any harm."

Elmo wished the day was over and he and Willy were in the movies. There was a George Raft show at the Bijou. He tapped the gauge with his screwdriver handle to make sure it wasn't sticking. He'd always liked Raft, he had a sharp, fast way with the women and didn't take any back talk. He wasn't as good with women as Cagney, but he was a helluva lot better than the monkeys in tuxedos who were always helping them out of cabs and opening doors for them and trying to kiss their hands.

Mabel said, "Well, I guess you know your business better than I do." She sat down on the sofa and began telling him about their new shipment of French candles and glass figurines from Sweden.

Sweat began popping out on Elmo's forehead and on the backs of his hands. A cold empty feeling was in his stomach and his throat felt raw and scratchy.

"Some of those little foreign things are so cute they'll just break your heart. Oh, I wish I could just show you how teeny they make them. Why, one little group has a whole family sitting down for dinner and they aren't any bigger than a minute. You could put three families in the palm of your hand." Mabel sighed. "I declare if they're not the darlingest things you ever laid your eyes on. You can see their little eyes and their ears and even the food on their plates. I swear if they aren't a prize."

Elmo wasn't listening. He was trying to figure how he could get her out of the house so he could take a drink of Joe's whisky standing on the sideboard. Maybe she would go to the bathroom. He would only need a few seconds. He wiped the sweat from his hands thinking of the women he knew and how they could drink him beer for beer right through the night and never have to go.

But Mabel had no plans to go to the bathroom, the kitchen or anywhere. She sat on the sofa fanning herself and eating peppermint patties. She told him about her new slip covers, her new frost-free refrigerator and her plans for wall lamps in the dining room that would match her Italian cut-glass chandelier in the hall.

Elmo stood up, announcing that he had to get something out of the truck. He returned carrying a forty-pound cylinder of sulphur dioxide gas. Pretending he was connecting it to the compressor head, he pointed the opening at the sofa and opened the valve. "Look out! Look out!" A heavy charge of gas spewed out and filled the room.

Mabel screamed, "Lord God! What's that?"

"It's an accident! It's an accident!" He fumbled in his tool box. "Go on outside! I'll call you when it's okay."

Mabel fanned her face with her hands, snatched up her purse and ran out the door.

Elmo's eyes were streaming with the terrible rotten-egg smell and the liquified gas from the open valve was dribbling down his hands. He held an oil rag over his face as he cut the valve off and pushed the draperies back so he could see outside. Mabel was standing on the front lawn frowning and crying and fluttering her hands. Elmo picked up a bottle of Joe's Scotch and quickly pulled the cork. Then he changed his mind. Mabel would smell it. He put the Scotch back and opened a fifth of vodka. Vodka didn't smell.

Elmo's throat pumped three long times and when he put the fifth of vodka back it was one-third empty. He wiped his mouth. The 100-proof vodka with no chaser made his throat tremble and his ears ring. But it soon stopped and the warm sweet feeling that he knew so well filled his stomach and began flowing down his arms. His fingers and hands felt strong, his arms and legs supple and smooth and he smiled softly as if he heard harps and wood winds playing in the distance. He moved over in front of the mirror and shook his right arm loose and began studying his windup.

Mabel came up on the front porch and sniffed in through the screen door. "It's better, isn't it? Isn't it? It seems a little better."

"Yes ma'am. It's fine. Fine. Couple more minutes is all she needs. It moves out pretty fast."

"How about my draperies and my slip covers? This place is going to be smelling like a chicken house."

Elmo leaned on the doorway. He was half drunk but he knew his breath was pure. He felt relaxed and confident. The world was easier for him when he was drinking. It was easier thinking and keeping track of things. Everything didn't get all blurred and fuzzy. It was even easier talking to women. He almost told Mabel that she worried and fretted and talked too much, but he settled for, "No, ma'am, it's going to be all right. Few more minutes and you won't be smelling a thing."

Mabel sniffed at Elmo. "What's wrong with you? You haven't been drinking? Maybe that stuff, what do you call it?"

"Sulphur dioxide."

"Maybe it's affecting you. You seem different. Kind of strange and funny-like."

"No ma'am, I'm fine. Fine." Elmo took two long strides and wheeled around slowly as if he were on the pitcher's mound. He rubbed an imaginary ball in his hands, and looking down the freshly waxed hallway at an oil painting of two cocker spaniels in a basket of flowers, he shook off his catcher's first call. Mabel was standing in the doorway with her glasses on her nose staring popeyed at him. He put his hand on his hip and nodding at his catcher he said, "Mabel, you and Joe got to come out tomorrow and see me work. I'm going to be moving that ball by them so fast they ain't going to even know where it's coming from." He nodded to his catcher, and stretching his six-foot-four-inch frame up until his fingers were grazing the ceiling, he took a long look toward second base. He rocked back and rared down deep. His right hand went to the floor, his size-14 foot reached for the ceiling. He paused as if frozen and uncoiled in a whistling windmill delivery.

Elmo's long reach was too long for the hall and on his follow-through his fingers nipped the chandelier. The rigging snapped, the chandelier vibrated and tiny tears of cut glass came raining down on the hard polished floor.

Mabel covered her face with her hands and peered through her fingers whispering, "Oh, my God! Oh, my God!" She slipped her shoes off so she wouldn't break the glass crystals and rushed for the telephone on the sideboard.

Elmo blinked and shook his head. The room stopped spinning and he focused on the swinging chandelier. The pieces kept falling and bouncing on the hardwood floor like icicles from a roof drain. He circled them cautiously, went back to the air conditioner and unhooked the gauges.

Mabel had dialed too fast and had gotten the wrong number. She was dialing again and watching Elmo as if he was a mad dog.

Elmo was rushing to get finished and get out. The gas was balanced, but he wanted to check out the compressor before lifting the unit into the casement. He plugged the cord into the outlet and threw the switch.

Mabel got through to Maynard. "Mr. Latimer! Mr. Latimer! It's me, Mabel Tatum!" She stopped talking. Her mouth opened slowly and she tried to scream.

Elmo had the air conditioner on full blast and the silk draperies were drifting like shadows toward the whirling blades of the condenser fan. He didn't see them. Mabel dropped the telephone as the blades caught the cloth. The draperies trembled and rippled. They bucked twice, and with a noise like rotten canvas tearing they ripped down from their traverse rods and were snatched into the unit. In two seconds the meat-grinder blades had cut them to long seven-foot ribbons.

Maynard's voice came from the dangling receiver. "Mrs. Tatum! Mrs. Tatum! Mabel! Are you all right? Mabel! Mabel!"

Mabel picked up the phone. "It's that fool Elmo you sent out here! He's crazy as a loon! He's tearing my place up!"

Maynard said, "Let me talk to him."

Mabel was white-faced and breathless. She handed Elmo the phone. "Go on! Tell him what you did!"

Elmo sat down on the coffee table. "Hello, Maynard. How's it going?"

"You bastard, you've been drinking."

The warm sweet feeling drifted over Elmo again. "Not so's

you'd notice it, good buddy. I'll tell you a little something, though. The old arm feels great."

Maynard shouted, "Elmo dammit!"

Elmo interrupted, "Easy, Maynard, easy now. Okay, so we've had a little accident; ain't nothing that can't be fixed."

"What happened?"

Mabel was standing in her stocking feet holding up the greasy shreds of her draperies.

"Oh, the old lady's in an uproar out here. I broke a couple pieces of glass from one of those doolollies they hang from the ceiling and a piece of one of her curtains got caught in the fan belt. Let me tell you how I'm going to pitch old Ben Giles tomorrow. I figure I'll. . . ."

"Dammit, Elmo, you're stoned."

"No, Mayn, hell, no. I ain't had a drop. I'll take an oath on that."

"Shut up a minute. Now listen at me. Don't you touch another thing. Just sit right where you are. I'll be there in fifteen minutes."

"All right, Maynard, anything you say."

Maynard Latimer slammed the receiver down and cursed. He clawed his fingers down his bald head and shouted for his secretary. "Call the Blue Velvet! Get me Willy!"

Willy answered. "What's up?"

"Plenty! Elmo's stone drunk out at the Tatum's. How the hell do I know where he got it? He got it, that's all I know. I'll try and catch him. Here's the number: A-X-four-nine-seven-oh-two. Call him up. Keep him talking till I get there. If he gets loose we'll never get him."

Willy called Mrs. Tatum but it was too late; Elmo had gone, leaving his tools and the air conditioner still sitting on the floor. He began calling the honky-tonks and the beer halls. No one had seen Elmo or the Mason Dixon pickup truck.

It was eleven before Willy and Maynard found Elmo sitting on the curb across the street from the Pentecostal Church on Spring Street listening to the Friday night sermon. He was dead drunk and had less than an inch of bourbon left in a fifth of I. W. Harper and had another full fifth in his hip pocket. He had bought and eaten four canteloupes and he had the eight rinds lined up in the gutter as if they were a baseball team. He was figuring out how he would play his infield against the heavy hitters from Moss Hill.

Willy leaned against a fire plug. "Aw, Elmo, why you want to go and do a thing like this for?"

Maynard was too tired to talk. He sat down on the curb and began spitting in the gutter and shaking his head.

Elmo hadn't heard Willy's question. He shifted his infield canteloupes to the right side and pulled his left fielder in toward center. "I tell you how I'm pitching Shag Dobbs? Low and outside. I'll keep him reaching out so far he won't be getting up enough traction to blow on."

Maynard shouted. "What in the hell gets into you anyway, pulling a fool stunt like this! That old biddy's soaking me a hundred and fifty dollars for that mess you made. If I had any sense I'd fire your ass right now and kick you off the team."

Elmo cocked his head at Maynard and then looked at his canteloupes. "Aw, lay off, Mayn. Feel that arm. It's like greased leather. I'll be threading a needle with my fast ball." He pushed his first baseman out from the line. "I'll be crowding that Lovelace boy. I'll give him a couple swifties by his ear. That'll keep him from digging in on me. Hey, how'd the Cards do today?"

Willy groaned, "Who in the hell cares!"

Maynard said quietly, "How much you had to drink, boy?"

Elmo's canteloupes changed for him from baseball players to places he'd been. He moved the rinds as he retraced his path. After the vodka at Mabel Tatum's he had bought two six-packs of Budweiser beer and driven out to Bob Dove's miniature golf course on Dexter Road. He had finished the beer there, and racing back to town before sundown, when the liquor stores closed, he had bought his two fifths of I. W. Harper Bourbon. He had then driven out to Mungo Peak's Blue Hawaiian Inn, where he had stayed and drunk and square-danced until he was hungry. Back in town at the Moon Mist Café they had refused to serve him and he'd gone down to the Farmer's Market and bought a bag of peaches and four August-ripe canteloupes. He had no idea of how or why he'd stopped near the church.

Willy whistled. "Twelve beers, a pint of vodka and a fifth of bourbon. It's a wonder you ain't drowned."

Maynard said, "We ain't got a chance. He'll be hung over so bad he won't be able to look at another drop." He dug his elbow in Elmo's ribs. "You eat all the peaches?"

Elmo smiled. "Yessir, and all the canteloupes. I been taking good care of myself. I'm in great shape. I feel fine. I swear I do."

Willy said, "We gotta keep him moving, Coach. We got to stretch him out till game time."

Elmo leaned forward and shifted his canteloupes again. "Low and outside to old Lefty Atkins. He's got to hit left side and I got him plugged." He raised his third-base rind and smacked it down on the black tar. "Right here!"

Maynard said, "Oh, Jesus!" The church service had ended and a big group from the congregation was crossing the street. Maynard ducked his head down as they passed. Elmo raised his hands and rocked back on his elbows. *"Hallelujah, brothers!"* The congregation passed by and headed for the bus stop.

Willy said, "Okay, Elmo, let's go."

Elmo lurched up too fast. He lost his balance, took two long steps that came too late and spread-eagled out facing the center line on Spring Street. He checked the I. W. Harper in his coveralls pocket and got up. "All set."

Maynard, Willy and Elmo started out before midnight and

stopped and drank at every honky-tonk on the Savannah Highway all the way out to Coopers Corners. After finishing off the I. W. Harper they bought a half gallon of bootleg corn whisky from Monk Phillips out at the French Quarter Motel. The corn tasted more like turpentine than whisky and Willy couldn't drink it, but Maynard and Elmo were too far gone to tell the difference. Willy switched to Pepsi-Cola and kept talking baseball trying to keep Maynard and Elmo from falling asleep.

By dawn Willy had drunk three king-sized Pepsi-Colas and had eaten five bags of salted peanuts and three packs of peanut-butter cheese crackers. He was sleepy, hot, itchy and irritable and fed up with trying to keep Elmo and Maynard going. They were in Hoot Conklin's Diner and Elmo was lying back against the booth wall with his mouth open. A fly was crawling down his nose. Maynard lay sprawled out with his head on the table. He had overturned the ash tray and matches and ashes and spilt Seven Up, which they had used to chase the raw corn with, were covering the table.

Pete the night counterman came over mopping. "He looks terrible, Willy. How you going to get him to play?"

Elmo was snoring. Maynard cursed in his sleep and raked his hand through the ashes and then across his head.

"Give me a hand, Pete. I got to keep them moving."

Pete leaned his mop against the counter, squinted his eyes and took his last pull on his half-inch cigarette. "Let me hit 'em with the old ammonia. That'll move 'em."

"I don't want them getting sick."

"Naw, it's safe, Willy, it's just like smelling salts. I use it on the drunks all the time."

Willy got out of the booth and put a penny in the gumball machine. He had to have something to take the peanut-and-cheese taste out of his mouth. "Okay, try it. But take it easy."

Pete emptied half a bottle of Dixie Belle ammonia on the floor around their feet and then poured a puddle over the

Seven Up and the ashes on the table. "There, now just give that a few seconds to work."

Elmo's mouth closed and his bloodshot eyes opened. He swayed forward. "What? What's up? I can't breathe straight."

Maynard mumbled and looked around wildly. Wet ashes and a match stem were plastered down the side of his face. "Hey! What's that smell? What's going on around here?"

Willy gave Maynard a handful of paper napkins. "Here, clean your face off."

Elmo frowned and shook his head as Willy and Pete steered him toward the door. "That's ammonia! That's what it is. That stuff will eat your shoes up."

Outside on the street Willy hooked his fingers in Elmo's back pocket to keep him from falling. Maynard sat down on the curb. His head slumped forward on his chest. "I can't make it. I've had it."

Willy turned Elmo loose and shifted the jar of corn up under his arm. "Come on, Coach, its' already five-thirty. Just a few more hours."

Maynard held his head and shook it slowly. "I'm fifty-six years of age, Willy. I'm too old for this route. I'm going on home."

A brown and white hound wagged her tail and rubbed up against Elmo's leg. He squatted down and cradled the dog's face in his hands and looked in her eyes. "What's your name, gal?"

Pete held the screen door open. "Queenie! Get your butt back in here."

The dog left and Elmo sat down on the sidewalk. He kept looking around. "Where'd she go, Willy?"

Willy helped him up and unscrewed the fruit jar lid. "That's Pete's dog. Come on, hit it again."

Elmo took a drink and wiped his mouth with his sleeve. "Willy, old buddy, I got that thin feeling right this second. I'm going to have my fireball going, I can cold tell it."

"Let's go, El."

It was eleven when Willy pushed Elmo through the tall weeds and the scrub oaks to the river bank. They stripped down, laid their clothes on a flat rock and dove in. Willy was too tired to swim. He floated and drifted downstream until he came to a path that ran into the water and climbed out. Elmo was shivering on the bank and trying to dry himself with his handkerchief and T shirt. His teeth were clattering, "I'm starving!" Willy gave him another drink and he began richocheting rocks across the water. "I'm going to be on top today, Willy. On top!"

At Bootsie Boyd's Diner Willy made him eat four fried eggs, bacon, a stack of buckwheat cakes and a malted milk shake. When the manager wasn't looking, he poured him an orange-juice glass full of corn. "Okay, Elmo, bottoms up."

The cold swim and the big meal began sobering Elmo up, but the 110-proof corn cut through and the sober didn't take. By one o'clock he was skinning rocks down the road and shouting, "We're gonna slaughter them, Willy! Eat 'em up! Hey, don't you be forgetting my puttees." He wore brown leather Western Union messenger puttees over his coverall pants when he played. He claimed they were good for sliding.

Willy gave him another big drink. "They'll be there."

The whisky was hitting Elmo faster. He dropped down in the gutter and did ten push-ups from the curb and jumped up into a series of side straddle hops. Willy said, "Slow down, Elmo. You going to wear yourself out."

At two Willy led Elmo across the infield toward the Green Wave bench and their fifty-eight fans sitting behind them and along the first base line on Coca-Cola crates and nail kegs. As they passed first base Elmo suddenly whirled around and at top speed headed for second.

Willy shouted, "Come back here!"

It was too late. He went into second low and hard, and hitting the dirt with his hip, his ankle and his outstretched arm, he laid out a perfect fall-away slide. Willy helped him up. "You crazy fool! You all right?"

Elmo grinned, "Never better. How'd you like it?"

"Come on, get ready."

Elmo changed his socks, strapped on his puttees, squared his double billed cap and began warming up. Maynard kept his cap pulled down low over his eyes to keep out the blinding sun as he gave instructions to Snow Folsom, his catcher, and Murphy Boatwright, the short stop. He hadn't been able to tie his shoes and he kept his hands in his pockets so no one would see how badly they were shaking. Snow said, "What's the matter, Coach? You look a little peaked."

Maynard moved out of the sun and stood in the shade of a Tube Rose Snuff sign near the bench. "I ain't been sleeping too good."

Elmo was taking his warm-up pitchs. The Moss Hill bench and their fans were shouting at him. "Hey, Elmo, who does your undertaking?" "Hey, Elmo, you look like death warmed over." "Hey Elmo! Elmo!" A loud deep voice came from the Moss Hill fans. "You got about as much chance as a one-legged man in an ass-kicking contest." The crowd laughed. The half gallon of moonshine was almost gone and Willy sent out for a fifth of I. W. Harper. The deep voice came again. It was Barrel Foster sitting on a cane-bottomed rocking chair. His brother Jim played left field for Moss Hill. "Hey, Elmo! Where'd you get those eyes? They look like piss-holes in the snow."

The game started. Elmo was half drunk, half asleep and completely wild. He threw two in the dirt and one so far outside Snow didn't even bother to try for it. He walked the first two men. The third popped out and he hit the fourth on the shoulder loading the bases. Elmo craned his neck forward so he could see Snow and home plate. Everything seemed to be sliding and shifting. He thought he saw the batter crouched over first base and then at third.

Barrel Foster had taken his shirt off. His foghorn voice boomed out. "Hey Elmo, you look a little green around the gills. Run your finger down your throat. Maybe you'll feel better."

Willy limped up to the mound with his head splitting and

his feet on fire. He only came up to Elmo's armpits; squinting up like a weary lizard, he patted him on the back. "Steady, Elmo. Steady now. Don't listen at that fool. You got them right where you want them."

Elmo frowned down. "How come the inning's so long?"

"You been throwing wild. Lots of walks. Ease up, quit trying so hard."

"Yeah, that's what I'll do. How many outs?"

"One."

Elmo wiped the streaming sweat from his eyes, pushed his hair straight back and adjusted his foot-and-a-half-long cap. He smacked the rosin bag into his glove and looked in at Snow. "Okay, baby, where you want it?"

Snow lowered his mitt and pointed two fingers straight down for a fast ball. Elmo saw the mitt but he couldn't see the fingers. He raised his arms and rared back. He pushed his foot at the batter's face and came down hard. The ball flashed out and the umpire shouted, "Steee-rike one!" Elmo fanned the batter with the next two pitches.

Turk Jones crowded over the plate and Elmo put a fast one right by his Masonic ring. "Strike one!" The team was excited, the fans started clapping and shouting and Willy's high scratchy voice began cutting through like a buzz saw. "Pick that chicken! Pick him, Elmo! Pick him clean!"

Elmo did. He retired Turk and then pitched no-hit ball for five straight innings. There was no score. At the sixth he began to flag and gave up two long singles. Willy poured him a three-ounce shot of whisky into a Dixie cup. "Here you go, El. Just what the doctor ordered."

He tossed it down and smacked his lips. He started to smile but stopped. His face flushed. He gagged, spat the whiskey out and began coughing. He wiped his eyes. "I can't, Willy. I'm full up. I'm about to have a whisky fit."

Maynard said, "Come on, try again, boy. You got a shutout going."

Willy was scared. "Maybe I can cut it with some water."

"I can't, Willy. I just can't. The stuff's coming out my skin.
I can't hold no more."

Maynard took the cup from Willy. "Let me try him." He
rubbed his hand in the small of Elmo's back. "Now just
relax, boy. Relax. Forget what it is."

Elmo took a deep breath and swallowed. He shut his eyes
and clamped his teeth together trying to hold it down. It was
no use. "I'm sorry, Coach."

He tensed and tightened up. He began twitching. His loose
whiplash delivery changed and he began aiming and steering
the ball over the plate. His speed and knife-edge control
vanished. Moss Hill picked up four hits and one run from
Elmo in the first half of the eighth. In the ninth they scored
again.

It was two to nothing and the Green Wave was batting for
their last time. Barrel Foster was booming through a rolled-up
newspaper and sounding like a bullfrog in a sewer pipe. "It's
all over, Maynard! All over, Elmo! Next year Little League.
Ain't that right?"

A dog crossed the infield.

Maynard went back and forth along the first base line trying to keep his throbbing head level and balanced and shouting hoarsely for a hit. "Let's go, men! Let's go!"

Elmo sat on the bench breathing deeply through his mouth
and trying not to be sick. He was batting third. The streaming whisky sweat had soaked his coveralls and made his socks
slide down into his shoes. The stiff puttees were chafing his
bare ankles.

Snow got on first with a scratch single and Maynard
crowded in tight to coach him. Willy was at bat. Maynard
shouted. "Look 'em over, Willy! Look 'em over!" He had one
eye on Snow and one on Willy, and every two seconds he
would glance back at Elmo, who looked as if he was having a
combination of dry heaves and d.t.'s. A hot-dog boy was behind the bench yelling for Willy to put it out of the park.
Maynard shouted, "Shut up, there! He can't hear me!" He

cupped his hands over his mouth. "Just get on, baby! Just get on!"

The first pitch to Willy was a ball.

Suddenly Maynard looked back at the hot-dog boy and then at the shivering Elmo. He limped and trotted over. "Give me a dog, son." After tossing the meat out and wiping down the mustard with a napkin he sat down next to Elmo.

The second pitch to Willy was a ball, the third a called strike. Maynard sang out, "Watch him, Willy! Watch him! Heads up Snow!"

Maynard picked up the fifth of I. W. Harper and poured three or four ounces into the hot-dog roll. "Okay, Elmo, here you go. Get it down fast."

Elmo's hands were trembling and his teeth sounded like small stones in a Prince Albert tobacco can. He swallowed without chewing and began breathing in deeply to hold it down.

In the batter's box Willy's count went to three and two and he dug in to guard the plate. The ball came in high and hanging and he spun his bat toward the rack and went down to first, pushing Snow on to second.

The whisky sandwich took, and Elmo felt a surge of power and vision sweep over him. He grabbed up five bats, and as he waved them around in a giant circle, he ripped out a rebel yell that was louder than the freight train going by. He tossed away two bats, grunted loudly and swung the remaining three back and forth as he staggered out to home plate to face Mule Higgins. He dropped the two extra bats, took a practice cut and lurched into the batter's box.

Barrel's deep voice swept across the field. "Hey, Elmo!"

Elmo looked around.

Barrel rocked back and forth. "You look like something the dog spat up and the cat dragged in. How you gonna hit if you can't even stand up?"

The Moss Hill bench and fans roared.

Maynard shouted, "Go to hell, Barrel."

Willy sang out from first base. "Don't listen at him, Elmo! Lay it out of here! Lay it out!"

Elmo pointed his bat at Barrel. "Listen you, you. . . ." He couldn't think of anything to call him. "You just watch where this here ball's going."

Elmo dug in and spat out at Mule, "Okay, Slow Motion, put something on it."

Mule Higgins grinned, cranked up and threw his hardest ball.

Elmo was ready for the fast ball. Had Mule thrown a slow ball, he would have broken his back, for he swung so hard both feet left the ground. The hit sounded like a double-barreled, twelve-gauge shotgun blast and the ball streaked out over the center fielder's head as if it was wired to the transformer on the top of the telephone pole six hundred feet away. Elmo knew it was long but he didn't know where it had gone or if it was fair. Spinning around had made him dizzy, and the stands, the fans, the noise, the sky and the field whirled by crazily. He didn't know where to run or where to throw the bat.

Maynard screamed and waved his arms and came running up. "It's a home run, you dope! A home run! This way! This way!"

Elmo shook his head, dropped the bat and went lurching and wheeling out around the first base line. "Where'd it go? Where'd it go?"

"Kershaw County. You done it, boy! You done it!"

Elmo was drunk enough to pitch and hit but too far gone to run. He tagged first and kept heading for right field. Maynard caught him and pointed him at second as Willy streaked over home plate and cut across the mound and met them. They loped and dogtrotted toward third. Elmo was wavering and swaying from side to side, Maynard was kicking the dirt and hooting at the sky and Willy was slapping Elmo on the back to keep him moving.

At third Elmo stopped and pointed at Barrel Foster. "Barrel!"

The fans stopped clapping and a single voice sang out, "Tell him, Elmo!"

Barrel was putting on his shirt and getting ready to leave.

"I know what I was fixing to call you. A suck-egg dog! That's what!"

The fifty-eight fans of the Green Wave, the hot-dog boy and the bench screamed, shouted and pounded on their Coca-Cola crates and nail kegs as Elmo with one long arm dangling over Willy and the other over Maynard threw his shoulders back and strolled home.

SOUTHERN FRIED

FLEETWOOD DRIGGERS couldn't stand the heat long enough for work on the big grill at Holly Yates' place in Moss Hill, but he had good soda-fountain hands and a nice smile. Customers liked him. They never tipped him, but they liked him. He was big and heavy-set for a soda-fountain man, six foot two or three inches plus a big blond pompadour plus his soda-fountain cap, which stuck up another four or five inches. His face was long and thin like a greyhound's and his ears were smoothed down at the sides of his head like he'd been raised at top speed or in a high wind. His face looked fast. He had a fast name and everyone called him Fleet and that made it that much faster. Fleet worked the same shift that Preacher Watts and I worked, from four P.M. to four A.M. With the exception of Blue, who worked on garbage and mop and ran errands, Preach was the only colored man on the inside at Holly's. All of the curb boys were colored, but Agnes the cashier, the five inside waitresses, Fleetwood and I were all white. Holly was white too.

Preach and I never had much use for Fleet. I guess it was because he hated the kitchen and anyone connected with it. Once in a while when things were slow on the fountain Holly would send Fleet back to help us get ready for the big after-the-movie rush. Fleet would curl his lip down and change into a kitchen apron. He would tell Holly how he couldn't stand the grease heat but Holly would insist. Fleet would come back and work near the door where he could feel the air conditioner from the front. The kitchen wasn't air-conditioned. We would let him do things like slice tomatoes or strip lettuce. We didn't want him back there any more than he wanted to be back. Holly knew this but Holly was always trying to make it a "Happy, family-type thing," as he used to say. After a few minutes on the big sandwich board slicing tomatoes Fleet would stick his thumb and forefinger in his eyes and pinch his nose. He'd make sure Holly saw him and he'd shake his head slowly. It worked every time and Holly would come back, "You all right, Fleet?"

Fleet would pretend not to hear him until he repeated the question. Then he'd say, "All I got to do is close my eyes and there that monkey is." Holly would reach up and pat him on his shoulder. "You better get out of here and get some air, boy."

Fleet would start untying his kitchen apron, which was always spotless. If Holly was still in earshot he would say, "Man, I don't see how you boys stand this grease heat—it must be two hundred right now." Then he'd put on his little white soda-fountain jacket with "Fleet" printed over the left breast pocket and his stiff white overseas-type cap with "Holly's" printed all over it, and light a cigarette. If Holly were still present Fleet would tell us how good we were. Like he would say, "Ain't no heat worse than grease heat. How come it don't bother you none?" Preach would say something like, "We use to it."

But the minute Holly would walk away from his little "Happy, family-type thing," it would change. Fleet made sure Holly was out of hearing range and then he looked at Preach. He screwed up his long face and tried to look intelligent with his jaw and his eyes. "Preach, you a college man, tell me something. Right or wrong, can a nigger stand more heat than a white man?"

I worked on the grill a lot so I spoke up. "It don't bother me, Fleet. Maybe it bothers you cause you got weak blood."

"I didn't ask you anything, runt. I asked that question to Preach."

Preach said, "I don't know, Fleet. I never gave it much thought."

"Well, I want you to take my advice and give it some thought."

About that time Holly smelled something was wrong and he came back. Fleet straightened his cap and went back to his fountain.

He'd check his vanilla, simple, strawberry and chocolate syrups, trigger his soda jet a few times to make sure the pressure was right, line up his whipped-cream cylinders in the slide-top refrigerator, arrange all of the maraschino cherries so the stems were pointing up and begin polishing the chrome and glass around the Pepsi-Cola, Coke and Dr. Pepper dispensers. He kept it spotless. He loved that fountain and he knew every square inch of chrome and every square foot of duckboard that ran the length of the long counter in front of the big blue mirror and the four jukebox stations. Fleet was good on the fountain and he had a big reputation. He worked smoothly on sodas and sundaes and on the small sandwich board. He was quick and kept his orders straight and had a nice movement for dipping ice cream.

But the soda fountain was one world at Holly's and the kitchen was another. Fountain boys could sit at the counter or in the booths during their breaks but in the kitchen we were always so greasy and streaked with ketchup and mustard that we had to go out back and sit by the barbecue pit. Preacher Watts was in charge of the four-to-four shift in the kitchen. I worked directly under him and directly above Blue. During the school term I only worked eight hours.

Preach was just between dark brown and blue black. He had a razor welt that looked like someone had laid a ruler from the tip of his left ear to the edge of his chin and carefully followed it. His hands were three times lighter than his face and his front four teeth, two upper and two lower, were framed in bright yellow gold. He was tall enough to reach the back of the grill without straining and he had long fine fingers that were callused with toaster and grill burns. He knew how to use the calluses and could pick up a toasted barbecue from a flat-bed toaster with his bare hand without changing his breath. Preach was thin for a cook and liked to keep by himself. He kept thin by never eating anything fried and he never ate his own cooking. Whenever he got hungry he'd go outside and sit in his 1939 Ford and send his order in to me. Everything had to be broiled or baked and he was crazy about salads and fruit. Preach was in his last year at the Bible College and during his breaks and dinner he'd sit out in his car and eat salads and cottage cheese and things like that and study. He wasn't studying to be one of those Jesus Screamers or Rollers, and he looked down on all of the Snake Handlers and Miracle Shouters that filled the tents along the Two Notch Road and out on the Winnsboro Highway.

He had a nice soft voice. He never used big words, and he made everything as simple as he could. Once in a while a member from the congregation where he was apprenticing would come into the kitchen with a problem and Preach would take him off behind the dirty laundry or out by the barbecue pit and they would talk it over. Preach was good like that.

Usually when Preach's break was over he'd come back in and start talking about what he'd been reading. Like he'd say, "You know anything about Immanuel Kant?"

I'd say, "No."

"How about Frederick Hegel?"

I'd say, "No."

"Which one you want to hear about?"

"Give me that first one."

I'd be slicing tomatoes or patting out hamburgers or skinning the big double grill down with a spatula. Preach would put his hands in his pockets under his apron and begin walking back and forth on the duckboards. "Well first off you

spell him K-A-N-T and you have to go for that long A. . . ."
'He'd shake his head and smile, "Immanuel Kant . . .
Immanuel Kant. . . . Yessir, that was one fine man. He was
born over there in Germany. You be surprised how many big
men in philosophy come out of Germany. Looks like they got
it in their blood."

Preach would keep walking back and forth on the duckboards and talking about his philosophy, and every few
minutes I'd say "I understand" or nod my head, but most of
the time I'd be grinning at my reflection in the big triple pop-
up toaster because he might as well have been talking in
Chinese. If I was on tomatoes I'd play a little game seeing
how thin I could slice them. If the tomatoes were firm and
the bread knife was sharp I'd get them so thin they'd roll up
like carrot curls.

Preach would always finish up by saying, "Well, that's
enough of him for tonight. You get too much thrown at you
and you can't swallow it. Now I'll tell you a little bit about
old Mr. Hegel and tomorrow we'll come back and visit Mr.
Kant again. . . ." Then he'd laugh like he knew I hadn't
understood a word and say, "Boy, when I get through with
you those high-school teachers are going to think you are
some form of genius."

Everything was going along smoothly between Preach, Fleet
and me until the first night Sonny Love came to town. Business had been fair during the afternoons and we had ourselves
geared for the one big rush from eleven-thirty to one when
the theaters let out. But no one had allowed for Sonny Love
pulling a big crowd on his first night in Columbia.

It was around midnight and Preach and I were in the
middle of the rush. The big grill was almost full; and I had
two three-basket French-fry pots going on potatoes and
chicken. We were about even with the orders and all of the
supplies were ready. Suddenly Holly came shouting into the
front. "Jesus Christ, you ought to see them! You ought to see
them! I can't believe it. Love's got eight thousand people and

every damn one of them is headed this way."

Fleetwood screamed. "We'll be swamped. I can't handle no crowd like that."

Holly stood in the door between the fountain and the kitchen. "I'll help you, Fleet. What am I going to do about hamburgers? What do you say, Preach?"

Preach said, "We got plenty everything, Holly . . . let 'em come."

Holly said, "You want to start frying now?"

"No, let 'em come. We got it down pretty good. You better get us up some more buns and meat, though."

Holly patted Preach on the shoulder. "Listen, you say the word and I'll close the place down."

Fleet spoke up, "How'm I going to get up enough ice? I'm already low on syrup. How about me, Holly? What am I going to do when they start ordering milk shakes? I'll get so far behind they'll walk out."

Preach laughed, "Don't worry, Fleet . . . that crowd ain't going to be ordering milk shakes. That's a Pepsi-Cola and Doctor Pepper crowd."

Fleet didn't like the way Holly was giving all of his attention to the kitchen. He stomped back to the fountain and began noisily checking and filling up his syrup stations. . . . He shouted out to the cashier, "Agnes, give the storehouse keys to Blue. Have him get me four simple syrups and about a dozen gallons of Pepsi-Cola syrup."

Agnes wasn't any more than ten feet from Fleetwood. "Do you have to yell like that?" she said.

"Damn right I do. If that stuff ain't in here we're in trouble. . . . And tell Blue to crank up that ice maker—we going to need another two hundred pounds. I knew I should have stayed home tonight. . . . Who in the hell's Sonny Love anyway?"

Before Agnes could tell him they were in the driveway and blowing their horns for service. In ten minutes every parking space was filled and the cars were backing up on the street for service. In each car there were four, five, as many as eight people. The Sonny Love revival had been from nine until midnight and they had been singing, praying, shouting and rolling. They were hungry. Preach was right about it being a Pepsi-Cola crowd, but Holly was wrong about it being a hamburger crowd. They ordered hamburgers, lots of hamburgers, but they also ordered chicken, steaks and barbecues. We'd been ready for a big rush on hamburgers. It came but with it came the other orders for steaks and chickens. At twelve-thirty we were at top speed. Orders were stacked a foot deep on the ice-pick spike in the window but we couldn't touch them until we had room. At twelve-thirty-five we were out of room. I counted quickly: sixty hamburgers, forty barbecues, twenty fried chickens and all the steaks the broilers could handle. Preach took over the incoming and outgoing orders and the finishing work on the big sandwich board. I fried.

All eight of the three-basket Fry-O-Laters were full and going, the big grill was packed solid with hamburgers, and every broiler had four steaks with the fat hissing and flashing. Preach kept saying, "Don't rush, boy. Don't fight 'em. I got everything under control. Just fry. . . . You see an empty space on the grill, fill her up. I keep track. Don't worry." And then he'd laugh. "If we get in real trouble we can always get old Fleetwood back here to help us."

But I worried anyhow. The ten curb boys were screaming at the window and slamming on the order bell, the four waitresses up front were pounding on the partition glass and Holly was chewing his cigar and shouting "Get it out, Get it out. Come on, Preach, get it out. . . ."

The French-fry pots were bubbling white as the fresh-cut potatoes and breaded chicken were scalded and fried at 380 degrees. The grease was so thick in the air you could write your name on the refrigerator door thirty feet away from the grill and fry pots, and the fat at the back of the grill flowed through the keyhole to the grill drain like water. The duckboards were beginning to get slippery. Flour and cracker meal from the chicken batter rose in the heavy grease-filled air and my hands and arms were white with flour and sticky with eggs. Preach went through a case of lettuce in thirty minutes.

The juke box was on full blast and everyone was shouting. Fleet sang out, "I'm almost out of Pepsi syrup. Agnes, can't you hear me, I need Pepsi syrup."

Holly shouted. "Give 'em root beer, they won't know the difference." Holly came back to the doorway and watched us. "Preach, you need any help?"

Preach smiled down at the sandwich board, "Where would I put any help, on my shoulders? Tell you what, though."

Holly said, "What?"

"You can screen these orders out. We can't be taking no more orders for omelettes."

"Jesus Christ, did you take any?"

"A couple—now we ain't got no room."

Holly picked up the P.A.-system microphone. "All right out there . . . listen a minute . . . no more omelettes . . . get that . . . no more omelettes . . . we're too busy for omelettes. Everything else is fine. We got hamburger, chicken. We got steaks and we got some nice fresh-sliced and minced barbecue. . . . But no more omelettes."

At one o'clock the rush had reached the peak and was holding on. The exhaust fan slowed down in the heavy air and couldn't pull the smoke and the heat out fast enough. The temperature was rising and I had to throw salt on the duckboards to keep from slipping. Holly opened the back door and put a twenty-four-inch Tornado fan on us. The smoke thinned out but the heat around the grill and the fry pots had risen and nothing would put it down. Sweat was running down Preach's nose and ears into the barbecue and lettuce and he couldn't stop it.

I tried to work back from the grill but I was too short and couldn't reach the back rows. The heat was getting to me. I

felt like dancing. I began to get delirious. The walls seemed
to be covered with well-done hamburgers. I began working
close to the fry pots—too close—I was taking too many
chances.

I was working too close to the fires. Instead of using the
long broiler fork for pulling out steaks I went in under the
flames with my spatula. The heat was getting to me. The
orders were still stacked in the window. Horns were blowing.
Fleet and Holly were shouting about ice and screaming at the
curb boys to pick up the orders and keep the big window
clear. The order bell kept ringing. Holly smoked his cigar
faster and faster and did nothing but shout and the girls in
the front were wild-eyed and slamming their open palms on
the big partition glass for hamburgers, barbecues, chicken,
steaks, anything you got. . . .

I wanted to stop and check supplies. It was my job to keep
Preach supplied on the big board. If I could only leave the
grill for a minute and check everything. If I could only leave
the grill and dance. I had a tremendous urge to dance. The
heat was making my ears ache and I could taste the heavy
grease on the back of my teeth. It tasted good. Everything
began to shift in the room. I was getting dizzy. I wondered
where the monkey would come from. I stared at the big black
grill now brown with hamburgers—well-done to the right
—medium to the left—rare in the middle . . . Keep your
eyes on the rare, the well-dones will take care of themselves.
Little faces began appearing in the hamburgers. Sixty little
faces all bright and clear. The well-dones looked older than
the rares. The mediums were all grinning. I began tapping
my spatula on the edge of the grill and doing a little delirious dance on the duckboards. Preach touched my spatula
with his bread kife. "Heat got you? Hey, boy, heat got you?
Tell me, you see the monkey?"

I think I said, "I hope so." I did a double shuffle salt dance
on the duckboards and went down on one knee. The monkey
rose up from the well-done hamburgers, turned into a gorilla

and wrapped me in his hairy arms. The next thing I knew Preach was shoving ice chips into my mouth. I always snap out of grease-heat attacks fast. The gorilla made a gargling sound in my ear, then laughed, turned back into a little thin monkey and jumped back up on the grill. He ran across the grill stepping lightly from the mediums to the well-dones and dived into the 380-degree grease. And then I felt better. The first noise I heard was Fleet shouting, "I'm out of Dr. Pepper syrup. Where in the hell is that goddam Blue? Blue, damn your soul, where are you?"

Preach was stroking my face. "You all right, boy?"

I sat up. "I'm fine now." I picked up my spatula from the floor. "Anybody see me?"

"No . . . no, boy. No one saw you 'cept me." He turned over two rare hamburgers with his bread knife. "Boy, you gave me a real scare there. If I had to work this with Fleet or Holly I wouldn't have made it."

That little compliment brought me around sharp and clear and I turned over nine rare hamburgers with a nice rolling wrist movement that he had taught me. Preacher smiled and pulled down another handful of orders. "Here we go."

Preach shifted back to the sandwich board. He was working eight sandwiches wide and six deep. I began talking out loud in case the monkey started climbing out of the grease. "Barbecue sliced, thirty-five cents with a side of potato salad and three pickle chips . . . one chicken in the rough . . . a piece of breast, a piece of thigh, a leg and a tender, juicy, always-fun-to-eat wing . . . a lettuce cup, two slices of tomatoes, a dab of mayonnaise and a serving of salt and pepper . . . two large and generous handfuls of French fried potatoes and here you are, sir, for only one dollar and twenty-five cents . . . cost you a dollar fifty at Ed White's and he gives you two wings and no thigh. . . .

"How we doing, Preach?" I felt great now.

"We doing fine, boy. You just fry . . . I got everything under control."

I looked down at the next order . . . four bacon, lettuce and tomato sandwiches on whole wheat toast. "You see this?"

Preach looked at it. "Send it back."

I kept my little singsong going. "No, Preach . . . let your old daddy handle this . . . I got something I want to try out. . . ." I threaded twenty-four slices of bacon onto a skewer fork and lowered it into the deep bubbling fat.

Preach said, "Boy, that ain't going to taste like nothing."

"I know but look how fast it cooks." It was done. Crisp and sere with about a thousand per cent shrinkage. Preach punched the whole wheat bread down in the toaster. "Well, normally I wouldn't let you send it out. But seeing that it's for Sonny Love and his crowd I guess it won't do any harm. I bet that crowd don't know bacon from pork liver."

As Preach finished up the bacon, lettuce and tomato sandwiches he said, "We need some tomatoes."

My heart dropped like a stone. I couldn't leave the grill to slice tomatoes and he was working six deep on the board. He didn't have time or room. I said, "You want me to call Holly?"

"Man, no. . . . we'll be all right. Just let me get some room here. Hand me some tomatoes when you unload the potatoes." He began laughing. I thought the monkey had made an appearance on the sandwich board.

I got the tomatoes from the refrigerator and gave him seven. "What are you laughing at?"

Preach took the bread knife and began fanning it through a tomato. I'd never seen him work so fast, but all the time he was laughing. "That Sonny Love crowd is as bad as the Jehovah Witnesses. They don't tip a dime. Old Blue out there says all Jo-Jo got tonight is forty cents and a hatful of religious tracts." And so Preach sliced tomatoes while he worked and if I've ever seen anything prettier than that it never registered. He didn't seem to be hurrying but he was efficient and every time he moved something got done. A few empty spaces began to appear on the grill around two-thirty and within the next half hour we had caught up on the incoming orders. I cut back to two French-fry pots and was able to open up the back of the grill, where the grease was as thick as chicken batter. We had been going steady for four hours when the orders in the window were all gone.

Preach said, "I got to have a break. . . . Okay?"

"Fine with me . . . you must be pretty tired."

"No, nothing like that . . . I been thinking over that Immanuel Kant and I'll be dogged if that rascal ain't got me stumped. I thought I had him a few nights back but I let him get away." He took off his apron and wiped his head with the inside of it. "I won't be long."

"Take your time Preach. You deserve it."

When Preach came back from his break Fleetwood drifted into the kitchen. He was fanning himself with his little cap. "What a night . . . Jesus, what a night. What does that Sonny Love do to the . . . my damn back is almost broke." He sat down on an empty beer case. "Christ, doesn't it ever get cool back here?"

Preach was cleaning out his condiment containers. He was quiet and kept staring at the sandwich board trying to figure out his problems on Kant. Fleet said loudly, "Hey, Preach, how 'bout if you fry me a steak?" Preach snapped out of his problem. He didn't want any trouble.

"Sure thing, Fleet. You sure you want it fried? I can broil him for you. No trouble at all . . . make it more tender."

Fleet looked him in the eye and said, "Listen, dark meat, if I wanted it broiled I would have said so."

I reached in the refrigerator and pulled out a nice gristly steak. It had been in the back of the refrigerator for months and was darker than the rest and the edges were curled up. I tossed it out on the center of the grill where it was the hottest. Fleet got up from his beer cases and looked down at the steak. "God almighty, what kind of steak is that? It looks like a piece of tire boot."

Preach walked over to the refrigerator and pulled out a big
T bone. . . . "How's that?"

"That's okay." Preach put it on the side of the grill and
began salting it down. He speared the curved dog steak with
his fork and dropped it in the garbage. "You like anything
else, Fleet?"

"Yeah, gimme some fried onion rings."

I said, "Come off it, Fleet. Eat some potatoes. We haven't
got any onion rings ready and you know it."

Fleet didn't look at me. He looked at Preach and said
slowly, "I don't want no potatoes."

Preach hung his big fork up and said, "Give him the
rings . . . I'll make the batter."

It was two nights later that Fleet got a raise and Preach
and I didn't. I heard it from Agnes. She told me how Fleet
had put it to Holly that either he got more money or he was
going to work for Ed White across town. Holly Yates and Ed
White were the big grill enemies in Columbia and throughout the three counties. I told Preach about it but he didn't say
anything. I kept after Preach about how we should see Holly
and talk it over. I said, "Preach, either of us could handle
that fountain and that two-bit sandwich board and you know
it. All that Fleetwood's got is a reputation."

Preach said, "Listen, if you want to see Holly about it you
go ahead. I got too many problems to be worrying about
money right now. Besides I don't want no trouble."

I kept after him. "Come on, Preach. Fleet isn't going to get
any easier to live with, and you know it. He'll probably get
worse."

Couple of nights later, after the movie crowd had left,
Preach and I were standing in the doorway cooling off and
watching Fleetwood work. The fountain was busy with a lot
of teen-agers. I began to study Fleetwood's style. There
seemed to be a lot of wasted motion but he got things done
and he looked good. He looked real good. Every movement

[159]

was finished as if he were on camera. Nothing jerked or jarred and he seemed to be inscribing circles and beautiful parabolas around his work. He did a lot of pivoting and knee bending and got his body into a lot of the action.

Fleet's best move was on banana splits. Customers would come in and order the thirty-cent split just to see Fleetwood work. This always pleased Holly and he'd sit up on his high stool where he'd watch Agnes and see that the curb boys didn't steal anything from the order window and beam down at Fleetwood as if he were his own son. Tonight it was heavy on banana splits and they had him working pretty steady. Most of the time that Fleet sliced bananas for splits he'd turn his back to us when we were watching like a plumber will do in front of a journeyman or a carpenter when he has a little something he doesn't want you to see. But tonight there were too many banana splits and he had to work out in the open. Most of us followed the classic pattern on slicing bananas. We'd peel it, lay it on the bread board, hold it up so the hump was on top and press the knife down. But Fleetwood had a one-handed method that none of us could copy. Here's how he did it. He'd lay the banana in his left hand and slice it with the peeling still on. Then he'd nick it on the side. This was a little grandstand effect. He claimed it let the air into the banana. Then without touching the banana with his right hand he'd squeeze it in some mysterious way so that the perfectly sliced banana would come sliding out into the banana split tray just as pretty as you please. Whenever Preach or I tried it we'd go too deep on the incision and cut our palm, or else not deep enough and when we squeezed the banana would come oozing out along the entire edge of the top cut like thick mustard. Fleet was working on four banana splits at once and he knew we were watching him. He turned his back to us when he sliced but I could see him in the mirror. And he could see me. Preach wasn't really watching him. He had that glazed Immanuel Kant look in his eyes and

I'm sure he didn't know or care if Fleet was working on splits or milk shakes.

Fleet finished the splits and started on four more. Once again he turned his back and once again I watched him in the mirror. He caught my eyes in the mirror and I continued to stare. He was furious. I winked at him. He slammed down his knife and screamed. "Holly, Goddammit, I quit. I quit, you hear. I ain't going to stand up here and work in front of those two bastards back there."

Holly came out of a side room. He was eating and was dabbing a big napkin at his lips. "What's the matter, boy?"

Fleet shouted, "Look. . . ." He pointed at me and Preach in the mirror. "They dogging me. They stand there watching me. I can't work with them bastards watching me. They stealing my ideas. They studying me. I ain't going to do it, you hear. I'm leaving here and going to Ed White's." Holly took him out in the yard and quieted him down.

When Holly came back he took Preach and me out by the barbecue pit and we all sat down on the bench facing the fire. Holly did most of the talking. "Listen now, I'll put it to you straight. If Fleet leaves and goes to White's I lose the high-school trade in the afternoon. They come out here to watch him. They claim he's the fastest thing in town. They even make book on him."

I said, "What do you mean?"

"I mean they order four banana splits or sundaes and then time him. Then they go out to White's and do the same thing and then out to the Red Pig and do it all over again. Fleet's the best in town and he knows it. Now you see why I pamper him so. You think I like to work with all that hollering and shouting going on? He gives me a flat pain in the ass but I got no choice. So I want you boys to go back in there and apologize to him. I know it's going to be tough but I want you to do it for old Holly." He paused. "Old Holly would appreciate it."

I asked old Holly about the raise and without batting an eye, he said, "Okay, as of tonight."

Preacher spoke, "That's mighty nice, Holly, I could use that extra money."

"If anyone deserves it, Preach, it's you."

Preacher thanked him again and then said, "What if someone was to beat old Fleet in this race around town?"

Holly said, "Boy, would I love to see that. If I saw someone do it I'd snap him up so fast, at any salary, and fire that Fleetwood Driggers so fast it would make his head swim."

I leaned forward. My hands were tingling. I was beginning to drool. I knew Preach was going to say he could beat Fleet. I closed my eyes and prayed that he would drag it out slow and beautiful so I could wallow in every juicy second of it. I closed my eyes tighter and gritted my teeth.

Nothing came. Preacher sat back in the shadows on the bench and said nothing. I leaned forward and stared at Preach. "Weren't you going to say something, Preach?" There was a long pause during which I closed my eyes again and hugged my knees tenderly.

"No, I don't have anything else to say. I guess we ought to get on back inside. I don't want them orders to get too far ahead of us."

After Holly closed the cash register and turned the big neon sign off out front, he went home. Preach and Fleet and I were the only ones left. Blue was out back on garbage. Fleet had finished cleaning his fountain and had been hanging around waiting to talk to us. Preach finished filling up the condiment line for the breakfast cook and I was putting the last soapstone touches on the grill. Fleet came back and sat up on the sandwich board. "I suppose it's too late for bacon and eggs." It was four A.M. Preach didn't say anything.

I said, "You're damn right it is."

"Well, what if I said I wanted eggs and bacon and I wanted you to fix them for me?" Preach was putting the extra tomatoes in the refrigerator. He was staying as far away from Fleetwood as he could. No one answered. Fleet tapped me on the shoulder. I leaned on the big soapstone and counted to ten.

"How about the eggs?"

Fleetwood was too big to fight but I had the soapstone in my right hand and the rat-tailed knife sharpener was hanging on the edge of the sandwich board. I said, "Fleet, why don't you forget the bacon and just have the eggs?"

"How's that again?" He was dying to hit me. . . .

I held on to the soapstone. "You can suck the eggs, you rotten son of a bitch . . . that's what."

He jumped forward and I jumped back with the soapstone raised. He took a step forward and said, "I'm going to make you eat that brickbat."

Preach shouted, "Hold it, Fleetwood." I looked over at Preach. I figured he had a meat cleaver or something. I looked at his hands but he had nothing.

Fleet smiled and began pulling his little clip-on necktie off. "You're the one I really want, and you know it. You want it outside or you want it here?"

Preach's voice dropped back down to his soft and mellow range. "I ain't no fighting man, Fleetwood, and you know it."

I unhooked the knife sharpener carefully and shoved it into my back pocket. I still had the soapstone in my hand but I was beginning to feel foolish holding it up in the air. "We can both take him, Preach. We can kill the son of a bitch."

Fleet turned to me, "You shut up, you little bastard, or I'll dip you in one of those fry pots." Then he turned to Preach. He was a head taller than Preach and about forty pounds heavier. "No, Preach, I ain't listening to no sermons. I want your ass and I'm going to get it tonight. I saw you out there with Holly tonight. What were you telling him, you black bastard?"

"You want to know?"

"Damn right. And I'm going to find out before we leave this kitchen."

Preach ignored him and began walking back and forth on the duckboards. I thought for a minute he was back with his problems on Immanuel Kant. He spoke slow, "The way I see it, Fleetwood, you and me are going to have to butt heads sooner or later. I been trying to avoid it. I been trying real hard cause I know violence don't do any good." He walked back and forth some more.

Fleet sat back on the sandwich board and put his feet up on it. "Take your time, Preach. Take plenty of time."

Preacher stopped and looked at his feet. "Now why you want to go sit on my sandwich board like that and put your feet up on it? You know that ain't right."

Fleet laughed and lit a cigarette, "What you going to do about it, Preach?"

He walked back and forth a couple more times. "Ain't but one thing I can do, Fleetwood. I got to straighten you out."

Fleetwood laughed, "That'll be the day."

Preach kept walking. He spoke very slow. "Fleetwood, Holly tells me all about this bookmaking around town on your soda-jerking speed. He tells me that all the high-school boys and girls say you are the fastest thing going. He tells me how they put money on you and how they win and how it is you who keeps this place filled up with that high-school trade in the afternoons. He tells me if you were to leave and go to Mr. White's across town he would soon lose the high-school trade."

Fleetwood said, "He tells you a lot of things."

"Let me finish. I got to speak this out clear so there is no misunderstanding. All the time Holly is telling me these things I ain't saying nothing. The reason I don't say nothing is that I don't want no trouble. I got troubles enough in school and I don't need this kind of trouble."

"Preach, you taking too long to get to the point. If you got something to say, say it. I ain't going to sit up here and listen to no sermon."

"All right. . . . Okay . . . All right, no sermons . . . I'll put it to you like Holly put it to me. He claims that if someone in town beats you on the fountain he'd hire them in a minute and fire you."

I spoke up. "That's what he said, Fleetwood. I swear to God, that's what he said. I was sitting right there on the bench with Preach when he said it."

Fleet said, "This ain't no news. He told me the same thing. Hell, I know that. Listen, is that all you going to say, Preach? Let's go outside."

"Hold it. I'll get to my point right now. I been watching you in the mirror, Fleetwood. You were right about that. I was watching you all right. But you were wrong about the reasons. I wasn't trying to copy your style. I was just checking it. I'll tell you something about your style. You ready?"

"Yeah."

"You ain't got no style. You got a lot of big movements, but you got no style. You do a lot of wheel-spinning. You don't get nothing done. The only reason you been beating the other boys in town is 'cause they are just worse than you, that's all. You haven't run up against any competition yet, and when you do church is going to be out."

Fleet smiled, "You're all wrong, Preach. Those boys have timed me with a stop watch and I'm the fastest man in the county, with Spartanburg and Monck's Corner thrown in."

Preach looked at him, "I timed you too, Fleet. You look good but you're slow. I know a man in town that's about forty per cent faster than you and he doesn't even jerk soda."

"Who's that?"

I sat down on the beer case and looked up. I was in love with Preacher Watts.

Preach stopped walking. "You are looking at him."

"Don't make me laugh."

"No, I ain't going to make you laugh. All I'm going to do is straighten you out. What if I would take a job at White's for a few days? Just a few days, mind you. Just enough time to let the boys make some big bets on you and then lose. Why, Holly would have you out of here with the dirty linen and you know it."

Preach stood with his hand in his pockets under his apron and stared right at Fleet.

Fleet said, "Just assuming that what you say is true, you mean to say you'd go over to White's and do this just to get me fired?"

"I would, Fleet . . . I wouldn't like to do it, but you don't give me much choice. You see, Fleetwood, you just ain't a reasonable man. If you were reasonable you wouldn't be sitting up on my sandwich board and threatening me."

Fleet grinned. It was that nasty knife-edge grin. He reached way over and ground out his cigarette in the middle of my clean grill. "That's not very reasonable either, is it?"

Preach looked at him. He looked hurt. "No, that's pretty low-life, too."

Fleet started to get up from the sandwich board. "Let's cut this crap out and go outside."

Preach still looked hurt. "You don't want to see how slow you are?"

"You mean you want to race me now? We're closed."

"Would you rather I show you up tomorrow when the high-school crowd is here? Normally I work better in front of a crowd. But it wouldn't be too good for your name around town." Preach smiled. "You might even wind up back here in all this grease heat."

Fleet jumped down from the board. "All right, damn you. . . . Come on, show me something." He rushed to the front and pulled down the Venetian blinds and turned all the lights on. "Okay, dark meat, what do you want to make and how do you want to time it?"

He looked over his clean fountain. He knew every inch of it, where everything was, how the taps worked, which syrup dispensers were slow, which fast . . . everything.

Preach sat down at the counter. "Fleet, we both can't go

together. You go first. I'll follow. You write down what you want to make. Make four or five things, make more if you want. We'll keep time."

Fleetwood looked suspicious. "I don't trust you. Who's going to keep time?"

Preach said, "No one to trust. You begin when you want and when you finish, that's your time."

"Whose watch?"

"We'll use yours. Here, put it up on the counter."

Fleet laid his watch on the counter. He picked up a piece of soap and listed on the back mirror: two chocolate sundaes, four strawberry sodas, eighteen small Cokes and seven banana splits.

I said, "You better cut that down some. Holly will have a fit if he finds out you're wasting all that ice cream."

Preach said, "No, that's okay. That's better for me. I'll get the feel better. Blue will clean up for us."

Fleetwood said, "I'll wait until four-thirty sharp." He put on his little white jacket and cap and brushed the side of his hair away from his face. He looked seriously at Preach. "Listen, this doesn't mean you ain't getting your ass cut when we're through. 'Cause the minute you're through here we go outside. You understand?"

"I understand."

Fleet looked at me, "And I ain't through with you either."

It was four minutes before four-thirty, and Fleet began warming his hands together and flexing his elbows and knees. "Listen, I don't like this. How I know you ain't going to mess with my watch?"

Preach said, "Here, wait a second." He pulled out a roll of Scotch tape from under the cash register and tore off a piece. "Tape it to the mirror . . . up high where you can see it."

He taped it up high to the left of the list.

Fleetwood smiled and rubbed his hands together again. There was still two minutes to go.

"How about a little side bet?"

"Okay with me," Preach said.

Fleetwood dropped his wallet out on the counter. "There's a hundred and forty there. How much you want?"

I said, "I want forty."

Preach laid his wallet on top of Fleetwood's. "I got the rest."

There were ten seconds to go and Fleetwood said, "It's your funeral."

At four-thirty Fleetwood flung open the vanilla, strawberry and chocolate ice cream holes and went to work on the sundaes. At four-thirty-two he was on the sodas and by four-thirty-five he had five Coke cups in his hand at once and was filling them with ice.

He kept his head down and never looked at the clock or at us. He moved fast and his movements were shorter than I remembered. There was a jerky quality about his actions but I knew his speed had increased from the time we had watched him two nights back. He slid the Cokes out onto the counter and picked up five more in his left hand. He had big hands. He could hold seven empty small Coke containers in his left, but when he worked the Coke dispenser he preferred to hold only five. The eighteen Cokes were lined up on the counter at four-thirty-nine and Fleetwood reached for the seven bananas. Preach got up from his stool and walked across the room to the booths and sat down. He lit a cigarette. Fleet hadn't missed Preach leaving the counter and he figured it was a trick to make him slow down. He speeded up.

At four-forty-six and thirty seconds Fleetwood threw up his hands and shouted "Done!"

The entire order had taken sixteen minutes and thirty seconds. Fleetwood picked up a Coke and began drinking and sat down at the counter facing the fountain.

Preach went to the kitchen and put on his apron and came back out. He drank one of the Cokes as we all watched the second hand on Fleetwood's watch lift the minute hand toward five o'clock. At three minutes before five Preach said,

"That was the fastest I ever see you work, Fleet. You looked real good."

Fleet lit a cigarette. "Don't start brown-nosing me now. The minute you finish up here I'm taking your money and your ass. And that's final."

There was one minute to go. Preach said quietly, "Sun's coming up. I'm getting tired." He began walking back and forth on the duckboards as if he were in the kitchen. He didn't look at the watch until he had walked back and forth four times. When he looked up the second hand had two seconds to go. Preach winked at me and started. He started slow, much slower than Fleet. Fleet saw it and started grinning. By the time he was finishing up on the sodas he had lost a full minute and a half to Fleet. I was getting scared and started inching down the counter so I could get the knife sharpener and the soapstone. Preach only picked up three Coke cups at once. But he picked them up cleaner than Fleet and worked the dispenser faster. He gained a minute of the time back on the Cokes and went into the banana splits a half minute behind. And then an incredible thing happened. Suddenly he found himself. Everything began to fit into place and the old Preach that I had watched fan the tomato slices during the Sonny Love rush came to the surface and flashed there. He worked low near the ice cream holes and when he dipped and ejected onto the trays it was a solid continuous movement. No elbows or knees or pivots, just wrists and hands and head. He moved so surely that when one of the split dishes slipped from the fountain and bounced on the duckboards, he didn't even look down. There was no telling how much time he was using because he had started the splits all at once and they would all be finished at the same time. I thought he was losing until all of a sudden I noticed he had the whipped-cream cylinder in one hand and his left hand filled with maraschino cherries. Each split got three shots of whipped cream, one for each flavor ice cream, and each was capped with a bright red cherry. Fleetwood Driggers had taken seven and a half minutes to do seven banana splits. Preacher Watts did them in four minutes flat.

Preacher turned and pulled Fleet's watch from the mirror. "That's it, Fleetwood."

I screamed "Hot damn son of a bitch" or something and ran down the counter spinning the bar stools and doing my delirious dance again. I vaulted up on top of the counter and did a rapid heel dance and let out a rebel yell that made the beer glasses rattle. What a sweet victory. What a beautiful three and a half minutes.

Preacher took the victory quietly. Preacher had more class than me. When Preacher finally spoke he said, "Fleetwood, I could have made better time than that if I knew the syrup line better." He pointed to the wallet. "You want to do the honors?"

Fleet didn't say a word. He had another problem on his mind beside the one hundred dollars. He was thinking about what Holly would do when he found out. He took all of his money out of his wallet and counted out a hundred and forty dollars on to the counter. He had four one dollar bills left and his social security card. "I suppose you going to tell Holly first thing in the morning?"

I said, "You damn right we are."

Preach handed me up forty dollars and slipped the rest into his own wallet. "I'll let you know, Fleet. I ain't decided yet. You better be going on home now. You look tired."

I was still up on top of the counter when Fleetwood opened the door. I was too tired to dance now and I sat down on top of the counter and shouted, "Hey, Fleet, they got great eggs and bacon over at Ed White's. They might even make you up some onion rings." As he slammed the door and started across the yard I shouted louder so my voice would go through the window, "If they say onion rings are à la carte tell 'em to go to hell."

Preacher was sitting on one of the stools drinking a Coke. He looked tired. I sat down next to him and picked up another Coke. "What you going to do, Preach? You going to tell Holly? We're going to get rid of that bastard, ain't we?"

"Don't say ain't boy." He finished his Coke and picked up another one. There were thirty-one left on the counter.

"Why don't you go home, boy? I'm going to stick around and help Blue on this mess."

I turned to him. "Whoa now, I'm not leaving here until you tell me when you're going to tell Holly. I want to be there."

The sun was shining down Pershing Street and reflecting in the windows of the L & D Beer Hall. The barbecue pit was still in darkness but parts of the parking lot were beginning to pick up the sun.

We were quiet for a long time. We were both tired now. It was going to be a hot day and it would be hard to sleep.

I knew Preach was thinking about Immanuel Kant and now I wished I had listened to him when he explained Kant's philosophy to me. I spoke in a strangled voice. "What would old Mr. Kant say about a thing like this? What would he say to do about a bastard like Fleetwood Driggers?"

Preacher turned and smiled. His face lit up like a banana split. "How you know that was what I was thinking about? Boy, you're getting smarter every day. I was just figuring what he would say about a situation like this and I believe I got me an answer."

I jumped in. "He'd say to ram it to him."

Preach looked serious, "No, he wouldn't say that. But I know exactly what he would say, though."

I said, "What?"

"I suspect he'd rub his beard a little bit and then he'd say, 'Let him sweat.' "

COLEY MOKE

In order to get back to Coley Moke's place outside Monck's Corner, South Carolina, you have to run down a Peevy or a Taylor or another Moke and make him take you back. Charley, Jim and I got us a Taylor and went back one day.

There were too many dogs in the yard to count but there were four runty gray pigs who'd been talked into believing they were hounds. When we petted the dogs we had to scratch the pigs. It was hot and the dogs were panting so Coley led us into his front room. There was a bed and a wood stove in the room and nothing else. No tables, no chairs, no lights; it was the only room in the house.

"Make yourself to home."

And then, "You bring any funny books?"

Charley pulled a roll out of his back pocket. Coley thumbed through them and said, "Fine."

He emptied a Mason jar of corn whisky into a water bucket, placed a tin dipper in the bucket and set it down on the floor.

Three of the older dogs got up on the bed with Coley. One of the little razorbacks tried to make it but couldn't.

We sat down against the wall near the bucket and when we started drinking, Coley started talking.

"See this dog here . . . his name's Brownie."

He was a long thin brown dog; his eyes were closed.

"Well, when I tell him the law is coming he picks up that steel bucket and runs out into the swamp, and I mean he doesn't come back until I call him. Couple of the others would do that for me but they got so they were spilling too much.

"Brownie here knows I got me only one small still going now and he don't waste a drop. One old timer—Trig—he's gone now—would take it out there by the creek. He was a mess. He'd drink a while and then swim a while and then sleep until he was sober and then start in all over again. . . ."

Charley nudged Jim and Jim nudged me. We drank some more.

Coley laughed and rasseled the head of the red bone hound on his left. "This here's Bob, and they don't come any smarter than him. One day he convinced these Federal men he would lead them back to the house. And they followed him. He led them poor bastards between the quicksand and the 'gators and showed them every cottonmouth moccasin in the swamp. He got them so scared they were just begging him to lead them back on the road—any road. They promised him steaks and that they'd never raid me again. Well, sir, Bob kept them going until it was dark and after he walked them over a couple long 'gators that looked like logs he finally put them up on the road. It was the right road but it was about twelve miles from their car. Old Bob sure had himself some fun that night. He told Brownie here all about it and Brownie told me."

Charley took a big drink; Jim and I took a big drink. There was more. About how Spot and Whip would team up on a moccasin or a rattlesnake and while one faked the snake out of his coil the other would grab him by the tail and pop his head off like a buggy whip.

Jim said, "Man, that is some dog to do that."

Coley began to drink a little more and when he started talking about his wife his voice changed. "Yeah, I suspect I miss that old gal. Wonder what she looks like now. She was something, all right. Up at dawn, cook a first-class meal and then go out and outplow any man and mule in the county and every Sunday, rain or shine we had white linen on the table and apple pie . . . ain't nothing I like better than apple pie.

"Sometimes we didn't speak for a week. It was nice then, real nice. As long as I kept quiet and minded the still and my dogs everything was fine. But we started talking and then the first thing you know we were arguing and then she began to throw the dogs up in my face. Let's see . . . it was right in the middle of the Compression. Right here in this room. She had to go and try and turn me against my dogs. . . . Well, the Compression hit us bad—real bad. I had no money, no copper for the still, and no way of getting any up. I was doing a lot of fishing and hunting then. . . . Yeah, right here . . . oh, it was different then. There were four cane chairs and a dresser and a mirror from Sears Roebuck against that wall, and there was a couple insurance calendars from the Metropolitan Life Insurance Company hanging over there."

He took a big drink. The light was fading but we could still see his face. A bull alligator deep in the swamp rumbled once and decided it was too early.

"Yeah, I was lying here with old Sport. He was Brownie here's father. He was young then and high-spirited and, you know, sensitive. When Emma Louise got up from her chair and came over he must have seen it in her face. They never had gotten along. He crawled off the bed and went outside. If I live to be two hundred, I'll never forget those words. . . .

"She said, 'Coley Moke, you are the sorriest man on God's green earth. Here it is almost winter, we got no money, we got no food, and you just lay there and stare up at that leaky roof. And what's more, you've gone out and taken our last hog and traded it for another dog.' "

Coley smiled and leaned forward. Then his face set mean

and hard. " 'Emma, Emma Louise,' I said, 'if I told you once I told you a hundred times. . . . But since you seem to not hear I'm going to tell you one more time. I traded that hog and I got me a dog for the plain and simple reason that I can't go running no fox with no hog.'

"Come on men, drink her up. When that's gone there's more where it came from. And if we get too drunk to walk we can send my old buddy Brownie here."

He rasseled the dog's head. "How about it, boy, what d'you say?"

We drank until it was time to eat. Coley lighted a fire in the wood stove and warmed up some red-horse bread. He served it on folded newspapers and with the little light from the stove we sat back down where we had been sitting and ate.

Later he chased the two pigs outside and we heard their hooves clopping down the porch and on the steps. The pigs slept under the house with the dogs. Coley said they generally got to bed a little earlier than the dogs.

An owl sounded, a bull alligator answered, and the moon glided out of the tall cypress trees in the swamp and the room began to streak with silver light. We slept. . . .

It was raining in the morning and all the dogs and hogs were in the living room. Spot, Trig and Buckles were on the bed with Coley. The two hogs were under the unlit stove and the rest of the dogs were against the wall. Charley, Jim and I were sitting on the floor.

Coley was talking. "Bob's father—that was Earl Brown —he's been dead a long time now. Let's see, next month it'll be eleven years. It doesn't seem like it was that long ago. Eleven years, man, but don't it drive by?"

Charley took a drink and handed me the dipper. I took one and gave it to Jim.

"Buried him out on that hill knuckle in front. He always liked it up there. Some mornings I'd wake up and look out and there he'd be sitting up there just as pretty as you

[175]

please. All the other dogs would still be sleeping. But not Earl Brown, he was always the first one up.

"He wasn't like the others. Now I ain't saying the others weren't smart, but it was a different kind of smartness. You know how it is with hounds. They'll do anything you tell them. But there's a lot of them that just don't have any initiative. Now that's right where Earl Brown was different. Earl Brown was always trying to better himself, trying to improve himself, you might say.

"I could tell it when he was a pup. The other dogs would fall all over one another getting at the food and when they'd get to it they'd bolt it down like they hadn't eaten in a month. But not Earl Brown, no sir. He'd wait and let them take their places at the trough. Then he'd walk over, slow-like, and commence eating. He wouldn't rush. He even chewed his food longer."

Coley got down off the bed and took a drink. He studied the bottom of the empty dipper.

"Yeah, they don't make any finer dog than Earl Brown."

He put the dipper in the bucket of whisky on the floor and sat back down on the bed.

"That dog was a loner, too. The others would all sleep in the wood box. Sometimes there'd be as many as seventeen all flopped in there on top of one another. But not Earl Brown. From the day that scutter was weaned he slept by himself outside the box.

"I guess I miss Earl Brown as much or more than any of them. He was a marvelous dog, all right. Marvelous, that's what he was.

"I told you how he'd sit up on the hill early in the mornings. Well, he wasn't out there lapping the dew off the grass for nothing. He was working on something.

"Boys, I want you to know what that dog was working on. I wouldn't tell this to just anyone else. They'd say that fool Coley Moke has gone slap out of his mind, living out there with all them dogs.

"First of all I wouldn't have known a thing if it hadn't been for the chickens. But they started making a lot of noise during the night. I thought a weasel or a snake was getting at them so I started watching from the window. It wasn't no weasel and it wasn't no snake. It was two foxes. Big red ones, long as dogs, and five times smarter. But those foxes didn't go inside the coop. They just stood there. They must have been there five minutes and then I thought I saw another fox. I looked again and you know who it was?

"It was Earl Brown. Well sir, those two red foxes and Earl Brown stood outside that chicken coop for ten minutes. My other dogs were all inside the house and they were going crazy. The poor hens were clucking and screeching for help. I didn't know what to do. Finally I heard Earl Brown growl and then the next thing you know the three of them ran off into the woods.

"I kind of figured Earl Brown was setting those foxes up for me to shoot so I decided to wait until he gave me some kind of sign. Well, next night it happened again. Same time, right around three o'clock they came out of the woods. Well, they had their little meeting right outside the coop and then they ran off again.

"Of course, during all this I had to make sure Earl Brown got out at night and my other dogs stayed in. That took some doing. The others all knew that Earl Brown was getting special treatment and they got mad as hell. And they smelled those foxes on him and they wouldn't have a thing to do with him.

"But Earl Brown didn't care what they thought about him. He even liked it better that way. But he got to looking peaked and red-eyed. Like he wasn't getting any sleep. I put a couple extra eggs in his rations. That boy was on a rough schedule. He'd go to sleep around ten with the others but he'd be up at two and off with his friends.

"Things began looking bad. My dogs were giving me a fit to be let out at night. I wasn't getting any sleep. And those hens. Lord, those poor hens were going right out of their minds. They got so nervous they were laying eggs at midnight. The rooster worried so he began losing weight and limping. He got so he wouldn't even crow. They were one sad-looking sight in the mornings. Wouldn't eat, couldn't sleep. I mean it got so bad them hens were stumbling around and bumping into one another.

"I decided to give Earl Brown two more nights and then end it. I was determined to shoot those damn foxes and get my chickens back on some decent schedule.

"And that was the very night it happened. . . .

"Earl Brown stepped aside and let one of those foxes go into the coop. Those poor chickens were so scared and tired. I guess they were relieved when that fox walked in and picked one out. He took a Rhode Island Red. That hen didn't even squawk. Just hung there in his mouth and across that red fox's back like she was glad it was all over. Those chickens slept the rest of the night. It was the first good night's sleep they'd had in three weeks."

Coley stopped. "You boys ain't drinking."

Charley said, "I just this minute put the dipper down."

Coley drank again and hunched himself back up between the dogs. "Well, I figured that was the end for Earl Brown. I saw where he had thrown in with the foxes and I knew it would be best if I shot him and the foxes. I had it worked out in my mind that those three were going to take a chicken a night until I was stripped clean. So I loaded up my four-ten over and under and got the four-cell flashlight ready and waited. I was praying Earl Brown wouldn't run off that night. But two o'clock came and he sneaked out and lit out through the woods. . . . You know what happened?"

"What?"

"They never showed up."

"Never?"

"Never . . . but still every night Earl Brown would leave the house at two. About a week later, I followed that dog out through the woods. I was downwind and I stood behind a big sweet gum and watched them.

"They were out in this little field and the moon was good and I could see everything. They were playing some kind of game out there in that moonlight. The foxes would run and Earl Brown would chase them in little circles. Then the foxes would chase him back and forth. And then it all ended and Earl Brown started back through the woods home.

"Mind you, I said 'started back.' Because the minute that rascal figured those foxes figured he was going home, he doubled back. I tell you that was one funny sight. Here I'm behind one tree and Earl Brown is behind another tree and we're both watching those foxes.

"They were running around in circles and making little barking sounds like they were laughing. I tell you, I don't know when I've been so fascinated. I shore wish I had had me a camera about then.

"All of a sudden it hits me what was going on. Old Earl Brown was picking up the foxes' secret about running. That rascal had paid them foxes to show him something. He'd paid them with that Rhode Island Red and now he was checking on the foxes to make sure he'd got his money's worth. Well, by God, I thought I knew something about hounds and foxes but I was shore learning something that night standing out behind that sweet gum tree. And Earl Brown not twenty yards away tipping his head around his tree . . . man, that was one funny night.

"Well, that running secret ain't easy and Earl Brown had to go back several nights. And every night he went, I went. It took him, all told, about three weeks but I'll be dogged if he didn't finally get it."

Coley got off of the bed and squatted down by us. He took another drink and we followed. He spoke lower now.

"I don't want them dogs hearing the rest of this. They'll get out and try it out and wind up breaking their necks. It's too tricky. As smart as Earl Brown was he had a hard time learning it. He took a few pretty bad falls himself before he got it."

Coley stopped and let the bait trail. . . .

Charley rose to it. "Learned what, Coley?"

Coley spoke even lower than before. "How to run like a fox, that's what. Oh, that was one fine dog. He set his mind to it and he learned it. He was marvelous."

Charley was getting jumpy. "What did he learn, Coley? What did he learn?"

"Don't rush me, boy. You don't know much about foxes, do you, boy?"

"I guess not."

"Well you know a fox can outrun any living dog if he feels like it, don't you?"

"Yes."

"Usually they don't feel like it. They're too smart to just do straight running. Most of the time they work in pairs and they get the dogs so confused they don't know what's going on. They'll be running one way and then all of a sudden the other fox will pop up from another direction. Hell, they have signals. Sometimes they'll run the dogs through briar patches, skunk cabbage, anything, and lots of times round and round in the same circles. A good fox will give a pack of dogs a fit. Lot of times a fox will hide and when the dog pack comes by he'll jump in and run along with them. He'll be barking and carrying on and having himself a marvelous time and the dogs won't know a thing.

"Oh, them red foxes are smart. And a good running fox on a straightaway, I mean, no cover, no nothing, can burn a dog down to the ground. He can run that hound right into the ground and he'll be as fresh as when he started. He won't even be breathing hard. You think back. You ever seen a tired fox? No. They don't get tired. And it's all because they got this secret way of running."

Coley was whispering. He really didn't want the dogs to hear. "It's like this. When a fox runs he only uses three legs.

Next time you see one running, you watch. You gotta look close, those reds are smart devils. They keep it secret and they only do it when the're off by themselves or when they get in trouble. Kind of emergency you might say."

Charley said, "Whoa now. What do you mean three legs?"

"They rotate, that's what they do. They rotate. They run on three and keep rotating. That way they always got one resting. That's why they give the impression that they're limping all the time and got that little hop in their run."

"Coley," Charley said, "I just can't believe that one."

Coley jumped up and walked across the room twice. He raised his hand. "The Lord will snatch out my tongue and strike me dead right here and now if that ain't the God's truth."

It continued raining . . . and the Lord didn't make a move. . . .

YOU DONT' SMELL IT:
YOU DRINK IT

FERLIN PERKINS was talking.

I drove all the way from Monck's Corner, South Carolina, to New York City with no stops except for gas so I was a little tired when I got in to the parking lot on Forty-second Street.

I told the man I was going to sleep in the car and he agreed that that would be fine. He said there wouldn't be any extra charge.

But let me tell you why I came up to New York City.

First of all I'm in the wholesale corn whisky business and what with taxes on legal whiskey getting higher, we've been doing a right smart business up here.

Well, business has been good lately and we been getting ahold of a lot of that Depressed Area Free Kennedy corn meal and sugar. So the profits, well, they've been right good too. The only problem is, and that's why I'm here, is the problem of packing.

Now it might not sound like much of a problem to you but when you stop and think about moving several hundred gallons of whisky at a time it gets a bit tricky. Normally we use fifty-five-gallon Coca-Cola barrels. They're made of good wood, they hold up in shipment, and they also give the whisky a chance to age a little. Takes the edge off, you might say. You know, when you put your whisky in metal or glass that's the end of the aging.

My father used Coca-Cola barrels and I been using them

for a long time and, well, frankly, we're used to them. Anyhow, we been getting these complaints from this chain of bars up here. They claim they want their whisky delivered in glass jars or five-gallon tin cans. Claim their men can't lift the big barrels.

Now I say, first off, that that's a helluva reason to want to change. So I'm pretty mad having to drive all the way up here just to tell this Mr. Murphy (he's the man that owns these bars) that we are going to keep right on using Coca-Cola barrels. And if the men can't lift them they can damn well roll them, and if they can't roll them they can siphon it off and carry it in their hats for all I care.

Well, I took off my shoes and shirt and stretched out on that back seat and got me some sleep. They have a radio station in New York that doesn't play anything but slow string and piano music. Oh, once in a while you might hear a clarinet but never any singing or anything like that. Well, this station doesn't have any commercials; they just play that music and every once in a while they tell you the news. I can't say I liked that music—it sounded kinda strange what with no singing and all—but I'll have to admit one thing: it was right restful.

The parking-lot boys were real concerned about me too and every half hour or so they'd come by and see how I was making out. You know, I never have liked New York City. It's just too big for my liking, but I've always believed that it doesn't matter where you go, you're going to run into nice people. When I checked out that evening I gave those boys two half-gallons of whisky to split up amongst them. They really liked that.

Well, I'd slept pretty well and I felt good so I decided to check a few of the bars and see how they were serving my whisky. Let me tell you, when I saw those prices printed on those little foot-high cards across the top of the back bar I dern near fell dead. Forty, fifty cents for blends and fifty-five for Scotch. And I mean it wasn't no three- or four-ounce shot.

No siree, it was that little dinky one-ounce magic glass. You know, it looks like it's a big drink but it's all in the way they magnify it. You can't put your little finger in that glass when it's empty. Oh, they give you ten cents off if you drink before ten in the morning. But, you know yourself, that's too early to do any drinking. And like they got a big free tray of pickles and sauerkraut and you can eat all of that you want. But, my Lord, if I charged forty cents a shot down home I'd be giving fried chicken and dancing girls and I don't know what all.

Well, I ordered me a drink in this Broadway bar. The minute he put that drink before me I knew it was from my last shipment. I could smell it, you know. The bartender was keeping it in a quart bottle with a yellow label on it. Called it Lord Calvert's something. Lord Calvert is standing there with one of them old-timey uniforms on. You know, green and red with kind of golden-colored pants. Had himself a big fluffy white collar and a long wand or stick of some kind. Had something in the background but I couldn't make it out.

Anyhow, I began to feel right proud. I was figuring on having some of those labels printed up and taking them back home. Yeah, I got me a nice feeling going there. Almost like patriotic, you might say. But all this was before I tasted it. Man, it didn't taste like nothing. That was the sorriest excuse for whisky I've ever had and I started raising hell.

I called this fat fellow over who was minding the bar and I asked him what he'd done to the whisky. He gave me a real dirty look and said that's the way he gets it and if I wanted to see the government tax seal I was welcome.

That was kind of funny but I didn't laugh. I told him how when I let that corn whisky out it was proofing at a hundred and twenty and had a half-inch bead.

He didn't know what I was talking about 'cause the next thing, he asks if I was accusing him of watering it.

I said, "Yes."

And then we went at it. . . . .

He said he'd been serving and drinking Lord Calvert for twenty years and that this was pure Lord Calvert blended whisky.

I got a good one in then 'cause I said the only thing pure around here is the pure horse (you-know-what) you're throwing around.

He told me that I didn't know one whisky from another. I came right back at him and called him a dog-faced liar. I don't let no one tell me I don't know anything about whisky.

Then he said something about putting your money where your mouth is.

I always like to carry plenty of money to New York City. I like to buy things from those Forty-second Street auctions and all, mostly gifts, you know. Anyhow I had a roll so thick it bounced twice when I flopped it down on the bar.

I told him to cover that.

It was four thousand dollars.

Well, he dove into his cash drawer and under the counter and got his wallet out and all he could cover was eleven hundred. When I started to pull the twenty-nine hundred back this little man with a mustache and dark glasses says he would cover the rest.

He was a funny-looking devil. Had on a black silky-type coat with no pockets or lapels. I didn't mind that so much but that business of wearing those dark glasses in a dark bar like to throwed me.

Someone told me how this little fellow was the owner of this string of bars. I started to shake his hand and forget all the betting and start discussing business. But he was kinda nasty, you know, and well, I just didn't like him. He finally tells me to put up or shut up and that did it.

Well, sir, the word must have spread faster than a skunk smell in a high wind 'cause the next thing you know this bar was one packed place. The television was off, the bar was closed, the door was locked. I mean those New York boys, they don't fool around.

Well, we kept arguing about how we were going to bet and we didn't get anywhere. Finally a fellow starts shouting he's from Queens and he's a lawyer and how he'll hold the money and how he'll make up the ground rules.

Well, we all listened and it sounded right fair to me so we agreed.

Now here's how they set it up. . . .

The lawyer and some other men were to pour four ounces of whisky into each of five glasses. They did this out back so I couldn't see. Then they set the five glasses on the bar in front of me. They marked each glass and each bottle out back with a number—that was for identification purposes. There was to be no foreign whisky, no Irish or Scotch or anything like that. They were to be blends or ryes or bourbons or sour mash or corn. Or any combination.

I told them I wasn't familiar with the brands and the labels but I could break down the blends, you know, like naming how much straight, what kind of blend, how much neutral spirits and what proof.

The lawyer was right nice about here and he said it would be fair if I had a little tolerance, say one point on the proof.

I said that would be fine but in exchange for that tolerance I'd also name all of the neutral spirits unless they were using synthetics. In case of synthetics I'd call the percentage only, give or take one per cent.

The crowd gave me a little applause when I announced this which I thought was right nice.

Oh, something else. There was a lot of betting going on all over the room so almost everyone there seemed pretty interested.

Well, sir, I started on the left. It was a simple cheap blend. I called the proof at eighty-six point five and that was right on the head. The blend broke down to sixty per cent rye at three years old, twenty per cent bourbon at four years old.

The other twenty per cent was neutral spirits with a real nasty echo taste.

I told them my boy down home was seven years old and he could make better whisky than that. That struck the crowd right funny and they all laughed a lot.

The second glass was a good Tennessee sour-mash whisky and the proof was a good ninety and every drop was between six and seven years old. Then I said I can tell you a little more about this whisky but it ain't in the bet.

The lawyer said go right ahead, there, you keep on talking, it might relax you. He must have figured I was pretty nervous and I thought that that was right considerate too.

So I told them how this whisky was made in Moore County, Tennessee, or pretty close by, 'cause I was familiar with the water there. Then I told them how they drip the whisky over a special hard-maple charcoal, also how their kegs were all center-cut maple.

You know that crowd was real impressed with that. Like you'd think them being from New York City and all, how they'd want to stick together and take up for their own kind. But no sir, they were real gentlemen and sports and I'll be dogged if I didn't get a little bit of applause.

Well, the other three whiskys were all simple blends and one straight rye and I went through them pretty fast. I mean there wasn't any question about who had won the bet. The lawyer counted it out in thousand dollar piles and it was all mine.

I gave the bartender two hundred dollars and told him to buy drinks for the house. Then I sat up on that bar and the crowd started asking me questions. You know, like how much corn meal to use, how much sugar.

But it was kind of funny too. 'Cause all the time I'm up there eating sauerkraut and potato chips and talking, this bartender keeps telling me his boss—you know, the one with those silk clothes—wants to see me in the back room. Well, I wanted to go back and see him and all that because I wanted to get that business of the Coca-Cola barrels straightened out but I guess I just got carried away with all those questions. Man, you never heard so many questions about whisky-making in your life. How much? How fast? How long you let it work? How much yield?

That was fun, though. I mean talking like that in front of an interested group like that. Every one of them had pretty good questions. Like one fellow said he understood that since the Federal men are watching the sugar purchases so tight he heard some crowd is using corn syrup. Now you think about that for a minute. That's right good information. We been using corn syrup in some stills for only a few months now but we thought we had ourselves an exclusive.

Well, that bartender finally grabbed me by the arm and said the boss insists I come back. I don't take that from no one so I reached over and fropped him alongside his head and he backed off. Man, I hate someone to grab me like that.

A couple of other fellows were going to help him take me back but the crowd wouldn't let them through.

I didn't want no more trouble so I said you tell the man I'll be back directly. 'Cause I didn't want to sit up there and talk myself out of a big customer like Murphy. Maybe he had a legitimate complaint. Maybe his boys had a hernia or something. I've been in this business too long not to listen to the other side.

But then I got to answering some more questions. Someone gave me a piece of soapy chalk and said, "Let's see a still." There was this big dark mirror up over the back bar. It must have been eight feet long and five feet high. I asked them what kind of still they wanted to see. They wanted to see the biggest one I had.

Well, we'd just erected this big one up on the Congaree River so I had it pretty fresh in my mind. Man, I stood up on that bar and drew up a storm. I put my steam boiler on the left. Told them how I fired it with coke or gas to keep down the smoke. Told them how it was a tight five-horse boiler and how I'd had it specially made and welded.

Then I drew over the steam pipe into the still. Told them how the still was made by jamming the center of one steel barrel with the top and bottom of another. Showed them the drain off and the septic tank arrangement we had. I always try to put the sour-mash slop in the ground. That way the sheriff can't spot the waste in the water and I just never liked the idea of killing fish like that. It cost a little more to do it this way but it's really better in the long run. This still uses a crew of six men and, well, when they can fish a little at night it works wonders with their morale.

Next I drew the preheater and the scaffold. You know, I like plenty of elevation under my heaters. When I showed them where the still was eight feet high and the heater fifteen feet high, some of them didn't believe me. I had to explain how we have to rely on a gravity feed from the heater to the still 'cause that live steam pipe gets pretty fierce and a man won't stay with a force pump long.

Well, next I drew the mash box and the mash pump. They all seemed to understand this part. You know, I guess all those boys knew something about making whisky. But the problem was they all thought the still was a little jug-shaped copper pot with a condenser coming out.

Well, I had to get kind of technical when I came to the doubler. This is a straight steam-rigged barrel with a drain valve. The doubler redistills before you hit your condenser box. This eliminates "low-wine." Low-wine is when it finishes off too low in proof and has to be rerun. Well, by this time I just about had covered that eight-foot mirror.

I got the blending tub on the mirror but I had to put the bench for the sampler and the water pump on the woodwork. When I stepped back and looked I couldn't believe it. It was really nice. You know, of all the stills I've erected and all the stills I've torn down and abandoned, I think I was as fond of that still on the mirror as any of them. I mean it. I guess being in front of that crowd had a lot to do with it.

But there's something about a well-planned still. Something real nice like every part does something. You know what I mean? There's no frills and decorations and every part does something. Functional, that's what it is. That's it.

Well, we discussed this still for another thirty minutes or so. I told them how I also designed a portable pot still with no preheater or doubler. Combining the steam boiler in a kettle and set it up inside a big truck. You had to stir the mash with a boat paddle to keep from scorching. We got it worked out so we could pull up to a farmhouse or even a trailer park, pipe in gas and water and take the slop out in barrels. The portable type has problems of too much heat inside the truck for the crew, too much low-wine and not enough room to store mash. But its main advantage, if you can stand the heat, is the secrecy. There's about fifteen of these rigs working around Richland County right now and I mean they're giving the law a crying fit.

Then I drew them another little sketch showing how they could build a little four-gallon still and make their own whisky at home. They liked that too.

Well, the last question and the one I really got rolling on was how much whisky my big still put out a day and what it cost. When I told him between five hundred and six hundred gallons a day they almost fell over.

I started to go into cost and pricing when I felt someone tug at my cuff. . . .

I looked down and here was the owner, only now he's got his dark glasses off and, man, don't he look scared? Then it dawned on me what was going on. This rascal was taking my ten-dollar-a-gallon corn, cutting it in half and selling it for forty cents an ounce. That comes to around a hundred and fifteen dollars a gallon.

So I leaned down and asked him if he was *the* Mr. Murphy

and he said he was. And boy, that was one funny spot to be in. He was scared to death I was going to announce that Lord Calvert and all the bar whiskys were corn and not government-bonded and -taxed whisky. He was scared and he was sweating and he was kind of smiling. Only it wasn't quite like a smile.

So I let him hang there for a while. I could hear him wheeze and sigh. He began drinking.

I told the crowd how good corn is the best whisky made when it's made right. How to make a mash box, how to make the mash, when to mix the yeast in, how you taste it, what you look for, how to pick out neutral spirits. How you should never smell corn whisky, you should drink it.

And then I got on to packing.

How glass and tin are dangerous for shipping. How they spoil the aging. How good wooden barrels, good fifty-five-gallon wooden barrels, are expensive but ideal for shipping and storing.

Mr. Murphy was smiling and nodding and every minute or so he'd touch my leg, you know, light like as if there's no hard feelings. Man, I had him running and he knew it.

I announced how the Federal men and the State men were getting rougher. How they're using helicopters to spot stills. How they watch the copper you buy and the sugar and the meal you buy.

Mr. Murphy was wiping his face with his silk handkerchief and nodding his head. I kept on about how good help is hard to come by and how the Baptist Church will knife you in the back and tell the law where your stills are.

My voice was getting bigger and deeper and I got so I could pause and let certain things set in. Like how transportation and gas and everything is sky-high and how we are being squeezed out of profits.

Mr. Murphy nodded again and did a little yodel and sigh all mixed together.

I took another shot at that Tennessee sour-mash stuff and

went on about how everything from now on is cash in advance and how we're raising the price on a delivered gallon from ten dollars to twelve dollars.

Mr. Murphy was playing with his checkbook. . . .

And finally how my father pioneered the use of fifty-five-gallon Coca-Cola barrels and how I been doing it for eighteen years and how I wasn't about to take any of my good corn and pack it any other way but in barrels.

Mr. Murphy was right obliging. . . .

MONCK'S CORNER

WHAT I REMEMBER most about Monck's Corner, South Carolina, is leaving it. . . .

Two were in the middle of the road, three were lying alongside the fence by the tobacco field, and Fred Peevy and Dean Brown were sitting down in the drain ditch eating sardines and Zu-Zus and drinking corn out of a half-gallon Mason jar.

Floyd Lovett stopped the car: "They get mad if you don't drink with them."

Dean handed Floyd the jar and he drank. He tried to speak but couldn't. He tried to cough but couldn't. He gasped, wiped his eyes, then closed them, wiped his mouth, shook his head and finally gasped, "Jesus, what is it?"

Dean handed the jar from Floyd to me "No name, ain't got no name."

Floyd said, "It ain't rub, is it?"

Dean said, "Man, you know I'd never give you any rub."

I took a drink and waited. It didn't taste as bad as it smelled, but I could feel the headaches moving down my arms and legs and inching around to the small of my back.

Dean was saying, "Dollar and a half a half gallon and we get a dime deposit back for the jar."

Floyd said, "Dollar and a half . . . let me see it again."

He closed his eyes and drank. He smiled and said, "Yes sir, it appears I've been too hasty. That stuff's got a nice taste.

Unique, that's what it is."

So we sat down there in that drain ditch and drank and spat and lied and ate Zu-Zus until it was dark. A breeze came up around seven, and later someone said: "Al's Place. . . ."

Bass fiddle, Hawaiian guitar, long-necked banjo, all-night square and round dancing. Mill workers, spinners, weavers, sweepers, wipers. Print dresses, straw hats, steel-heeled brogans. Room-shaking breakdowns, stomps, swamp shouts. No neckties, no socks, white or red Roy Rogers' scarves with cows' skulls or pairs of dice as slipknots. Thirty-five cents corkage. Room vibration keeps the bead bubbling on the 120-proof whisky standing in marked jars along the wall. Tall fellow on bass takes drink out of Mason jar. Needs both hands to hold jar steady. Uses back of hand for chaser.

We begin to dance . . . four hands across, promenade, all join hands, follow the leader. Intermission.

Catfish stew served in tin pie plates. Hot-peppery. Chase stew with cold beer, chase beer with 120-proof and back to stew.

Dean says stuff is as hot as a weasel's ass in a pepper patch. Sounds of fight outside.

Owner locks doors so no one can get out. No windows, can't see, don't care.

Music whangs up again. Return to dancing . . . new caller . . . tall thin ugly man, lips like two dimes pressed together, loud, nasal. Banjo solo . . . same chords only louder, flatter, madder, worse . . . more stew, more 120-proof, more dancing . . . hot, cold flashes. . . .

Palpitations. Lean against wall, can't understand it. It might pass . . . it might not. Head seems to be clamped in some gigantic squeezing machine.

Dean comes over, slaps me on the back. "Tell the truth, now, when you had so much fun?"

I can't think. It wouldn't have mattered because I couldn't speak. Dragged out onto floor . . . promenade . . . become bird in the cage.

Sneak out back door, pass table where catfish were cleaned, hold onto tree, to stomach, to head, try to vomit smoothly . . . pine needles, oak leaves, cool breezes. Lie down carefully and stare up through small trees at the autumn moon and swear I'll call Greyhound and see how much it costs to go north.

HAVE YOU EVER
RODE THE SOUTHERN?

CORA LEE and I had been writing pretty hot and heavy there while I was in advanced training, so when I got my commission, my wings and the thirty-day furlough that went with it I decided to get home and ask her to marry me before someone beat me to it. The planes were all booked up, so I got me a ticket on the Sante Fe. Now the Sante Fe is a pretty good line and even though it was day coach for sixty-eight hours I got into Dallas feeling pretty good. At Dallas we changed to the Texas and Pacific. It was forty-four more hours from Dallas to Atlanta, and while I didn't get much sleep I made that part all right too.

But at Atlanta we changed over to the Southern.

Brother, have you ever rode the Southern from Atlanta to Columbia?

The first fifteen or so miles went by fast. Then we started stopping. We made three stops out in the dark before we reached Buford, Georgia. There, a tall guitar player with a red bandanna around his neck got on. He looked at the seat next to me.

"Lieutenant, you mind if I join you?"

"Sure thing."

"That's mighty considerate of you."

I sighed to let him know I was too tired to talk and leaned against the window. I closed my eyes, but I was wide awake. I hadn't slept in I don't know how long, and now I was too tired to sleep.

He laid his guitar across his knees. It was an expensive Gibson with a vine of red roses and leaves painted around the edge. On the black frets down the neck he had a list of all the towns he'd been to; Atlanta, Savannah, Mobile, Charleston, Muscle Shoals, Columbia, Macon and Augusta.

I glanced at him out of the corner of my eye and that was all he needed. His Adam's apple rose and sank before he spoke. "This shore ain't much of a car, is it?"

I knew he was waiting for my answer. "Not much." I looked back outside. We were finally leaving Buford.

"Where you heading?"

"Columbia."

"That's a fine town. Fine." He moved his hand off the guitar neck so I could see all the cities listed. Columbia was next to Macon, near the bottom.

"You know, I've been riding the Southern since I could walk, but I 'spect this is the sorriest car I've ever seen. Look up there at those gas spigots. They made this car before they had electricity."

The train hit a bump and bounced. Ash dust from the big Ben Franklin stove in the middle of the aisle shot up in the air and drifted back over us. I didn't brush it off.

He went on, "Well, I reckon them boys overseas are riding in cars a heap worse than this."

I stared outside. The black fields seemed to relax me. I counted the hours since I slept last but I couldn't keep the figures straight. I figured five and a half more wouldn't matter.

"Lieutenant, I'd be obliged if you'd let me pick my guitar a little." He smiled. "My fingers are getting a little itchy."

I spoke at the window, "Go right ahead."

He looped the guitar cord behind his neck. He cocked his head to one side as he played and kept time with his big brogan shoe. He wore no socks. When he sang he looked at the red roses on the guitar. He seemed to be singing to them.

"I recommend the Lord to you." He sang in a low voice that carried the length of the car. When he finished the song he continued strumming. "How you like that?"

"Fine."

He looked around the coach and exchanged nods and smiles with the other passengers. The lights were on. No one was sleeping. A man in a glare-blue suit, across the aisle, had some whisky concealed in a brown paper bag. He offered us the bottle. I took a drink, but the guitar player shook his head and continued strumming and tuning up the Gibson.

The man took the whisky back. "Musician, you know any fast music? I don't mean any fast hymns. Something beside hymns."

The guitar player smiled. He picked the E string hard and listened close. He must have figured the guitar was in tune because he suddenly brought his brogan shoe down hard on the floor. "How about this?"

His fingers flew into "Won't You Be My Salty Dog." He played fast and grinned.

The man shouted, "Sing the words! Sing the words, guitar man!"

He played faster and shook his head in time with the music, "Can't do that. Ladies present."

The man said, "That's good! That's mighty good! Let's have some more of that!"

He strummed down to a whisper, "All right. Time for one more. Then I got to get me some sleep."

He nudged me with his elbow and smiled. "This one's for my friend the lieutenant here."

He tuned the G string. His smile faded. He looked white and dead serious. He began "The Air Corps Song." He sang the words in a low nasal tone right at the side of my head. "Off we go into the wild blue yonder. . . ." He sang the entire song. He knew every word, every word for three verses. He softened down toward the middle and then began rising until at the end he shouted, "NOTHING CAN STOP THE ARMY AIR CORPS!"

My head was splitting. The man with the whisky applauded and the guitar player stood up and beamed at the rest of the crowd. He sat back down. "I feel a lot better now. How about a little something to eat?"

I couldn't tell if I was hungry or not. He reached into his zipper bag and handed me a pepper-sausage sandwich.

"These biscuits were fresh-made this morning. I just can't sleep on no empty stomach."

We ate the sandwiches. The biscuits were heavy but the meat was good. He smiled as he wiped his fingers on the red bandanna around his throat and carefully laid the guitar across his lap. The neck brushed against my leg and I moved closer to the window. The minute he closed his eyes he was asleep. He slept sitting straight up with his hands on the steel strings.

The lights were still on in the car. It seemed warmer, and the smell of the ashes made me thirsty. The window began to rattle and I leaned against it to make it stop. I tried to sleep in the position he was in but the window noise was too loud. I shifted away from the guitar and tried crossing my left leg over my right. Then I tried crossing my right leg over my left. The window had to be held tight and my legs kept going to sleep.

The train kept stopping in the small towns and out in the dark between the small towns. I never saw anyone get on or off and I gave up trying to figure out why we made so many stops. I wedged my knees up into the seat in front of me, leaned hard against the window and kind of rooted down onto the bottom of my backbone. Somehow I got to sleep near Toccoa, Georgia. I don't know how, but I did.

We were coming into Greenville, South Carolina, and I had been sleeping for a half an hour or so when the train bounced hard and then stopped hard. We were both awake.

It was quiet and I thought we were getting some water or coal or something. All of a sudden the door burst open and this terrible racket came at me.

You know what it was at two-seventeen and fifteen seconds in the morning? It was a band. Must have been seven of them. They were all about ten years old and they had cornets and those little tambourines. They paraded up the aisle and back. You never heard such a racket in your life. They seemed to all be playing different tunes. One of them got up on top of the Ben Franklin stove and did a little dance while the others came around collecting money. They were a nice bunch of kids, and they said they needed the money for uniforms for their baseball team. Everyone was groggy; we all chipped in dimes and quarters.

The train started moving again and the kids jumped off into the dark. I tried the same sleeping position but the small of my back was too sore. The guitar player laid his hands back across the strings, smiled, and went back to sleep. We moved forward about five hundred yards and stopped. While the train stood still I began to doze. I slept sitting straight up with my head back. When the train started I leaned against the window and dozed in little short nervous snatches. The glass felt cool. We stopped at Piedmont, South Carolina, and a new conductor got on. He examined every ticket and every passenger. He got in close and peered into my face. He had a breath like a cat.

Another few miles and we stopped hard. I thought we'd hit another train. Everybody was wide awake and the lights were on full blast. Someone was shouting. A whistle sounded ten feet away. It was the new conductor. He shouted, "Belton, Belton, South Carolina! Everybody out for Belton, South Carolina."

I was delirious. My hands were wet and that whistle screeching had given me palpitations. Outside there were no lights. We were in the middle of a swamp.

I shouted back at him, "What do you mean waking us up

for this mudhole?" He looked me in the eye and shouted again. Louder, "Belton, South Carolina! Everybody out for Belton!"

I was mad and began getting up. He was too old to hit but I figured I'd shake him down a little bit. The guitar player touched my sleeve. "It don't do no good. He can't hear. He's deaf. Stone deaf. Don't do a bit of good to holler at him."

I was nervous. The sweat was streaming. The palpitations were stronger but I felt weaker. I knew I'd never get to sleep now.

It was three-forty-seven and I watched the minute hand on my watch heading for four o'clock. We were due in Columbia at seven-fifty.

The passenger in front of us got off and the guitar player swung the seat back. We each had a full seat now.

"You better lie down, Lieutenant. You look like you could use some rest."

Man, I did. I really did. The window was chattering away, but now it didn't bother me. I was desperate for sleep. I stretched out on that cane seat and hooked my legs in behind me. I put one hand under my head and one hand in my pocket. Oh, that is one tough position to sleep in. There's just enough room in that double seat to confuse you. You can't lie down, but still you feel something can be worked out. It can't. There just isn't any way unless you can go to sleep in a hurry. I tried to do that but I got confused again. I lay there a while with my feet and legs asleep and nothing else. I could feel the imprint of that woven cane seat on my hand and face, but now I was too weak to care. Finally I dropped off. I seemed to be sinking in some hot black well.

I wasn't asleep more than twelve minutes when the conductor started shouting we were in Shoals Junction.

It was four-thirty and ten seconds and it was still dark. As the train stopped, two colored kids came running through the aisle selling fried chicken in the box.

I was trembling now. I thought I was going to be sick. A

cold draft whipped the ash dust over us, but I was sweating. When I sat up my feet were all puffed up and bulging inside my jodhpur boots. They were prickling, and when I lifted my numb legs over and put my feet on the floor the pain was terrible. The bones in my face ached from the cane pattern and the hand I had held in my pocket was paralyzed there.

Before I knew what I was doing I bought a box of chicken. The train sat there in Shoals Junction for fifty-two minutes and twenty seconds on my new Air Force watch. The conductor shouted several times that a bull was sleeping on the tracks and they were having trouble finding the owner. The guitar player and I ate the chicken and the lettuce and tomatoes and the French fries. There didn't seem to be anything else to do. "Lieutenant, when you lay back down you better turn the other way. That cane stitch has kind of messed up the side of your face."

The train started again and I lay back down. I knew the chicken was a terrible mistake and for some strange reason I began to giggle. The heavy grease stayed on the roof of my mouth and I could taste it all the way down my throat. I lay back with my head on the armrest and my knees toward the window and watched the farms go by. It was peaceful. The moon was still up and I could see the tin roofs shining out in the black fields. I tried to think about Cora Lee, but when I closed my eyes I couldn't make her face stay in focus. I'd wired her from Atlanta and told her to meet the train. I was going to propose at the station. Right there on the platform at South Broad. If she accepted, we would be married in two days and we'd have twenty-two more glorious days and nights together. But I had to have some sleep. The guitarist was sleeping again. His mouth was wide open but he wasn't snoring. His left index finger was on the fret marked "Macon." I began to think. When had I slept last? I didn't want to count up the hours but I did; it was forty-seven. I'd be in Columbia in a couple of hours. It was getting light outside, I began to panic. *I had to have some sleep.* I felt like shouting it. I didn't want Cora Lee to see me like this. *I had to have some sleep.* My hands were soaking wet and I could hear my heart pounding. It sounded weaker. Every fourth beat sounded different, like it was leaking. Maybe I was dying. Everything seemed blurred. The lights looked orange with strange purple halos spreading out around them. The ash smell came back. The chicken grease thickened on the roof of my mouth and the whisky taste belched up. I was in a coma. My legs and left arm were sound asleep. Very skillfully I tried to figure how I could make the sleep come up from my legs to my head. It seemed simple. It was down there, sleep was down there in my legs, all I had to do was pull it up. I opened my belt to let it flow up. I was clean out of my mind.

I shook away the dizzy spell and tried to think. Lord, I was weary. I was so weary. I was so weary and tired and miserable. All I wanted to do was sleep or lay my head down and cry. But second lieutenants in the Air Corps don't cry. I tried to keep my eyes closed.

There was a light in the east and I tried harder to keep my eyes closed. I knew what it was in the east. It was the sun in the east and I didn't want to see it. But I did. It was tipping up beyond the cotton fields and I knew that the night was over. I began to pray. I actually began to pray. *"Lord,"* I said, *"Lord, please. Please let me sleep, Lord. Please, Lord. Please."*

He must have heard me right outside Dyson, for there a calm sweetness passed over me and I slept. Yes, the Lord heard me that morning and only He let me sleep on that Southern day coach. The sun was in my eyes and sparkling on the red and green shellacked roses of my guitar-playing friend, but I slept. My legs were jackknifed up in the air and my head was lolling out in the aisle. The taste of grease and ashes and whisky had miraculously been taken away and a lovely gentle sleep folded over me like freshly carded wool. What a fine, fine sleep. My head was in Cora Lee's lap and she was sitting under the big loblolly pine on Laurel Hill. There were soft clouds in the sky and a soft, sweet smile on her lips. My fingers were on the hem of her blue and white dress and her fingers were gently stroking the soft part over my eyes.

Yes, the Lord got on that day coach right outside Dyson, South Carolina, and he stayed with me all the thirty flat miles to Pomaria. But at Pomaria, that rascal got off. He left me. I woke up jumping. The train had stopped. A vendor was shaking me and shouting in my face.

"COFFEE!" he screamed. "Coming into Columbia! Get your coffee while it's hot!" I shouted back, "What's that?"

"Columbia, next stop! Get your coffee now! Last chance!"

I looked outside. The sun was high and hot. It blinded me and I couldn't see. Every bone and muscle in my body was jumping.

I was too nervous to speak softly. I shouted again, "How far to Columbia?"

"We're right at it."

I looked down at my hands. In my right was a Dixie cup of coffee, in my left a package of Del Monte raisins.

I stared at the guitar player, "How'd I get these?"

"You bought 'em, fifteen cents for the coffee, ten cents for the raisins."

He pointed at the coffee. "You better make haste and drink that. Them cups melt fast and you can't hold 'em too long."

And then I noticed my fingers were burning up. I dropped the coffee on the floor and watched it spread out into the aisle. I wiped my burning fingers on my socks and started to get up.

I looked outside, "Wait a minute. We aren't even close to Columbia. We're in Pomaria. We got another hour yet."

The vendor was leaving the car. I started to tell the guitar player that he had made a mistake, that we weren't in Columbia, we were in Pomaria. And then it dawned on me. I hollered at the vendor. "You told me we were in Columbia! You lied to me! I could have slept another hour."

"Lieutenant, where you going?"

"I'm going to fix his ass, that's where I'm going."

I took a step and had to stop. My feet were asleep and felt like a thousand needles were stabbing them. I stood in the coffee and held onto the back of the seat.

"Give me a second. Wait till I catch my breath. I'll be all right in a minute."

"Lieutenant, you better sit down before you fall down."

"No, leave me alone. I'm going to get that lying bastard. Only take a minute. I'll be all right in a minute."

But I wasn't. I tried again and almost slipped down. I was too weak to walk. My strength had been taken away in the night and there was no fast way of getting it back.

The guitar player took my arm and lowered me to the seat. I put my head between my knees and breathed through my mouth.

I shook my head. I couldn't believe it. I was too weak to get up. Tears were in my eyes, I looked up at the guitar player. "If I had any sleep, you hear, any sleep at all, I'd fix his ass."

I gritted my teeth and clenched my fists, but nothing happened.

The guitar player said, "He knows."

"He knows what?"

"He knows you been on this train from Atlanta and he knows you're pretty weak."

My head was clearing, "You mean he does this all the time?"

"He shore does. Oh, once in a while some young buck like yourself will jump up and raise hell. Usually he just touches them on the shoulder and they sit back down."

I saw the vendor out the window. He was coming down the platform towards our end of the car.

I strained at the window. "Give me a hand here."

We got the window open just as the train began moving. I stuck my head out and shouted. "Coffee vendor!"

He came back and stopped under the window. The train was moving out now.

"Listen, you bastard, I live in Columbia. You hear that? I

live in Columbia and I'm getting me a car and coming back here tomorrow and cut your ass. You hear that?" My strength was coming back now. "Just wait, bastard," I shouted. "Just wait. . . ."

He frowned and placed his coffee bucket and vendor tray on the platform. He then put his right hand on his left arm and raised a long hand and finger to the sky.

I stepped back from the window, wound up, and winged the box of raisins at his head. It missed. As the train picked up speed I watched him pick up the box, wipe the dust off and put it back in his tray. I turned to the guitar player. "And you say he does that all the time? Tells all those people that they're coming into Columbia so he can sell them coffee and raisins?"

"Before God, Lieutenant, I ain't lying. Lots a times he tries to sell the folks Cupid dolls."

He looked at the roses on his guitar and then back at me.

"Lieutenant, I ain't going to sit here in front of you and criticize the Southern Railroad. No, sir, I'd never do a thing like that. I been riding it too long and it's been right good to me. But I'll say one thing."

He traced his finger down the list of cities on the fretwork. He seemed embarrassed.

"I've been on every road on the Southern, the Seaboard and the Atlantic Coast. Every one of them, and I know every spur and roundhouse on the line. And all that time I don't believe I've ever had cause to enter what you might call a formal complaint. But it shore do look like those Southern Railroad folks could make some improvements on this Atlanta-to-Columbia run."

When the train arrived in Columbia, the guitar player helped me off and then got on the Charleston train across the platform. My feet were still asleep and my arms were so weak I dropped my B-4 bag. Cora Lee shouted and came running down the boardwalk. She was directly in the sun. I couldn't focus my eyes and I didn't see her until she stood before me. I knew my eyes were bloodshot; I knew I looked a great deal older than I really was. I looked around for some shade to stand in but there wasn't any. She took my hands in hers and looked at my eyes. She had to look away. Something in my eyes had frightened her. I started to say, "I haven't slept in five days," but I didn't. I waited to see what she would do next, figuring that true love would triumph. She looked at me again. This time something in her eyes frightened me.

"Oh, Billy, your wings look so nice." She looked at the wings and then at the Lieutenant bars and then back at the wings. Never in my eyes.

And then I saw the red Ford parked by the taxi stand. Behind the steering wheel sat a captain. It was Talmadge Kelly, an old flame of Cora Lee's. She talked fast. "Billy, there's something I been wanting to tell you. . . ."

I didn't want to hear it.

"Getting married tomorrow at the Green Street Methodist. And guess what?"

I didn't guess.

The guitar player was watching us from the Charleston train window. He had a drawn and serious look on his face.

"Want you to be our best man. Oh, please say you. . . ."

I had my right hand over her mouth. I didn't know what I was going to do. Just squeeze it shut, maybe. Then a whooshing cloud of steam blew out from under the train. When it cleared I looked down, and there was Cora Lee sitting on my B-4 bag, pulling down her skirt and starting to cry.

The guitar player leaned out the window. "Come on, Lieutenant. Come on down to Charleston with me."

He met me at the train steps and helped me with the bag.

As the train moved out of the station, the signs on the rat-colored houses that lined the tracks all ran together. Grove's Chill Tonic, Tom's Toasted Peanuts, Eat Bit-O-Honey, Chew Brown Mule, Drink Dr. Pepper. The guitar player began tuning up for the long flat stretch to Charleston. My head was clearing. "Play something fast."

He whipped into "Take Me Back to Tulsa, I'm Too Young to Marry," held it still for a minute, then stopped. "You like that?"

"That's fine. Perfect. Play it a couple times."

He smiled and leaned down close to the strings to watch his flying fingers as the train made a wide swinging turn through Colored Town and headed out for Charleston and the sea.

HELLO, NEW YORK

GOT A POSTCARD from my buddy Lamaar Peevy of Monck's Corner last week. "Bill, am coming up to New York. Leaving Tuesday, should be at the Dixie Wednesday. Will call when I get in. Lamaar." The Dixie is the Dixie Hotel on Forty-second Street.

Wednesday the phone rings. "Hey, hotshot."

"Peevy, you old dog. When'd you get in?"

"Ain't in yet. You know that road that runs up aside the river?"

"Sure, West Side Highway."

"Well. I got in the wrong lane and couldn't get off the fool thing. Damn near wound up in New England. I'm at a place called Van Cortlandt."

I gave him directions south and told him to get off at Twentieth Street. "Be careful now, Peev, the exit's on the left."

Two hours later he showed up. We parked his car and took a cab uptown. I have an extra bed, but he wanted to stay at the Dixie. "Where'd you stop last night?"

"Baltimore. Tried the slot machines for a couple of hours but couldn't do no good, so I came on through."

He checked in and got a room behind the neon. He liked it there. As he began changing clothes I saw he was carrying a .45 automatic. "That thing loaded?"

"Wouldn't be worth much if it wasn't."

"Well, leave it here. They'll burn you a new one if they catch you carrying it."

"Okay, baby, anything you say. It's your town. Getting fat, ain't you?"

"Little bit."

He was shaving with a straight razor. "Look over in that satchel. I brought something along."

Inside the bag were eight spider-webbed pints of red whisky. "You make it?"

He nodded. "Best run all year. See if it don't taste like the old man's."

I shook a bottle and watched the thick bead foam. "Looks good. Where you running with the Feds so tight?"

He laughed and finished his throat. "Stud, I've got me five hundred-gallon ground hogs working double shift right this second inside the city limits. Got them twelve feet down in fallout shelters."

"Hey, that's good moon!" I took another drink. "That's really fine stuff."

Lamaar took a long pull on the bottle and dropped it down about two inches and then smeared his face with a full ounce of Aqua Velva. He put his money belt on, checked the clip on his gun, slid it under the pillow, and began buttoning up his stiff starched white shirt. He wore a wild checkerboard jacket with black, browns and orange cutting through it. He changed his white socks and slipped on a brand-new pair of yellow dagger-pointed shoes, opened his collar over his jacket and pushed his flat porkpie hat to the back half of his head. "Let's go."

We were off. At Toffenetti's we had the breaded pork chops with tomato sauce and the foil-wrapped baked potato. Lamaar had two servings of strawberry shortcake and four cups of coffee. "Feel like a new man."

From Toffenetti's we walked twenty yards to a white-slave movie called *Naked Facts*. From there to a newspaper-headline shop on Broadway. Lamaar bought one: "Lamaar

Peevy Hits N.Y., Stock Market Trembles." To Birdland, Roseland, back to Birdland and then to the Metropole. All during the music Lamaar kept saying he was sure he knew Cozy Cole by another name and that he was from Savannah, Georgia. During the intermission he went up on the bandstand. He came back and said Cole looked like the Owens boy he knew in Savannah but he didn't talk like him. I took him back to the Plantation Bar at the Dixie and when I said good night he said he was going to sit up a while and watch the color television and have another nightcap.

Next day I met him at noon. He said he'd gone out again and met a sweet little girl over at the Travelers Aid station in the Greyhound Bus terminal and how you could always meet nice gals there if you knew how to act like you were from out of town or like you were lost. Said she was from Ames, Iowa, and she knew a lot about Big Ten football. He had another headline: "Lamaar Peevy Makes A Killing in the Stock Market."

We did the Empire State Building, Radio City, the Rockettes; he couldn't figure out how they all kicked to the same height each time if they were different sizes. It was cold but he wanted to eat at a sidewalk restaurant. Ate on Forty-second Street overlooking the Vim discount-store lights and the comfort station at the Public Library. A bum came up and tried to panhandle us while we were on the shrimp cocktail course.

From there, two auctions, Hector's for cherry cheesecake, saw the Hermaphrodite, tried a knish, saw the human mummy, the wax museum showing the death of Dillinger and an original oil painting of Pretty Boy Floyd. Walked to Fifty-fourth Street to shake hands with Jack Dempsey and promised him we would eat all our meals there. Lamaar made him show us his Firpo punch. Had a beer at the Cross Roads. Lamaar said he had heard if you sit there long enough every one in the world will eventually walk by and that he was beginning to believe it. He took out a black notebook and after counting all of the cabs he saw in five minutes he wrote down "67." After that he went out in the street and counted all the movie marquees on Forty-second. There were twelve on the blocks between Sixth and Eighth Avenues. He wanted to know how many bars, movies, cathouses in town? Where do the bums sleep? Where do the taxicab drivers go to the john? We took six twenty-five-cent photographs, all leering, squinting, or cross-eyed, and then recorded our voices in a duet of "Get Up, Get Out, You Whorehouse Bum."

Had tickets to a play and caught a cab up to Fiftieth Street. Lamaar said he would pay the cab fare. Pulled out a two-fingered country clip purse and counted out five dimes and two nickels to the driver. The cabbie held out his hand and asked if he was getting any tip?

Lamaar looked in and said, "What did you say?"

"Up here we generally get a tip from a fare."

Lamaar handed me his hat and leaned on the window jamb. "Listen, you bastard, if you don't put this coffeepot in gear I'm going to pull you out of there and kick your ass until your ears ring." He meant it. The cabbie saw it and moved out.

"I don't hold with tipping."

After the play we walked across town. Passing Bill's Gay Nineties we heard the banjoes going inside. Lamaar took my elbow and said, "Now, there just ain't no way in the world for us to get by here."

We went in and started drinking and singing along. Lamaar kept requesting songs, but they didn't know them.

"How bout 'Wreck on the Highway?' "

"Don't know it. Listen, mister, this isn't a folk-song place; we're playing vaudeville music."

"Okay, okay, keep at it. I like it fine. Tell you what, you know 'Georgia Brown?' "

"Now you're talking."

Lamaar sang so loud I thought they were going to throw us out. He gave the man five dollars and then another five to play it again. Told him it was his absolute favorite song and that he had spent a good deal of time in Georgia. He winked at me when he said Georgia because I knew he meant Atlanta and Atlanta meant the Federal pen where he had spent over three years for bootlegging.

He called the waiter over and asked what would happen if he brought in his own whisky and just bought ice and Seven Ups. The man said he would ask his boss but he didn't think he would like it.

Went back to the Dixie and made some phone calls. To a Village party where no one seemed to know anyone else. There was no heat, no place to leave coats, no ashtrays, no glasses, no ice or host or hostess. Lamaar said this was the damnedest party he'd ever been to. He put two fingers in his mouth and blew a screeching whistle. They gathered around him like he was crazy while he sat down on the floor and opened up his zipper case with four pints of corn and a dozen fresh lemons. He opened all the bottles and began cutting the lemons.

The crowd tightened in around him and began asking him questions about where he was from. He didn't answer any questions but he told them how to make whisky in the kitchen, about red horse bread, about the men's game played with six half dollars at the edge of the table; how to load dice, how to throw dice, how to mark cards and the great secret of the shell game, and finally how if anyone of them ever got into South Carolina to be sure and come out to Monck's Corner and just ask anyone in town for Lamaar Peevy, and he would put them up for a weekend of the best fun they ever had in their lives.

A tall fellow from C.C.N.Y. who pronounced every letter in every word began discussing segregation. So Lamaar, poker-faced, told him how where he lived there were only a few slaves left, but the cost of living was just too high to keep them, and how the unions have gotten in and now you can't trade beads and mirrors for skins any more.

[213]

The lemons ran out and a very thin and very pretty girl began to get sick. Lamaar tried to talk her out of it but she was too far gone. When he saw it was too late he gave her his zipper case. . . .

A fellow dressed in charcoal gray hat, shoes, socks and tie kept shouting he was from Rego Park but that he was educated at Harvard and that he didn't like Norman Mailer. Lamaar said he did and they argued for a while. Lamaar finally said there wasn't any use arguing with a fool and that where he was from, when they couldn't decide an argument they generally went out back and rasseled. The crowd backed up and Lamaar and the man from Rego Park got down on the floor with a headlock on one another and rolled around. There was nothing to break in the room and after they both had sore ears and sore heads they stopped, smiled and shook hands.

Lamaar offered free whisky, said he would mail it up in a special container. Rego Park promised free legal advice for life and invited him to lunch at the Harvard Club. Lamaar said he had planned to go to the Statue of Liberty and the Brooklyn Navy Yard and take the boat trip around the Island.

Left party at three and went back to newspaper-headline shop: "Lamaar Peevy Leaves Sophia Loren for Brigitte Bardot."

Nightcap at the Plantation Bar and watched twenty minutes of the Late Late Show, Brian Donlevy in *Wake Island*.

Next day, early start. At Statue of Liberty climbed to top and looked out. Freezing. Brooklyn Navy Yard, Circle Line around Manhattan, all before noon. Had lunch at Jack Dempsey's, good food, Lamaar wanted to ask him about the Long Count but Jack was too busy with a convention. Saw a film on Broadway, *White Slave Goddess;* short subject, *Confessions of a Mau Mau*. Lamaar said the last dirty picture he had seen was *Birth of a Baby*. Didn't like it. Went to an auction . . . bought a comb and brush set in a velvet box for $6 and two wrist watches for $7 each. One was marked Bulova but where the "u" should have been there was an "o" (Bolova).

Souvenirs: pornographic playing cards, stink bombs, fake snakes, life-sized photograph of Anita Ekberg, plastic dog mess. Another headline: "Peevy Steals Elizabeth Taylor from Richard Burton."

I'm having visions and getting shin splints. Not Lamaar; he looks great. He seems stronger, eyes shining, pelt shining, long legs striding and never tiring. Up Broadway to Fifty-ninth, down Broadway to Forty-second; east on Forty-second to Fifty, west on Forty-second to Eighth Avenue. Up and down, across and back; we passed the Cross Roads and *The Times* news flashes every forty minutes.

A bum catches us on Sixth Avenue at Forty-second Street. "Listen, mister." He's talking to Lamaar. "You look like a fellow who's smart enough to move in on some easy money. Am I right?" He doesn't wait for an answer. He pulls out a ring with a forty-carat something in the middle. "Now you're probably saying to yourself, 'How's an ordinary-looking bum going to be walking around with a rock the size of the Hope Diamond unless there's something wrong?' Okay, I'll level with you. There is something wrong. Right this minute I'm being shadowed; I'm getting so I'm afraid to go anywhere. My life ain't worth a plugged nickel until I get rid of this thing." He slows down. "If you're as sharp as I think you are, you'll take this baby out of town and break it up. It's too famous to go like it is. You do it right and you're a rich man." He edged us over to a window. "What's the sharpest thing in the world? A diamond, ain't that right? And if I can take this diamond and cut through this plate glass that's probably a half inch thick, that ought to convince anyone that this is the genuine article."

He scratched the diamond on the glass and it cut deep. "See that? See that? If this were glass or one of those zircons, it would bounce right back and wouldn't even dent it. Go on, take a look. I can make another pass at it and take the window out if I want to."

Lamaar said, "What you asking?"

"Five hundred dollars."

"And you figure I could pick up maybe fifty or sixty thousand when I have it broken up and all?"

"Yeah, that's providing you can get it out of town fast." He kept looking around behind him and off in the distance toward the library. "I don't like the look of that crowd coming out of the men's room over there."

Lamaar looked at me, "I'd like a little something for my niece and I kind of like this fellow." He reached in his pocket and pulled out a roll of bills. "I'll give you three dollars. Take it or leave it."

The bum looked around at the shadows and back at the library crowd. When he handed Lamaar the ring he looked like a man who had just lost $497. "If I wasn't being followed so close I'd tell you no, but that's the way it goes in this field."

Lamaar put the diamond in his back pocket and we headed back to the Metropole.

Except for the Village party, we hadn't been south of Thirty-fifth Street, east of Fifth Avenue or north of Fifty-ninth. But we'd been thorough. We'd had pizza, coconut juice, pastrami, pig's feet, paella and Him Soon York, and Lamaar had been sick on the corner of Broadway and Forty-fourth Street.

Lamaar carried his bags across the lobby at the Dixie, waved a bellhop away and checked out. We went into the Plantation Bar for our last drink. After the drink we set the bags on the sidewalk and waited for a cab. The neon was coming on and the thick smoke from New Jersey was losing itself in the dark. The flames from a charcoal grille flared and a circle of pizza dough rose and spun in the air and floated down. The cabbies were cursing, the blind woman on the corner was singing louder, the bums were talking faster and the I.R.T. jam for tokens had started.

"Man, I really enjoyed this little visit. You sure got yourself a mighty fine town here. Yessir, New York City is really one great town to visit." Lamaar checked his hip for his .45, picked up his bags and gazed into the neon and the night. "But just the same I can't feature myself living here as a permanent thing."

PINEHURST, DUE SOUTH

I WAS IN the golf department at Abercrombie & Fitch looking over a set of Bobby Jones irons when he came in blowing on his hands, snapping his fingers and smiling as if he knew me. He wore a baseball cap, a light house-painter's-type jacket, low-cut sneakers and a pair of khaki trousers.

I was holding an eight iron. He took my elbow.

"Chief, you really look like a golfer."

He'd been drinking something like Helena Rubinstein's hair set. He took the club from me. He had a sing-song in his voice and a little two-beat rhythm.

"This is perhaps the finest set of irons made."

He gripped the club tenderly, as if it were revealing some secret to him it had withheld from me. He kissed the Bobby Jones inscription.

"What a sweet, sweet club."

He addressed an imaginary ball and looked out over the skin-diving equipment at some phantom green.

"Feels good, feels great. I tell you, I woke up this morning and my hands felt so thin they began to hurt. I put cold water on them but it didn't do any good. I had to come up here and get my hands on a club. You know what I mean, you're a golfer. It's freezing but you know how it is. You've got to get a club in your hands."

He waggled the club, took a short swing. "Ah, that's better. I'll be all right now."

[218]

He took my elbow again.

"Listen, Chief, I can tell you're not the kind that goes for the straight beg. Don't ask me how I know, but I do. You wouldn't be looking at Bobby Jones equipment if you did. And I'm not used to asking. I can't do it. I'm a golfer, not a panhandler. Chief, I've played them all, Winged Foot, Pebble Beach, Pine Valley, you name it, I've played it. The name's Peters, Charley Peters. You probably remember me from a few years back. Won sixteen thousand dollars in fifty-seven and took a few of the big ones in the Spring Circuit. You understand, I'm a pro. I can't ask for handouts. That's why the straight beg is out with me.

"But here's what I have in mind."

He squeezed my elbow, and looked me straight in the eye.

"I'll make you a genuine business deal. We split down the middle after expenses, fifty-fifty. You heard of owning half interest in a horse or a piece of a Broadway show? Well, for a little investment now, you're in the real money. You own half interest in a touring pro. I need a little roll to get a few meals, get the clubs out of pawn, get some golf shoes and head south. The Winter Circuit is in Tampa now. The way I have it figured we can catch them about Orlando, maybe Tallahassee. Maybe the first three or four weeks I play them cozy. You know, down the middle, go for the fifth and sixth prize money, take no chances. Pick up, say, four or five hundred for a few weeks. Get the wrinkles out of the belly, get the old swing grooved. Then about Greensboro, that's where the big money is, and that's the course I know like the palm of my hand. Ten thousand top money and I go for it. I go all out, go for the long ball, the stiff shots to the pin, aim for the back of the cup. Chief, we can make it, and I mean it's good living, alpaca sweaters, Foot Joy shoes. Have Palm Beach make up some special wardrobes, and all that big money."

He gripped the club again. He was smiling. He saw it all. He was shaking hands with Bobby Jones at the Master's in

Augusta. He had the green championship jacket on, and was telling the television audience what wonderful fellows Nicklaus and Palmer were. He had the $25,000 check in his pocket and his agent had already signed him with Spalding, Palm Beach, and Liggett & Myers.

"I'll get hot. I know it. I feel hot just talking about it."

The management was gathering and looking over at us. He began talking faster.

"What do you say? A hundred dollars and it's fifty-fifty after expenses."

He knew the "after expenses" had hooked me. He coughed, smiled, dried his hands and flexed the club again.

"And no more booze. Not a drop. You got my word on that."

I told him a hundred sounded cheap for a deal like that, and I meant it, but I couldn't afford it.

"That's all right, Chief. We can cut some corners. I can make it out of here with the clubs for fifty."

Two salesmen were walking toward us. His sing-song stopped, his words raced together and he moved me toward the door. I had swallowed the lure, the hook, the leader, and the line; all he had to do was get me to the door before the salesman got to us.

"We'll put it in writing over a cup of coffee."

One hand was on my shoulder, the other on my elbow. I felt warm, weak, buoyant, and strangely benevolent.

"Chief, this is one day you're going to remember. Maybe you can join me when I hit Pinehurst. I'll fix you up with a nice room at the Carolina Inn. Yeah, you'll like that. They take good care of you at the Carolina."

I could see the white portico, the azaleas, the liveried doorman at the Inn. A harmonica was playing and colored caddies, greater than Snead and wiser than Hogan, were crooning near the caddy shack. There were pink clouds low on the shortleaf pines, and against the deep and dappled green of the first fairway on Number Two course I could see my fifty dollars rising slowly on majestic flamingo wings into the blue reaches of North Carolina.

The street noise on Forty-fifth, the revolving door, the tennis shoes, the Helena Rubinstein breath, the salesman broke the spell. I shook my head, but before I could say my embarrassed "No," he squeezed my elbow.

"It's all right, Chief. I understand. I understand. Don't feel bad about it. I know how it is. Anyhow, it was nice talking to you. I really enjoyed it. I really feel better."

He smiled, tapped me on the shoulder, and with the same hand waved away the salesmen. He was still in charge.

"Tell you what you can do for me, though. Can you see your way clear of four bits? I'd like a soup and a sandwich over at Chock Full O' Nuts. You know, pick up the old spirits, that's all I need. I'll go ahead and catch a freight down to Tampa. Maybe get a driving-range job and get in shape. Little sunshine, orange juice, greatest thing in the world for the old short game. Yeah, that's what I'll do. I'll pick up the Circuit in Tallahassee. I can borrow some clubs when I get down there."

I felt ashamed only giving him a dollar and a half.

"That's great, sport. I won't forget it. Listen, I'll be playing them cozy for a few weeks until I get a little roll going. Just a few weeks. And then, watch out. . . ."

His feet were so cold he limped, but when he got through the door on the Forty-fifth Street side he called out,

"Keep that backswing slow and watch out for me on the sports page. . . . Don't forget the name now. It's Peters, Charley Peters."

200,000 DOZEN PAIRS OF SOCKS

DOUG CRAWFORD was the New Jersey salesman for the Triple A Folding Box Company, but his heart was never in it. Doug's heart belonged to golf. He had won the club championship at Twelve Oaks seven times, the county championship four and the state twice. Three times he had qualified for the National Open. Every fall when the northern courses began to freeze and the birds and the pros headed south he would try to decide between staying with his $17,000, expenses-paid-plus-Christmas-bonus job and playing professionally on the winter tour. Every year for the past eight he'd come up with the same decision. His game wasn't quite ready; he would stay with Triple A one more year.

It was warm for late September, and the air conditioning was on in the club bar. The bartender had gone to the stock room, leaving Doug sitting alone cracking and eating pistachio nuts and waiting for his two guests, Hilton Wren, the sales manager for Loomis Socks, and Leo Maddox, the chief buyer for the Butler Brothers chain stores.

As the company golfer for Triple A Folding Box, Doug had played with most of the purchasing agents in the New England territory. He had played with men so wild and strong they would hit a full foot behind the ball, plough up the turf and finish the swing with the heavy earth dripping from the quivering wood. He played with men so slow they would have to let foursomes of women go through. One client, who bought toilet-tissue boxes, would, when the club hit the ball, stop the swing, drop the club, grab his hair and scream "Oh, no, Oh, no." The caddies had called him "Oh-no Burnside." Another guest of the company had been a purchasing agent who had arrived at the first tee with the leather handles of his clubs sticking out of the top of his bag and announced that this was his first game of golf. He had hit his first tee shot off the neck of the driver. The ball came straight back and struck him on the ankle, fracturing it. Doug and the caddies had to carry him to his car and drive him to the hospital. Later, Triple A lost the account. Doug was bitter after this and every time he played with a new purchasing agent he was afraid something would go wrong.

As the clock at the end of the bar chimed ten-fifteen, Hilton and Leo entered the room. Hilton was always on time. Leo shook Doug's hand limply and looked around the wood-paneled room. "So this is Twelve Oaks? Heard a lot about this place. Pretty fancy." Leo was a short, heavy-set man with long black hair on the back of his hands and a thick pelt on his head combed straight back. He was perspiring. He looked from Hilton to Doug. "I could use an eye-opener. Can we get a drink around here?" The bartender came over, and Leo ordered a dry Gibson. Hilton joined him; Doug ordered a sherry on the rocks. Leo drank rapidly and ordered another.

On the second drink Hilton's eyes began to water. He was telling Leo about his promotional idea called Sockorama-Unisphere. Socks from all of the nations of the world would be hung from a big plastic copy of the World's Fair Unisphere with Loomis Socks blanketing the entire United States and part of Canada. If Leo bought the idea it would mean a floor model in each of his 660 stores and an order for 200,000 dozen pairs of socks. It would also mean an order for over 2½ million folding boxes for Doug. Hilton said, "I checked the Fair publicity boys and they said okay on the Unisphere. They figure it will be great publicity for everybody." Hilton had a thin nervous face. He sipped at his Gibson and kept watching Leo. "Wait till you see it, Leo. Just wait. I figure it will pay for itself in a week. And we'll be getting all that overflow advertising from the Fair. I tell you, it's got to work."

The two Gibsons hadn't fazed Leo. "Let me think about it, Hilt. You know how crowded my aisles get. Main problem is space."

"I already worked that out, Leo. You've got to see the model. I got the space problem all licked."

Leo finished his drink. He looked at the bottom of his glass and decided he didn't want another. "I'll give it some thought, Hilt." He turned to Doug. "Let's see your course."

Doug had always been a careful dresser. If he appeared on the first tee wearing white slacks, he also had on white shoes. If black slacks, black shoes. His golf glove always matched his hat, and his Izod socks and shirts seemed to be cut from the same bolt of cloth. Today Doug wore all white.

Leo wore grey-and-red-checked pleated Bermuda shorts. They were too long at the knee and too tight across the back. He didn't wear a belt. He had on a beige fishnet shirt, without an undershirt. Tufts of heavy black hair stuck through the big openings in the net, as did one dark nipple. He wore short elastic-topped black socks with a red clockwork pattern down the side and light tan ripple-soled golf shoes. He stuffed three golf balls into each of his tight back pockets and said, "Okay, I'm ready, let's go."

On the first tee Doug carefully put on and smoothed out the fingers of his white golf glove and looked down the fairway. The wind was riffling the leaves in the tall oaks at the side of the tee and the bright sun dappled the high spots on the fairway. It was a perfect day. Leo pulled out all four woods and gripping them all together began swinging them back and forth, loosening up the deep muscles in his back. He grunted as he swung. Leo was a powerful man with big forearms and enormous legs. He began swinging the four clubs in a circle, as if winding up to throw a hammer.

Doug nudged Hilton at the ball washer. "What's he shoot?"

"You mean his handicap?"

Doug nodded. Hilton was stretching his golf glove on. He was wearing bright red slacks and a blue-green long-sleeved shirt. "Says thirty-five. I've never played with him before."

Doug tried not to flinch. Hilton smacked his right hand into his left and wiggled his gloved fingers. He lowered his voice. "And for every stroke of that thirty-five, he's got over twenty retail outlets. You just keep thinking about that."

Leo handed the four woods to the caddy and pulled out his putter. He placed the club across the small of his back, locked it on the inside of his elbows, and began swaying back and forth.

Hilton lit a cigarette. "Two hundred thousand dozen pairs of socks. That's a lot of boxes, Doug."

"We could use the business. It's been a bad quarter."

They joined Leo by the tee markers. Hilton said, "Okay, Doug, it's your club. Show us the way."

Doug teed his ball and pulled a few blades of grass up and tossed them in the air. The wind was crossing from the right. He swung easily and finished the shot high. Out beyond the 200-yard marker the ball rose and curled into a high rising fade and came to rest within ten yards of the 250-yard marker.

Hilton said, "Nice shot. Okay, Leo."

Leo squatted down and pressed a tee in with his thumb.

Hilton said, "Like this, Leo." He held up a ball and a tee together. "Make the ball do the work."

"I forgot. I'm used to the automatics at the driving range." Leo gripped the driver and took four more lunging practice swings; his neck, arms, and leg veins turned a deep blue and bulged out. Then he stopped and backed up, wheezing. His hands were wet from the practice swings. Hilton started to give him a towel, but before he could get to him, Leo had dried his hands on the back of his pants and was ready to hit.

He swung viciously, missing the ball completely. The heavy swing jerked him forward and he took a quick step to keep from falling down.

Hilton said quickly, "Here, Leo, dry your hands. Take a Mulligan. It's okay on the first."

Leo tossed the towel back and lined himself up. He swung again. The club whipped back in a blinding backswing and whistling through grazed the top of the ball, trickling it out ten yards beyond the tee markers. Leo whirled around and slammed the driver into the ground. "Can't understand it. Can't. Hit 'em a goddamn mile at the driving range."

Hilton said, "Don't worry, Leo. You got it out of your system. You'll be okay now." Hilton drove 180 yards down the right side of the fairway.

Leo addressed the ball again, this time at the front of the long tee for his third shot.

Suddenly the public address system from the pro shop crackled and a voice announced: "Will someone in the three-some on the first tee tell the party about to drive that he must tee off from between the markers."

Leo was furious. He glared toward the pro shop.

Hilton looked at Doug. "What's going on?"

Doug shook his head. "Must be some mistake."

Hilton said, "Don't let it bother you, Leo. Go ahead."

Leo spat on the ground and went back to the ball. The announcer spoke again. "Will someone in that threesome *please* tell the party about to drive that he must tee off from between the markers."

Leo stepped back from the ball and cupping his hands shouted, "You stupid son-of-a-bitch, I'm shooting three."

Hilton laughed quickly, trying to turn the incident into a joke, but seeing that Leo was still mad, he covered his mouth with the corner of his towel and pretended he was coughing. The coughing rattled him and he felt a headache rising and beginning to pound behind his eyes.

Leo finally hit. The ball hooked sharply toward the hurricane fence beyond the narrow rough, hit the fence, and bounded back onto the fairway.

Hilton said, "Okay, Leo, it'll play." They started off. On the first hole Doug sank a six-foot putt for a three. Hilton had a six, Leo an eleven.

On the second hole Leo's swing was even faster than on the first tee. The ball hooked quickly into the tall grass and pine trees. Hilton watched it disappear. His headache was getting worse and he could taste the Gibson at the back of his throat. Pinching his nose and eyes with his thumb and forefinger, he decided he'd better stay with Leo as much as possible to discuss Sockorama. Hilton's game had once been a sound ten handicap but since he had been playing with customers so long and so regularly, it had gone to a seventeen. It had changed from a long, bold game to a timid, chameleon-like affair that adapted itself to any purchasing agent. If the purchasing agent sliced, Hilton sliced. If the purchasing agent hooked, Hilton hooked. Hilton looked toward the woods where Leo's ball had gone. He groaned, without making any noise, turned his right hand back, swung and followed Leo into the trees.

On the fourth hole Doug drove almost 280 yards. No one spoke. Leo hit. The ball hugged the ground and bounced out 170 yards into the middle of the fairway.

Hilton said, "Okay, Leo, right where you want to be. I'll take those all day, any day. Right, Doug?"

Doug smiled, "That's the place to be."

As they left the tee Hilton put his arm on Leo's shoulder, hoping to ask about Sockorama. Leo pushed his hand off. "Cut it out, will you? I'm sweating too much already."

Hilton joined Doug in the middle of the fairway. "I shouldn't have had those Gibsons. It's crazy to try and drink with Leo. He's got a cast-iron stomach." He watched Leo flog at the ball, sending it scuttling into the trees again. "Christ, if he'd only hit a few good shots."

Doug shook his head. "He swings too fast."

Hilton went on, "I know him, I know his type. If he gets off a few good shots he's a different man. I bet you a hundred dollars the minute he starts playing better he'll feel better about buying."

On the sixth hole Leo hit a solid spoon shot almost 200 yards to the back of the green. Hilton moved in quickly and shouted, "Beautiful, Leo! Really beautiful! Quail-high, all the way. That's what I call a golf shot. You see how she sat down?"

Leo smiled and lit a cigar. Hilton was afraid the shot would be Leo's only good one of the day. "Leo, I wish you'd fill me in on the Sockorama decision. I got the artist's sketches all together and the models practically built."

Leo's smile vanished. He kept his cigar in his mouth and spoke around it. "As of right now Sockorama is dead. Now leave me alone. Let me play my game. I'm just beginning to loosen up."

"But Leo, I got the sketches and the model is. . . ."

Leo walked off and joined Doug. "I can't concentrate. That bastard won't get off my back. He never stops selling."

Doug didn't answer. He was four under par and every shot he'd hit had gone exactly where he wanted. He watched a low wedge of Canadian geese sweep before them and settle behind the trees in the lake on the twelfth hole. His feet felt light on the springy fairway, and as he inhaled the heavy smell of the fresh-cut grass, he thought of his father and recalled the day they had seen the men's tennis finals at Forest Hills. When it was over, and after the applause had stopped and the crowd was leaving, his father had turned to him and solemnly said, "Son, it's a nice game but there's just no game like golf."

Leo touched Doug's elbow and spoke again. "You know something?"

"What?"

"I like you. You know why I like you? I like you because you ignore me. I like that. I come out for a little fun and a little relaxation and what do I get? Hell, I might as well be in the office. I tell you, I work harder out here fighting off Hilton than I do in town. At least there, I can tell the girl to get rid of him. Out here I'm trapped."

He pulled out his handkerchief and wiped his face. "It's like when I go to the golf outings. Every time I look around or go to the toilet there's a salesman grinning at me, wanting to do me a favor, or buy me a drink or ask about how my wife and kids are. They treat me like some kind of prince. Ha, that's a laugh. Leo Maddox, the prince of Butler Brothers. I tell you, Doug, it's relaxing being around you. You're different."

Hilton came over. He put one hand on Doug's shoulder and one on Leo's. "How you two getting along?"

Leo said, "We're in love. That good enough?"

Hilton barked a short laugh and crossed over to his ball. He lit a cigarette with the butt of the one he was finishing. He was afraid Doug's smooth game might be upsetting Leo. Still, they were walking together and Leo was talking, even joking. Maybe Doug had given Leo a lesson. If Leo would only change his mind and buy the Sockorama! Two hundred thousand dozen first-line socks. Maybe that would convince Loomis he was needed on the inside of the company. Twenty-four years in sales; he'd been out in the field too long. His nerves were beginning to show through. A man can sell only so many years. Maybe some day he would be vice president in charge of sales; then he could use his experience with the younger men. Go out in the field with them, show them the tricks of the trade. How to look the buyer in the eye. How to amuse him and then switch over into straight business. He could tell the younger salesmen how not to smoke unless the buyer does, and then to be careful where the smoke drifts. How to watch for nervous mannerisms, toe-tappers, finger-snappers, facial tics. How to apply sales psychology. How to find out if the buyer is Catholic, Jewish, Mason. How to feel them out about jokes, religion, women, maybe kickbacks.

Hilton looked out across the fairway. He would be firm to the younger men and keep their respect. Check everything on expense reports. Great idea: put phones in the salesmen's cars. Like a taxi fleet. That way he could always find them. It would keep them on their toes and out of the movies and the whorehouses. All he needed was the Sockorama job. With that he would be on top of the world. Maybe he could get the publicity boys at *Men's Hosiery Review* to have a page showing him and Leo and the Sockorama promotion. He would put the Unisphere in between them and have Leo and him shaking hands across it. Leo would love to have his picture in *Men's Hosiery*. He would need a slogan to go under the picture. "Hands Across the World." No, he would have to do better than that. He would think about it later.

They were on the eighth tee in the shade of a big oak tree. The wind was stronger. Doug teed his ball low and hit his longest drive.

Hilton said, "Nice shot, Doug. Okay, Leo, you can let out here."

Leo's dark eyes narrowed as if he were going to try to drive the green 520 yards away. He shifted his hands to the very end of the club handle for a fuller swing and crouched over so he could generate more power. It was the fastest backswing Doug had ever seen. Leo missed the ball completely. The flying club shot out of his hands. It whistled up into the oak tree and wrapped around a big limb above them. When it stopped vibrating the leather handle hung down on one side and the driver head hung down the other. No one spoke. Leo's face was white with red splotches. Hilton was dead white. One of the caddies vanished into the bushes cramming a towel into his mouth to keep from exploding, while Doug and Leo looked up at the club above them draped over the limb like a weary cobra.

Doug stepped forward and pulled out a brand new Titlist ball, teed it up, and handed Leo his own driver. "Forget it, Leo. This time I want you to lock your head down and take the club back nice and slow. Keep your head down, now; I'll watch the ball for you."

Leo hit the drive down the middle, 210 yards. Doug walked along with him.

Leo handed Doug his club. "It's that lousy Hilton. He got me all upset with that Sockorama idea."

Doug didn't hear Leo. He was planning his second shot. He felt enormous power and leverage in his legs and wrists and a fine sensitive control in his fingers. Every shot he had hit had been perfect. His game was finally right; it would never be better. He made up his mind. If he tied or beat the course record for eighteen holes he would quit Triple A and take his chances with the professionals. He could pick up the tour in Louisiana. Yes, it would work. If he could keep his game around 70 he could do it. Maybe not the big money at first, but he would be learning the ropes and the courses. And if he got hot? Maybe he could get on "All Star Golf on television. Each appearance meant $3000. A couple of those and he would be all right. He wondered if he could still try it. He was only thirty-four. How old was Boros? Snead? How old was Hogan? A gloomy thought rose behind his eyes. He could always go back to selling boxes if his game went sour. He shook it away.

Leo hit again. Again it was straight and down the middle. Hilton called out from the deep rough. "Nice shot, Leo. Nice."

Leo looked at Doug. He laughed. "You hit a ball three hundred yards and Hilton doesn't say a word. I hit one a hundred and fifty and he says 'Tremendous.' I ask you, what kind of salesman is that?"

Leo walked close to Doug. "You play a lot, don't you?"

"Quite a bit."

"You know, I can't see why this game's so tough. Chances are if I took it up seriously, you know, went out to the driving range a little more, maybe took a few lessons, I might get so I was pretty good. I like to bowl a lot. Now there's a game you'd like, Doug. There's a man's game. I bet you'd be pretty good at it. I'll tell you something, it's got a lot of advantages when you stop and analyze it." He relit his cigar. He was sweating, and the black hair on his chest and back glistened. "There's never any trouble about the weather, that's number one. Number two, if you're in the right crowd there's always a few laughs. Then if you get hungry or want a drink, that's right there too. And once in a while there's a broad in the next alley throwing pretty hard and you get a chance to see a little leg. These things add up. Yeah, you'd like bowling, Doug. You ought to look into it."

They were at Doug's ball. The green was over 250 yards away.

Leo said, "Tell you what, you teach me golf, I'll teach you bowling."

"This is an important shot, Leo."

"Okay, so hit it. There's no one on the green."

Doug hit a full brassie shot. He knew it was good. It traveled low all the way and settled on the right side of the green about twenty-five feet from the pin.

Leo said, "Okay, what do you think of my offer? Me teach you bowling, you teach me golfing?"

Doug didn't hear Leo. He was thinking about his score. If he could two-putt for a four and then par the ninth he would have a 30. No one had ever shot below a 31 on the first nine. He began walking fast. He wanted to get away from Leo so he could think and plan the next shot carefully. He couldn't let anything upset him; there was too much at stake.

Hilton joined him. "Listen, Leo says no on Sockorama and I can't tell if he means it or not. We got to have the business. We were shut down fourteen days last month."

Doug was planning his long putt.

Hilton said, "Maybe you can help out. I think he likes you. Maybe you can give him a few more pointers." Hilton dubbed a nine iron. He stabbed the club at the ground and looked at Doug. "You know my game, Doug. You know I play better than this. It's this pressure. It's having Leo along and that Sockorama hanging over my head that's making me press like this."

"You're too tense, Hilton."

"I know. I know. Listen, if Sockorama is dead my forecast for the year is shot. Maybe me too. You might as well know it, things haven't been going too great for me this year. Those Japanese socks are murdering us on price and I don't know where the orders are going to come from. Besides that, my best purchasing agent over at Long and Vogel's up and died on me and the new man they put in won't see me." He shook his head. "Two hundred thousand dozen pairs of first-line. That's a month's production. You any idea what kind of profit that means?" He gritted his teeth. "No man should have that kind of power. They become dictators."

Doug lined up his long twenty-five foot putt and without giving himself a chance to think about it, hit. The ball held the line for half the distance and then slowly curved in. As they left the green the caddies began whispering about the course record.

Leo stood near the apron taking a practice swing. "Hey, Doug, what else am I doing wrong? I got the head and the backswing all set. Give me something else to work on."

Doug walked over. "That's all for now, Leo. Just stay with that. I'll show you some more later."

Leo grinned. "You're the boss."

On the ninth tee Leo hit his finest shot. It carried over 200 yards and rolled out another twenty-five. He hit his second shot to the edge of the green. As Leo and Doug came up to the apron Leo said, "It's really great; I think I got it. I really think I got it. Just keep the head locked down and swing easy. Wonder why nobody ever told me that before?"

Doug was thinking about the southern courses and how much money he would need to break even for the rest of the year. He decided he could do it with $4000.

Leo said, "If I give Loomis this Sockorama, you get the box

business, is that right?"

Doug barely heard him. "Yeah, Leo, I get the boxes."

Leo slapped him on the back. "Okay, I'll give it to them. I don't like it. I don't like it at all. Matter of fact it stinks, but maybe it will move socks. American public is crazy anyhow, they might buy anything."

Doug smiled. "Thanks, Leo."

Leo said, "Don't say anything about it to Wren. I want him to sweat a little more."

Leo lagged his putt up six inches short of the hole and tapped in his first par of the day. Doug was thirty feet from the hole. He putted quickly. The ball was in all the way. He had a 29, two strokes below the record 31 for nine holes. He handed the caddy the putter and took the driver. All he needed now was a 36 on the back nine to break the course. record. He started for the tenth tee. He was sure now, he would definitely go on the tour. Leo spoke. Doug didn't want to talk or listen to anyone. He wanted to be alone for a minute. He had to make plans. He had to play the back nine carefully, not take any chances. Maybe he would use his spoon from the tees and play it safe.

Leo called out again, but Doug kept walking.

Hilton shouted, "Come on, Doug."

Doug stopped. They were standing on the far side of the green. Hilton said, "Come on, Doug. We're having one for the road."

Doug wanted to pretend he hadn't heard. If he stopped now he would never be able to keep the fine putting touch and the perfect game he had going. He couldn't stop now. Even a few minutes' interruption would break the spell. Hilton had removed his golf glove. Leo was peeling his off and grinning.

"Come on, Doug. Just one, that's all."

Doug handed the caddy his driver and slowly followed the two men toward the club house and the bar. He couldn't believe what was happening.

Leo said, "You see how that five iron sat down?"

Doug nodded. He was afraid to speak.

Inside Leo ordered three Gibsons. As the seconds passed Doug felt the fine putting touch oozing out of the tips of his fingers. He shoved his fists deep into his pockets hoping to stop the leak.

Leo proposed a toast. "To Doug Crawford, a great golfer, a great teacher."

They drank.

Leo continued, "You know, I learned more about golf today than I have in my whole life?" He smiled and laid his hand on Doug's arm. "Okay, Doug, you propose the next toast. Tell Hilton here what I told you."

Doug looked down at Leo's fingernails. They seemed to be as thick as oyster shells. He raised his glass. "To Leo and Sockorama." He looked at Hilton. "Leo's giving us the Sockorama job."

Everyone shook hands. Hilton beamed. His arm shot up signaling the waiter for another round.

The Gibson hit Doug like an axe. He stood up. "I've got to play the next nine. I can break the course record." There was no conviction in his voice and Leo pulled him back into his seat.

"Come on, drink up. You can always break the record. Come back and do it tomorrow." He took a big drink, spread some cheese on a cracker and laughed at Doug. "How many days in your life do you see a dog like Sockorama-Unisphere sold? Jesus, what a lousy name."

Hilton said, "Maybe we could change the name."

"Naw, leave it. Probably sell socks like crazy."

Doug said slowly, "All I need is a thirty-six and I got the record. No one's ever had a twenty-nine on the first nine."

Leo slapped him on the back. "You still talking about records? Come on, drink up there, lad. We're lapping you."

Doug's hands were cold. The putting touch was gone. He gripped the stem of his Gibson glass and raised it to his lips.

Maybe next year was the right year for the tour. He looked at the Gibson. It seemed greasy on the surface. Two and a half million four-color rotogravure boxes with no chiseling on price; it would be the largest piece of new business of the year. He could stay with Triple A through Christmas to pick up his holiday bonus and then join the tour in Florida. Maybe he could play until then. The courses might not freeze so early this year, the winters seemed to be getting milder. Doug finished his drink and swallowed the onion.

Hilton made him a double-decker cheese and cracker sandwich. "Here you go, Doug boy. We've got to keep you in good shape." He slapped Doug on the back and grinned at Leo. "Didn't I tell you he was the greatest golf teacher in the world?"

Leo ordered another round and bit off the end of a fresh cigar. Doug finally removed his golf glove and watched Leo blow his first puff of smoke toward the ceiling. After the third round of Gibsons had been served, Hilton pushed the cheese-and-cracker tray to the far side of the table and, clicking his ball point pen down, he began sketching the Sockorama-Unisphere model on the tablecloth.

ROOM 306
DOESN'T TIP

AUGUST 10TH, 101 degrees and even the dogs are off the streets. It's Graduation Day and I'm ninety-fourth in line. Have nothing under my black robe except pants and T shirt. The hot cotton feels like it's just been ironed. Wonder if Coke machine is empty.

The senator speaking wipes his face, takes a drink of water and drones on about opportunities, challenges, new horizons, and facing the future undaunted. Plan to go to Miami to work until sailing for Venezuela in October. Job lined up in iron mines, teaching. Two-year contract, $600 a month plus living expenses. Will save every penny, come back with $14,400 and a thousand pages of the Great American Novel.

The speech ends. The honoraries and Ph.D.'s are first. My hand's wet when I shake the senator's. Dean sees I have no shirt on. Full-fledged Bachelor of Arts of philosophy and history; have $36.14 and a Greyhound ticket to Miami in pocket. Owe the dry cleaners $3.60.

Greyhound to Miami takes seventeen hours. Once past St. Augustine it's all like Daytona Beach: white sand, bright sun, gliding gulls and lunging pelicans. Miami, next stop. The Golden Strip—City of the Sun—America's Playground. Have a milk shake and a pack of Fig Newtons at the Greyhound station and check the classified ads.

Short-order Cook, $60, no drunks.
Service Station Man, $60, must be willing to work.

Day Laborers, $1.50 per hour, white/col., no drifters.
Car Washers, white/col., $1.25 per hour plus tips, steady.
Bellhops, Miami Beach, heavy tips, no salary.
Counterman, nite shift, $55 per week.

At the Royal Garden Hotel, a three-story 300-roomer on North Beach.

Manager: "Did you ever bellhop?"

"Yessir."

"Where?"

"Dixie Belle Hotel in Columbia."

"This is a little different."

"I understand."

"You in the Service?"

"Yessir. Second lieutenant, Air Corps."

"Then you know how to wear a uniform. Right?"

"Right."

"Okay, you're on. Eight to eight, half hour for lunch. You can sign for your meals in the coffee shop. Report to Jerry on the door. He's the super. He gets your first ten per cent."

"Thank you, sir."

"The name's Sherman. Are you broke?"

"Yes."

"Here's ten bucks. Sign here. Pick up your uniform from the housekeeper. She's in the basement. And listen, something else."

"What's that?"

"No hustling women."

The superintendent: Jerry Rafferty, a short red-haired race-track-tout type who could get a tip out of a stone. "There's no real money down here till December. I usually don't come down till November."

"But how much now?"

"A hundred and fifty, two hundred tops."

"A month?"

"You crazy? A week. Hell, I pull a grand down from

December on. Hit fifteen hundred during the February action."

"Jesus, how do you do it?"

"Different ways. Check-ins, check-outs. Laundry, dry cleaning, car wash, repairs, rentals, reservations, tours. Anything that comes up. You name it, I got a piece of it. That includes you."

"Yeah, I know."

"Listen, don't try taking luggage out of the cars. Your territory ends at the door until I signal you down. Got it?"

"Okay, but what if you're not here?"

"I'll be here."

"But what if you're not? Hell, you can be in the john or something. I'll look like a damn fool standing inside while they're blowing."

"I'll let you know when I'm leaving. Then we split down the middle. If I catch you holding out you're through."

A black Fleetwood Cadillac pulls into the circle. Jerry: "It's a rental. Probably good for a deuce. Okay, get back inside." A short man in a Chesterfield coat with a tall wife who isn't speaking to him gets out. Jerry takes the car keys, unloads the trunk and stacks the luggage on the steps. He sells the man a car wash and an oil change while he makes out the car ticket. Two one-dollar bills flutter and Jerry tips his hat with his left hand, which is my signal to come out for the luggage.

Put three bags under left arm and two heavies under right. Push open glass door with hip. While they are at desk I pile bags at elevator, get it down and lock it with inside trigger. They sign up for a $12 room facing Collins Avenue. Rooms facing ocean are $20 until December, then everything sky-rockets. Ocean singles go to $46 a day, two-room suites $110.

In elevator. Man is wearing a glare-blue business suit under Chesterfield. Woman has a small fur piece. It's 90 degrees outside.

"Did you have a nice trip down?" (Don't say flight; may have taken train, driven, or ridden Greyhound.)

They're from Chicago. He's in the meat business. Woman silent and furious. In room, pile luggage on racks. Hang fur piece and Chesterfield on curved wooden hangers. Big motion in bathroom, checking towels, window, air conditioner. "Well, it looks like you're all set. Everything seems just right. My name's Bill, and if there's anything I can do for you, just pick up the phone." He tips me a dollar bill rolled up around a fifty-cent piece. My first tip. Not bad for three minutes' work. Strange pair, though. Could have been brother and sister instead of man and wife. Wonder how Jerry spotted them for two dollars.

Jerry: "Aw, you can tell how they drive and walk and everything. Read them; you've got eyes. That monkey's used to a compact. He's got no business in a Caddy. He almost fell on his face climbing out of it. They get down here and store their cars in town and rent the hearses. Check that right rear tire, all whacked up from the corners. He's been clipping them all day. That's why he went for that wash job. Lot of tricks in this field, buddyroll, but you got to keep your eyes open and stay sharp. Okay?"

"Okay."

First day made $16. First week cleared $92 after ten to Sherman and eleven to Jerry. Beats "Day Laborers, $1.50 per hour, no drifters," and I'm beginning to like it.

Jerry's price for what I learn is cheap. During check-out we work together on loading luggage. Touchy moment. Some sharpies will rush around pretending to be in a hurry and made each boy think the other has the tip. No chance with Jerry. He holds the driver's door, I hold the other door or the trunk lid. Pretend it's stuck if necessary. Doors or trunk not closed until one of us touches hat with left hand. If no tip, door stays open and Jerry bold-faced, says. "Isn't there something you're forgetting?" I can't do this. He can and it doesn't faze him. Earns more than his 10 per cent right here.

Jerry: "Never let them get too far behind. If they say I'll

take care of you next time, let it ride once. But only once. Next time tell them they said that last time. That usually works. Keep your eyes on their foreheads. Don't try to out-stare them. Lots of them are in sales and they know the ropes. That'll just make them mad and they'll tell you to go to hell. I got one in now. Benedetto, room 306. I've already called him on it, but he gave me some cool British swill about tipping at the end of the fortnight. Wears a two-hundred-dollar pair of slacks and a hundred-dollar shirt and he hasn't reached for the first dime."

Benedetto, room 306, three pieces of matched black kangaroo-skin luggage from Mark Cross with stickers from Rome, Athens, Oslo, is tall and tailored. His hairbrushes, nail brushes, shaving gear, pipe rack, pipes and shoe trees are from Abercrombie & Fitch. He stands in lobby and prowls pool. Never in bathing suit, always in chartreuse slacks with matching ascot carefully folded at neck under a wine-colored, long-sleeved silk shirt. He dresses and stands like a successful poet or a captain on leave from the Coldstream Guards, but with his slick hair and narrow eyes, he looks like a tap dancer. After each service—getting him a gin and tonic, ice, tobacco, baby club sandwich or grilled cheese—instead of tipping he smiles and touches finger to forehead. This suggests he is keeping tab of what he owes us.

Jerry says, "File that move under 'fat chance.' He'll probably sneak out carrying his own bags and take the bus at the corner."

"But he's loaded!"

"Doesn't matter. He's a no-tipper. I've got to think of some way of shaking him up."

The pool is off limits for the bellhops except when they're serving food. All pool concessions—mats, chairs, towels, oils, lotions, foil reflectors, eye cups and nose guards—belong to the cabana boy, Phil. Phil is a six-foot-two golden giant who can swim the length of the pool twice under water and knows how to smile. Calls everyone by their first name and is a real suck. He passes himself off as a health faddist. Practices yoga, eats soybeans, organic foods and yoghurt. Stands on his head in the morning for ten minutes to clear it. Jerry says he could do that by spitting. Sits straight, walks straight. Verges on being muscle-bound but laughs at weight lifters. Probably curls and presses secretly. Tells everyone he wants to be an advertising executive in New York City and is looking for the right contact. Cabana boys have shorter careers than middle weights. Guests like them young and supple. At twenty-seven he'll be over the hill. Has executive job hedged by being a masseur and a pimp. Will go far down here. Will never leave. Constant battles and jealousy between bellhops and cabana boys on whose rights end where. He can get drinks and soft drinks from bar but can't serve food. We can't serve drinks except with meals. Every tray I take out to pool, he checks to see if I'm faking a grilled cheese in order to move in on the martini crowd.

A specialty of the hotel is serving meals on floating tables to bathers in shallow end of big, double-kidney-shaped pool. Pot cheeses, cream cheese, swiss cheese, pastrami, tongue, corned beef, sauer-kraut and sour tomatoes. Cream cheese and bagels, cream cheese and lox, cream cheese and jelly. Dr. Brown's Celery Tonic, sour cream and borscht very big. Light eaters, average eaters and heavy eaters, intrigued by floating tables, overorder. No appetite from lying around like logs in the sun all day, but they try anyway. A duty.

One heavy-hocked size 18, corner view of ocean, $26-a-nighter with four pieces of matched red leather luggage and a sable coat with a Neiman Marcus label, groaned two low notes. "Oy, oy, so it's time to eat again."

Fifty to a hundred foil reflectors under the sun bathers' throats are blinding. Have to turn away when you walk by to serve. The sun crowd are lined up on a long curved duckboard rack with red and green pads under them. A timer goes off every five minutes and they turn over like knockwursts on a spit.

A stout lawyer with calamine lotion on his nose is on an inflated plastic dragon holding a prune Danish up so it doesn't get wet. Drifts near the edge talking to a friend. "You think I'm relaxing. You're crazy. I never relax here. Here I do business. They break their humps in New York on the I.R.T. and the B.M.T. I do it here. So who's smarter? I get them when they're relaxed. But me relax? Come off it. Only time I relax is when I'm on my boat in my lake. I get out in the middle and cut the engines and let her drift. I let her drift and I just lay back, smoke my cigar and say screw them all. Otherwise, it ain't worth it."

Rich foods, rich sun, rich hours. Meal times are any time. Breakfast is served until four in the afternoon, lunch and dinner any time. The pastry cook works a 12-hour shift and he barely keeps up. Peanuts, pretzels, cheese-flavored popcorn pour through the bar in ten-gallon tins and the wastebaskets and ash trays are loaded with Hershey, Butterfinger and Milky Way wrappers. At night the cool breeze sharpens the appetites. Manny Wolfe's is packed until 5 A.M. The orchestra leader playing in a glassed-in restaurant broadcasts that when you drive down Collins Avenue for your midnight snack, blink your lights and he will wave back. There's a traffic jam on Arthur Godfrey Boulevard.

Early morning. Sounds of the retching and the dying. Alka-Seltzer, Bromo Seltzer, Pepto-Bismol, Kaopectate. Doctor nearby services three hotels. Carries a stomach pump in his leather sack. Keeps busy.

Jerry: "You can't figure them all. But you'll get the percentages if you stay with it. Take the gambler. He's in from Las Vegas. First thing he does in the elevator is rattle his silver dollars. He wants you to know what he is and he doesn't want to talk."

"I see."

"Okay, so right away you don't try to outguess him. He spends his life outguessing. He doesn't want to be hustled.

But he doesn't want to be tabbed some shoe salesman either, get it? So you play it close. Very close. If you press, you lose. If you don't, you lose. You got to cut it right. Listen, this ain't no romance. The more you make the more I make. That's why I'm bringing you along."

I nod. "I understand."

"People think this racket's a snap. That all a bellhop does is smile and hold out his claw. Boy, they know a lot. The super up at the Beverly pulls down sixty thousand a year. Got a Chris Craft and a Lincoln Continental. You don't live like that with your hand out. Anyhow, take the gambler. He's in the elevator riffling his silver dollars. Right away you know he's studying you. Your tip can run from one to twenty, but he's running up and down the stack trying to figure out what you're worth and where he'll cut it off. So what do you do? I'll tell you what you do. You watch him but you don't watch him. You wait for him to make a move and you key in on it. If he wants to keep quiet, keep it quiet. Joke, joke. Talk, talk. Just let him start it. And for Christ's sake don't let him know you're listening to the money. One stud man caught me and tapped me. Said he'd give me seven to two I couldn't call it. Broke me up. Him too. Came across with a sawbuck and a fiver for every pitcher of ice. They're right guys but they don't want nobody hustling them. You know something? If I had it to do all over again I'd start out in Vegas. If you can read that crowd you're home free.

"Tell you something else. Never hand a guest his change. Lay it down on the dresser. Make him pick it up. Get him reaching for it and crowd in there close where he can see you in the mirror. You've got to keep reminding them what you're there for. And watch the wife. She knows the man's going to overtip. So stand with your back to her, or between them, to give him a chance. He's going to lie to her anyway.

"Women tippers, that's different. Men I can read. I keep drawing blanks on women. Most of them go the flat twenty per cent Schrafft's tip on everything. But they'll cross you up.

I've gotten as high as twenty bucks for buying a pack of cigarettes and twenty cents for moving up a steamer trunk. You
never can tell about them. I had one up in the Catskills
figured for at least a sawbuck and she gave me a god damned
apple.

"You take a bellhop working one of those mom-and-pop
South Beach flea bags. Right away he's in the john with his
big motion letting you know you've got hot water and a couple
towels. Then he rushes out and breaks his ass pushing up the
windows. Wants you to think he's responsible for everything.
That's the way to starve up here. When a man puts down sixty
bucks, for a damn room, he's got to figure the sheets are clean
and he's got toilet paper. Just go in the john and cut the lights
on. Maybe show them where the switch is. If you want something to do with you hands, flash those curved hangers when
you hang up their coats. I'll sell you a few extras. Women
love them. And when they check out, make sure you give
them a couple. It'll cost you but the extra tip will cover it.
Don't carry a cigarette lighter. Always carry matches.
Lighter's too fast and might not work. Light the match and
let them see you fan the flame to get rid of the sulphur smell.
They like that. And don't let them see you slouch or lean on
anything or get tired."

The light and the buzzer went on. It was Benedetto in 306.
Jerry: "There's that bastard again. I gave him a pitcher of
warm water last night with one ice cube in it and a dusty
glass and he didn't bat an eye."

"What're you going to do with him?"

"I don't know. But let me handle him."

Jerry comes back from 306 waving Benedetto's $200 char-
treuse slacks like a flag. Trying to decide what to do with
them to scare him into tipping. Considers jamming the
zipper, breaking the zipper handle, tearing off a belt loop,
removing the front pockets. Decides to decide later.

To Jerry's advice I add my own notes: don't tell a piece-
goods salesman that you're in philosophy or interested in

teaching school. Tell him you're in insurance, accounting, advertising. Relate your ambitions to his career. Plenty of time to discuss schools and writers when the teaching crowd comes down in the spring. Be surprised, astonished when weather is cloudy. Act bewildered, even shocked, when it rains.

Miss Avril: "So where's the sun?"

"I'm, sorry, Miss Avril. I just can't understand it. This is the first time it's been like this. It can't last much longer."

"What do you mean it can't! It is! It's raining cats and dogs and I'm stuck in a thirty-six-dollar-a-night room. I can't go back to work like this. I've *got* to get a tan. How'll they know I've been here? That creep Mildred Geddings lived off Metrecal and didn't spend a dime over the package and came back black. Look at me. I'm like an oyster."

"You can get a tan in the solarium."

"Hell, I can do that on Lexington Ave at the Y.W.C.A. for fifty cents. I flew two thousand miles and I'm dropping six hundred dollars just to sit out here with the potted palms and write postcards? Well, at least something's free around here. Is the bar open?"

"Yes, ma'am."

The heavy drinkers stay in the bar all day. It's a dark mermaid-type lounge with an undersea panorama in blues and dark greens. The hostesses wear transparent Bagdad-Valentino pants and the place is so dark they need flashlights to make change.

More notes: find out about people and introduce them around. Find out where they live, even street, if possible. Keep notes. Two men from 168th St. in Manhattan will pound each other on the back as if meeting in a foreign country. Others are scornful of this and looking for escape, but not many are looking very hard. Usually a pose. Neighbors will have a good time if thrown together. They sit in lobby and pick apart the others. Wives throw off Saks Fifth Avenue accent and stride, and discuss Macy's and A-and-P prices. Men discuss territories, their cars and how they get from Van Cortlandt to Canarsie. The car and mink renters look self-conscious. Walk stiffly as if shoes hurt or they're being followed, or they go overboard and try to casual it like Dean Martin. Beware of change rattlers but don't let them scare you. The noise works both ways. They're scared you've heard and are insulted, and often will overcompensate and overtip.

Sherman, the manager: "Here's the problem. Julian Vogel is coming out to look the place over. He's a big shirt manufacturer, one of the biggest. I want him to stay here. He's an ocean suite for a solid month, and the salesmen stick with him like fruit flies. Last year twenty followed him into the Blue Hacienda and they stayed all month. We've got to get him. Show him the place. Give him anything he wants. He's crazy and he doesn't trust me, so stay on top of him. I'm counting on you."

Julian Vogel arrives. Short, thin, neurotic. All nerve ends. Unusual head shape, seems to be two differently shaped lobes joined together by an operation. No hair. Rimless, steel-framed glasses as thick as Coca-Cola bottle bottoms. High-strung and wretched. Slightest noise makes him jump and quiver. Should be in rest home, not here. I show him the entire hotel. Room by room. Hotel has 300, horse-shoes toward Ocean, backs up to Collins Avenue. Night club at bottom corner of one wing, kitchen at the other. Julian has moist suffering eyes, wants peace, quiet, can't stand noise or smells or vibrations. Show him all available rooms and suites.

Says no to all rooms on ocean side. Surf too noisy.

Says no to wing near night club. Too noisy. Claims he can hear the bass vibrations when the orchestra's playing. I can't.

Says no to wing on Collins Avenue. Traffic too noisy and exhaust fumes.

Only wing left is on kitchen side. We walk down padded hallway sniffing the kitchen odors. Vogel keeps walking, keeps sniffing. Finally finds a suite near front which he claims is odor-free. No noise, no smells, no vibrations. Ideal room; top floor away from surf, traffic, kitchen and night club. It has taken two hours to find it, but we have. He likes it. He likes the foam mattress, windows. Air conditioner responds to all settings. John flushes quietly. Water pressure fine. Even likes the salmon and tan coloring and the bullfighter motif over the headboard. All set, smiling, delighted, rubbing hands and crossing and recrossing room as if he's measuring it. I call manager.

Sherman comes up beaming. He starts to seal deal with handshake but suddenly Julian pulls back. Something is wrong. He acts like he's been tricked.

"No! No! It won't do."

Sherman: "But Mr. Vogel, it's perfect." Runs through qualities of excellence. "It's perfect, perfect. I'm sure you'll be happy here."

Julian smiles, "Perfect, yes, but wrong nevertheless. I'm too far from the kitchen. I'll get my breakfast cold."

"But Bill can get it here in two minutes from the kitchen. Less than that."

"Not fast enough. If the elevator is busy he has to wait. If he climbs the stairs, even if he runs, it's too late. Everything gets cold. Sorry, I like the room but I can't live like that."

Sherman is dumbfounded.

I speak, "What do you have for breakfast, sir?"

"Oatmeal, prune juice. Hot toast and coffee. It's no use, I like the butter brushed on my toast and after a couple minutes it gets soggy."

"But what if I set up a Sterno unit in the linen closet? It's only twenty feet away. I'll do the toast there and keep the oatmeal hot for you. I'm sure I can handle it."

"My boy, you can." Julian smiles, turns to Sherman. "This boy's a genius. I want him to wait on me personally on everything. I'm staying."

In hall, Sherman has arm around my shoulder. "Great going. Great. Stay with him, you can clean up on him.

And listen, I want you on the split shift. There's more action at night around here. Should be worth another hundred."

Summer weeks of $150 now peanuts. If I don't make $50 a night am upset. Venezuela 10,000 miles away and getting farther. Will do novel in Miami. Need a title for it.

"Hi, buddy, got any girls around here?"

"No, sir, check the cab man at the corner."

"I gotcha."

Jerry: "Leave the broads alone. Trouble, nothing but trouble. They'll spoil everything. They get to hanging around and then it's too late to get rid of them. Give me a car wash and a grease setup anyday."

More notes: off duty don't mingle with the guests. Cabana boys can, but that's another horse. They lock themselves to guests and build sick patronizing friendships. Introduce men to women, women to men. Their tip builds until it's no longer called tip but a going-away present. Where cabana boy's tip builds, bellhop's does not. You must make it fast on each call. A bellhop who drinks with guests breaks down distance barrier. It's like tipping a friend. Familiarity Breeds Contempt.

Jerry calls me over to his desk. Tourist guide books piled on desk a foot deep. Brochures on everything: Everglade cruises and fishing trips. Rent a car, a boat, an Indian. Buy fruit, candy, flowers. Benedetto's slacks are back from cleaners. Jerry has spent hours figuring what he is going to do to them. Takes out Parker pen, wiggles valve and drops a single tear of ink on the middle of the fly.

Benedetto is in lobby. All-black ensemble, looking out through plate glass at the pool. Jerry takes him over to his desk, whispering.

Benedetto screams, "What in the hell happened? Those are my slacks!"

Jerry: "I'm really sorry, sir. Looks like marking ink. I raised holy hell at the cleaners. They'll make it good."

"But they're special-made in Jamaica. Jesus Christ, they set me back two hundred dollars." All trace of the British accent is gone.

"They got to get the adjuster out. I put the value at two fifty. That way if they cut it down we can slide back to two hundred. Listen, Mr. Benedetto, why don't you let me put a good tire on your front left for you? I can get it recapped cheap right up the street."

Benedetto 306 sees the handwriting on the wall. "Recapped!"

"Yessir, only fifteen dollars."

"I want a new one. A good one. I want the best."

"How about a nylon one? Then you don't have to ever worry?"

"Okay."

"And I'll get her washed and greased for you. All right, sir?"

"Okay, okay. . . . Dammit, I liked those slacks. You can't match that color in this country. I'm going to the bar."

Sherman: "I've been thinking how you handled Vogel. You're really shaping up. Maybe even superintendent material. Tell you what, you ride it out here till the season breaks, then I'll shoot you up to the Catskills. We own a big place there. Get this same crowd in the summer. That'll give you May off and you'll be ready to start in June."

"Sounds good."

"Sure, and you can spend your vacation there at no cost. Lots of college girls helping out in the restaurant. That isn't bad duty."

Thoughts of Venezuela have long gone. Will now do first draft of novel in Catskills, finish it here next winter. Have quit looking at used-car lots. Decided to drive someone's Cadillac to New York, where I'll buy a new convertible. Have saved $2,040.

Miss Avril in bar: "Doesn't anyone ever go in the ocean?"
Bartender: "Not many."

"Oh, they're all so sick. It looks like a meat rack out there. How do they stand that sun? It's so close you can't breathe. And all that oil and foil and those awful nose guards. Oh, I shouldn't have come down."

"Haven't you met anyone you can talk to yet?"

"They're all drags. They're from the West Side and Queens and they're all millionaires. Who needs them?"

"That was gin, wasn't it?"

"Yeah, and a little easy on the vermouth this time; okay."

The long and the short and the tall. Clothes to cleaners and laundry. 54 Stub Short. Stylish Stout. Size 18. Size 20. Heavy girdles, boned bras and supp-hose. One pair of pants for a man with a stomach like a globe consisted of a yard-long zipper with two stubs for legs attached. Couldn't hang it on hanger; folded over my arm like a tablecloth or a coat. Extra charge at cleaners. They couldn't lay it on ironing board.

Dry cleaning and laundry comes through Jerry marked up 40 per cent on cleaning and 50 per cent on laundry. Company does a good job and Jerry watches that nothing gets stolen or swapped. Jerry also keeps whisky in back of his car along with razor blades, shaving cream, Kotex and prophylactics. Resells everything at double price. Seven-dollar Cutty Sark goes for $18. Jerry: "Tell them you have to run across town in a cab to get it. Don't worry, they're used to it. The whole Beach does it."

Julian Vogel. Sterno cooking every morning. Hot toast and butter and oatmeal. Every morning smiling over the steaming Quaker Oats. "You're a good boy. I'm going to take care of you." No tipping. Another Benedetto?

May have made a mistake. Have gotten too close to him and there's no backing off. Should have called him earlier, but backed out thinking there was big tip coming eventually. Maybe a hundred. Maybe two. Will soon see.

Two weeks later and still only $5 for checking him in, and his fatherly smiles over the steaming porridge. Nothing for the breakfast. Nothing for the ice, the lunches, the midnight snacks. He seems to be gathering himself for one big present. Maybe he thinks of me in cabana-boy terms?

On Friday, Vogel wants to see me. Long personal talk. What do I want to do with myself in future? Could work for him. Would be a good shirt salesman. Good Manhattan territory, throw in part of Connecticut so I could get a company car. Says he feels like a father to me. Has no son. Big tip coming, I can feel it. He's building up to something. It comes. His daughter is on school vacation and is coming down tomorrow for a week. He wants me to take her around town in his Cadillac. Grins. All expenses on him. Slaps me on back.

Gertrude Vogel arrives. Tall; sad, tubelike face. Julian gives me $200 and keys to Caddy. Wants receipts for tax purposes. Three red-hot, ice-cold nights. Gertrude keeps talking about her economics examination. I'm glad because I've got nothing I want to talk to her about.

Julian is complaining to manager that kitchen smells are seeping into his room. I spend hour trying to find where they're coming from but can't. Tell Julian must be from restaurant down Collins Avenue. But wind is from ocean. It doesn't make sense. Try again later. Smell is Campbell's Chicken Noodle Soup coming from room 202. Knock on door. Two good-looking blond college girls. They are sneaking in Metrecal and fruit, and cooking soup and corned-beef hash on a Sterno setup. We laugh about Julian Vogel sniffing down hall trying to find where it's coming from. Wind up giving them three fruit baskets, more Sterno fuel and sneaking them hot Danishes up in the morning. Romance doesn't get a chance to blossom because of pressure of $24-a-day room. They have to leave. I drive them out to airport in Vogel's Cadillac, no charge. Will look them up in Greenwich Village when I come thru N.Y.C.

December bleeds into January. The boat to Venezuela has been gone three months. The heavy action begins. Package plans drop off and the big spenders arrive. We give each couple checking in five curved wooden hangers and a $2.50 basket of fruit. Camels'-hair coats, vicuña coats, vicuña with fur-trimmed collars. Women look taller, longer-legged, smoother, well-cared-for and moneyed. Are used to having doors opened for them and gazing into middle distance while husband or boyfriend signs register. Wear chinchilla hats, full-length mink coats. Seem to be taller than the men. Bigger, heavier luggage. Have to use dollies to carry the big upright steamer trunks in. Women want to know where the hair-dresser is, not where the beach or the sun is. Nine, ten, eleven pieces of luggage. Suitcase for just cosmetics. Husbands cutting Corona-Coronas with small pearl-handled silver knives. Diamonds on fingers and in stickpins in $15 Sulka neckties. Soft, easy-fitting, tailor-made clothes. Cashmere blazers. Expensive shoes, long socks. They tip $5 and $10 as easy as if they're buying a paper.

A joy to work with them. Know what they want and when. Have been here before and don't flinch when you say $24 for a bottle of Pinch (Jerry has raised the price from $18). They encourage no closenesss, which is good and means tips will continue. All seem to be selling but don't seem to be pushing or hustling. Pressure but no pressure. Can't tell the salesmen from the buyers, which means they are all owners or executives of the companies.

Tips soar. . . . First week February, $442. Second week, $506.

Alky in room 109. Woman forty-six or so, six feet tall. Rough Texas face, has seen many terrible things. Drinks gin and sucks lemons. Eats chocolate-covered cherries. Leaves money crumbled in balls on dresser top with paper cups from candy. Gin and lemons on night stand in reach of bed. Lies around in bra and half-slip. Ice melts every hour. Constant service.

"Take five dollars, sonny." There must be four hundred on the dresser. It looks like a trash pile. "Just don't get sticky fingers. Hand me a couple of those cherries. Take one yourself.

Funny, I used to eat these things when I was a kid and now every time I go on a bender I have to have them. That ought to be worth a session on the couch. Back home I'm a big society gal. Art shows, benefits, cotillions, the works. Down here I'm a drunk. You understand?"

"Yes, ma'am."

"Okay, no violins. No sad songs. Just keep the ice coming and keep everyone out of my hair. What did you take, five dollars?"

"Yes, ma'am."

"Okay, take five more. If I don't eat one meal a day I get sick. So right around eight bring me up a steak rare and some fries and ketchup, a green salad and a glass of milk. Don't call me and ask if I want it. Just bring it up. And if I don't eat it, don't worry about it, okay? Bring it every day around eight. *Dinner at Eight;* that's a Noel Coward play. You want a drink?"

"No, ma'am."

"Do you have to call me ma'am? I'm not that old. Call me Bunny."

"Okay, Bunny."

Julian Vogel is checking out. Eleven pieces of luggage. Daughter is tan and looks better but still bad. Julian looks like he's still smelling the chicken noodle soup. The salesmen have gotten to him and he's had a bad time fighting them off. Tips me $10. Fair but disappointing. The Sterno and the oatmeal brought us too close together. Must learn to keep distance.

Third week in February, $568. Fourth week, $587.

March begins and as if on a signal the vicuñas and chinchillas are leaving. The migration is over. They are due someplace else. The hotel is jammed with check-outs. Very few check-ins. Then a rush of check-ins.

The package plans are flooding the Beach. The cloth coats are returning. Somehow I resent them. The men look out of place here after the rich have left. Seem louder, more vulgar;

want to carry their own luggage. Shoes are tan, brown, ripple-soled and unshined. Socks are short, elastic-topped argyles, athlete's-foot white or forty-cent ice-cream colors with clock patterns down the ankle. Pants are too long at break, too loose or tight in seat. High or low in crotch. Suits are from racks, and have ridges and bulges on shoulders. Women look better than men, but not like the tall, furred goddesses of February. Strange and unfamiliar labels on coats. No more brass-studded leather luggage. No steamer trunks. Now composition, pressed cardboard. Old B-4 bags from the Army and oily hang-up Vinyl sleeves. Too much talk. Too many question. Everyone is too nice.

"What time do you serve lunch?"

"It's served all day."

"My name's George and this is my wife Alice. We drove down from Akron, fifteen hours at a stretch. Made it in thirty hours. So you're Bill; well, that's fine. If we need anything we'll call."

Wife says, "George!"

"What?"

She nods at me.

"Oh, sorry." Pulls out a 6-inch-long, 3-inch-wide suede purse with a double snapper on top. Snap. Snap. Long fingers wiggle down the sleeve. He brings out a quarter and a nickle, another quarter and then a dime. He puts one quarter back and gives me the forty cents.

The season is over.